MY OBSESSION

Love at First Sight

By Dare 2 Dream

In remembrance of Malaysia Airlines Flight 370

March 8, 2014

My Obsession
Book Series

Love at First Sight
Our Feelings
Never Stop Loving You
Giving You Reasons
In Our Dreams
Nothing Can Compare To You
Grateful

DISCLAIMERS

MY OBSESSION

Time—only valued when there was not enough. Often un-appreciated because we had too much. Unvalued because we believed there was plenty of time, we had nothing but time. Never grateful for the time we had, but for sure when two people fall in love, they would forget that time ever existed.

Love—never enough time for it!

If time could freeze for all eternity, what kind of feelings would time transform into? Would these feelings of forever become essences for a love that never changes? Or has love changed to become eternal?

For now, as he held her deep in his arms, one second would be enough. Satisfied for those brief seconds when she was in his arms, even when the thought of letting her go hurts him inside.

The man stood tall as he embraced the woman in his arms; he squeezed her tight. She was much shorter than him, so her head reaches to his chest. He inhaled the sweet scent of her hair and listened to her angelic voice when she asked, "Are you okay?" He realised, he couldn't live without her. Someone he thought he could never love, an unreachable artifact he could never own. The one person who—he thought, *It's better if I hate you.*

CHAPTER 1

When I first met you

He remembered back to six months ago when he met *her* for the first time. It was mid-April, and the sky was as bright and beautiful as it could be after the rain. The grass was wet, but a refreshing vivid green and the air smells like spring.

He sat near the window inside a coffee shop that day, and the shop was closed by his office. His full name was Yang Tian-Xu. Yang was his surname, and his birth name—Tian-Xu.

As a direct descendant of the Yang Family, he knew his burden. Many remembered the 'Generals of the Yang Family' to be nothing but folklore. The Yang family's histories were long forgotten by many, however, their descendants still remembered and worshipped their family's history.

It took no effort for him to keep himself busy when he stared outside the window. The busy street kept him entertained as he sat across from Jin Qi-Long, who was both his friend and business partner.

Jin Qi-Long and Yang Tian-Xu were childhood friends with different personalities. Yang Tian-Xu was always the serious type, never mixing his personal and business matters together. His friend was more playful and liked to goof around, be it personal or business. Amazing how they remain as friends since they were five.

Today's meeting was to discuss a new product that Jin Qi-

Long's company were supposed to release in August.

Yang Tian-Xu's company was a family business, known as Yang Corps. They were a large corporation in the country, but their main office was in a city known as City Y. Legal offices, medical walk-in-clinics, hospitals, banks, and real estates were a small portion of their operations. But if the business they invested in could gain them wealth, Yang Corps would invest.

Despite not needing to provide for his family, Yang Tian-Xu was a workaholic. Wealthy, but he still had goals to have Yang Corps become even more prominent. He took over the marketing and advertising departments of Yang Corps.
They scheduled a meeting today, to discuss the auditions plans for the commercial. However, Jin Qi-Long's only interest was women. He wanted the famous singer, Lee Yin-Yin to become the lead actress in the commercial for his new product.

Yang Tian-Xu just sat and listened while the guy rambled on about how beautiful this actress and singer was. Yang Tian-Xu had a suit on, and he looked dashing and handsome as every girl that walked by would sneak a glance at him.

A handsome young and successful businessman—he sat with his back straight, he had an aura around him that showed his confidence. He had everything anyone ever wanted: money, power, even women if he desired. He listened to Jin Qi-Long talk as he sat still. The discussion was about random things—where it wasn't essential or business related. The topic did not interest him, and he stared outside the window, *again.*

Outside on the busy street, with plenty of people moving back and forth. He stared at a homeless man who sat there with his pet dog across the street. They both looked as if they had eaten nothing for days and were dirty. Yang Tian-Xu stared at them with pity in his eyes.

Life must suck for them, he thought. Then a girl—who looked like she was still in High School—walked by—dressed in a simple light-blue T-shirt and a pair of ripped up dark-blue jeans, her shoulder-long black hair dangling in the wind.

She didn't just walk past them, she smiled and gave the homeless man a bag. Grateful for anything he could have, he nodded in appreciation as he opened to see it filled with food. He hurried to grab a bite, snatching a sandwich from the bag, munching it fast as he thanked her.

The girl gave him another bag. Pet food, it was the one with balanced nutrition for dogs. She then smiled at the dog as she bent down to pat its head. She got up and left with a sweet innocent smile on her face, she waved farewell to them both. Yang Tian-Xu did not notice, but his eyes followed *her* for a minute or two before he turned his attention back to Jin Qi-Long.

The guy continued his talk about how great this Singer was as if Yang Tian-Xu cared. Because they had been friends for a long time, Yang Tian-Xu let him continued talking nonsense. The two spent at least two to three hours at the cafe, but it was just the chattering voice of Jin Qi-Long as he rambled on about the super-hot girl: Lee Yin-Yin, who was also an actress and a model, however, Yang Tian-Xu nodded—not giving a care about anything else.

The time passed by slower than he wanted it to as he saw the time displayed 1:35 p.m. on his cellular phone. Yang Tian-Xu ended their meeting, "Hey, it's getting late. I have to go back."

Jin Qi-Long protested and complained, "Aw! But why? We can go out for a drink, it's rare for us to hang out, and you've been so busy." He wanted his friend to stay with him, hang out, grab a bite to eat and talk about girls. But Yang Tian-Xu rejected his offer as he got up from his seat.

"Yeah, I have a lot of documents to look over and sign." Going their separate ways, Yang Tian-Xu left the coffee shop.

A busy day in the area meant no parking space close by, so he parked at a park-aide up the street from the cafe. As he walked over, he passed by the homeless man and the dog. However, just like anybody else he passed by, he ignored them and only took a glance.

He climbed into his expensive looking car and left the park-aide. As he drove out, the road packed with ongoing traffic, he waited another three minutes before squeezing into the main street. During the three minutes he waited, he saw *her* again. This time she was helping an older lady as she pushed a cart of recycled bottles—trying to cross in front of him. The girl up close looked so petite, yet she acted as if she could push the whole cart herself, not allowing the old lady to help her.

Once they crossed over, the girl would smile and help the woman secure the cart before leaving. Watching her somehow made his heart skip a beat.
What the heck am I thinking? The corners of his lips curled up, and he surprised himself with his thoughts.

He drove out as soon as he got his chance, sometimes he would look at his rear-view mirror hoping to catch a glimpse of her. The drive back to his office building wasn't long, he got off his car, and his assistant—Tseng Kuan-Yin went to the driver's seat and drove the car off a parking spot for him in the underground parking lot.

The prized company name, Yang Corporation, also known as 'Yang Corps'. The proud and majestic logo of Yang

Corps hung outside of their headquarters. The two security greeted him, "Good afternoon, President Yang!" as they stood guard outside while Yang Tian-Xu entered the building. Inside the building, as he got in—the staff greeted him.

There were two other security guards on duty inside the building. The older looking man greeted him with a simple, "Good afternoon, Mr Yang." The other guard looked younger, he was nervous as he bowed his head down and shouted, "Welcome back, President!"

He got inside, and the front receptionist greeted him with a bow, he walked his way to the elevator. An elevator-greeter lady was standing there to welcome him. Instead of asking him, "Which floor?" she decided he would go to the highest floor. A man with such superior status within his own family-operated company, his final destination must be at the top, she imagined.

With eight floors total, starting at the bottom at ground level, the lobby hosted the customer service counter in the building's centre. It allowed the staff to greet the customers or clients as soon as they stepped foot inside.

At Yang Corps headquarters there was only a limited amount of office space available for rent, with a high rental price. However, Yang Corps had other locations and malls as well for small business owners to rent. Yang Corps was a huge company, and they had the lion's share in Real Estate Development.

The first and second floors were a part of the shopping centre while the third floor was the food court and an extension of the shopping mall. The fourth and fifth floors were office spaces, (like lawyers' or doctors' offices, and so on). Marketing, Advertisement, and Human Resources were on floors six and seven.

Employees had access cards for their respective level, and Visitors must sign-in at the reception desk. The final floor belonged to Yang Corps and functioned as its Headquarters, it was inaccessible to the public, and only people of importance within Yang Corps had access to it—no exception.

The lift attendant instantly thought he would go up to the eighth floor. However, as she pushed the button, he immediately reached out his index finger to push the button for the seventh floor.

She quickly apologised. Yang Tian-Xu remembered a Chinese idiom his grandfather once used, so he told her, "It's alright, it's not like you're a worm in my stomach, how could you know what I want?"

The girl was embarrassed as she blushed, she stood by his side through the entire trip up, it was a good thing the whole journey was 30 seconds long. However, she could feel the pressure of standing next to the only heir of the Yang Family. The elevator reached the seventh floor. Yang Tian-Xu got off, and she bowed her head to see him off. Yang Tian-Xu walked with complete confidence, as always.

It was 2:00 p.m., the office was busy, and the staff greeted Yang Tian-Xu as they saw him passing through. It didn't take long for him to reach the office on his long legs. The sign on the office door display was 'Manager Jiang Fei'. He was the manager in charge of this floor. However, with his sudden disappearance, it gave Yang Tian-Xu a colossal headache.

It could be possible for him to leave all work to Assistant Tseng, but he wouldn't do that and neglect his duty as Yang Corps' President. Yang Tian-Xu was an extreme workaholic, it's never his nature to do something like that. Also, his assistant might end up hospitalised with all the amount of duties and responsibility—he would get stressed to death with all the other workload related to the different departments of the company.

Nothing was missing or stolen, and it wasn't like Jiang Fei ran away, he was a trustworthy and well-organised employee of Yang Corps. The manager, Jiang Fei's disappearance was a misfortune. Missing for two years on a plane along with 239 people on the flight, he disappeared without a trace. No one knew for sure what had happened, but everybody wanted answers.

Families and friends continued searching for the truth but found nothing. People wanted to know, hoping that their loved ones would return home safely. With those thoughts, they did not give up, missing them every day, hoping for a miracle. However, they had to carry on with their lives. Yang Tian-Xu needed to find a replacement, but for now, he couldn't find anyone he could trust as much as he did with Manager Jiang.

When he got inside the office, he pulled out the chair and sat down at the desk. He didn't immediately work on the computer. He sat there and closed his eyes as he felt all the anxiety from the piles of documents on the table. Suddenly, the images of the girl appeared in his mind.

He found himself thinking again, If it was me... Would I have been so kind?
A corner of his lip curled up again. Then he shook his head as he said. "Why did I think of her!?"

Time quickly passed by before he realised it was already late. The staff went home, one by one, while he remained in his chair, lost in his thoughts. A knock on the door and his assistant —Tseng Kuan-Yin's head popped in. "Hey boss, if there's nothing else, I'll leave for the day, okay?"

"Sure thing." He said, Yang Tian-Xu was a man of few words, but he was competent in his line of work. He had a lot of work as the president of a significant enterprise company.

Although his assistant helped out a lot, he did most of the work; Yang Tian-Xu needed to read over the documents—sign them. Once he could find a proper replacement for Manager Jiang, his workload would lessen, but for now, he had to monitor the projects on the seventh floor.

The plane disappearance was massive news in the country, but people's lives must go on; with work seemingly endless, Yang Tian-Xu needed a break for a minute. He thought about how it could have been, if he were on that flight instead of Manager Jiang Fei, he would have been the missing one.

"Life is too short." He thought—as her smile reappeared in his mind.

By the time he realised how late it was, he took his laptop and a USB drive and placed them in his suitcase as Yang Tian-Xu left his office, the entire floor was already empty as he walked out.

The current time was 5:32 p.m. as he walked into his car in the underground parking lot. He got in and started the engine, and drove out to the gate, he paused for a minute to remember the girl from this afternoon. He thought about how bright her smile was as she helped the elder-lady push the cart, and how sweet her smile was as she patted the dog's head.

He shook his head, bothered by his thoughts as he said, "What the heck am I thinking about?!" Feeling a little frustrated with himself, he lifted both his hands up to ruffle his hair. Then he closed his eyes for a minute. He calmed down and continued to drive home.

An expensive car, with a costly mansion at the top of a hill with the most beautiful scenery of the city, he looked as if he was born of a wealthy family—which he was. Yang Tian-Xu, the only heir of the Yang Family household with a heavy burned on his shoulders.

The Yang Family dates back during the Song Dynasty period. Their family had become the most potent family again since Ancient China. Carrying the family's name had more pressure—ten times heavier on his shoulders compared to his work.

Among these powerful families—three of them had power and status equal to the Yang Family. These families were the Tong, Pan, and Cheung. Since the Song Dynasty, the Pan and Yang families were like enemies. Although it had been thousands of years ago; they still remained as enemies. A thousand-year-old grudge could not be resolved with ease; enemies remained as enemies no matter how long time passed.

When comparing the Cheung Family and the Song Dynasty's emperor would be a little far-fetched comparison. However, as the mayor of City Y, their influence in political matters within the city would be like a king. City Y's current mayor was Cheung Wai-Ma, who was the head of the Cheung Family, he was also Yang Tian-Xu's grandfather.

The Pan and Yang families were both semi-related now through the Cheung Family. Mayor Cheung's first daughter, Cheung Yun-Er married Pan Rong; who was head of the Pan Family, and Yang Tian-Xu's father, the eldest son—Yang Fei-Hung married Cheung Lan-Er, who was the second daughter of Mayor Cheung. Cheung Lan-Er gave birth to Yang Tian-Xu, which made Pan Rong—Yang Tian-Xu's uncle by marriage. Although considered as families, the Pan and Yang Family still harboured secret hate between each other.

Yang Tian-Xu was the mayor's grandson, and the relationship gave the Yang Family a significant boost in power. The Pan Family had the same amount of power and wealth as the Yang

Family. However, unlike Cheung Lan-Er—her sister—Cheung Yun-Er was in fact childless; even though she was the eldest daughter of Mayor Cheung.

Mayor Cheung and his second wife had a son, twelve years older than Yang Tian-Xu, named Cheung Yun-Bo. Yang Tian-Xu was still the mayor's only grandson. Cheung Yun-Bo was someone unmarried for the moment and had no intention of getting married any time soon.

Cheung Lan-Er worried about her son, what if he wishes to stay unmarried like his uncle? She wanted her Tian-Xu to marry someone she could be proud to have as a daughter-in-law. Someone like Tong Yue-Yan—who belonged to another powerful and wealthy household that could match the Yang Family.

The Tong Family had more power in City A than they did in City Y; however, they were still thriving in City Y as one of the four largest family-operated businesses in City Y. And their family head was currently the Mayor of City A—the second largest City in the Country. If Yang Tian-Xu married Tong Yue-Yan, it would be like a cherry on top of a cake. It would be *just* too perfect.

Yang Tian-Xu opened the front door and was greeted by his mother as he entered. Cheung Lan-Er had Tong Yue-Yan with her as a house guest. Both his parent and Tong Yue-Yan sat together in the living room chit-chatting while having tea and biscuits that Tong Yue-Yan had brought with her as gifts from City A.

"Tian-Xu, my son. You sure are home late today." She gave him a disapproving look for being so late, "Did something happen at the company?"

"Mother, it's only 6:00 p.m., it is still pretty early. I have a few urgent contracts I need to go over before returning home." He said, as he hugged his mother, she would give him a peck on the cheek, as he was her one and only child.

Even though he was a little later than he should have been, but that was because Yang Tian-Xu had been busy with the thoughts of the girl he had met today. And he had kept dozing off at every red light—consistently being honked at. However, that reason, he would keep to himself.

CHAPTER 2

How I dream of you

Cheung Lan-Er—known by many as Mrs Yang. She was in her late 40s, however, she still looked young and had taken care of her beauty well. She asked him, "You remembered Yue-Yan right?" as she placed her hands on the girl's shoulder. Mrs Yang smiled at the girl next to her as she continued, "Yue-Yan arrived from City A today, and dropped by to give us a visit." Tong Yue-Yan smiled at him and gave a slight nod as a greeting.

He slightly nodded back at her, and his mother caught his father by surprised as she blames her husband, "This is all your father's fault! Yang Fei-Hung!"

Mr Yang choked on the tea he took a sip of—coughing as he put the cup down on their maple coffee table, he asked, "Why is it my fault?"

"Yes, it's your fault, you let my poor Tian-Xu work late every night! If you have been the President instead, our Tian-Xu would have opportunities to find himself a lovely girlfriend and get married by now, the reason he's still single is all because of you."

"But! Honey, if I took the job as president, I won't be able to spend as much time with you!" Mr Yang acted like he was a child—almost married for 30 years made him unwilling to separate from his wife.

"You are not as important as our Tian-Xu," she said as she

turned her sight to Tong Yue-Yan, "Don't you agree with me, Yue-Yan?"

Tong Yue-Yan understood what Mrs Yang was hinting at—when Mrs Yang complained to her husband in front of her. "You should come help at the company sometimes so that our Tian-Xu can spend more time with his personal life. Right? Yue-Yan?" Mrs Yang intentions were obvious, she wanted to play match-maker.

Tong Yue-Yan sat next to Mrs Yang, and she was blushing a little as she nodded in agreement, she had a lovely gentle voice, "Yes, it is imperative not to overwork yourself."

"Definitely!" said Mrs Yang, as his mother: she often worried about Tian-Xu. "I'll be glad and content if he married someone who is not only smart, beautiful, and understanding. Like you—*Yue-Yan*."

Tong Yue-Yan blushed redder when Yang Tian-Xu's mother complimented her.

"Honey, you will embarrass the kids." Mr Yang looked at the embarrassed Tong Yue-Yan as he apologised on behalf of his wife for attempting to match-make the two, "I'm sorry, she always liked you to be our daughter-in-law."

Tong Yue-Yan face grew hotter as she heard Mr Yang said those words. She was glad that both his parents seem to like her. She remembered back to when she first met him. It was her ninth birthday, and they came all the way to City A to help celebrate her birthday. Yang Tian-Xu had given her a music box—which she still kept to this day.

"Now look at who's embarrassing whom. You're making Yue-Yan's face all red." She said as they teased her about her being their future daughter-in-law.

Yang Tian-Xu remained calm. He said in a steady voice, "Mother, father—you two shouldn't have to worry too much,

I have my plans for the future, so please stop teasing and embarrassing Miss Tong. Excused them, Miss Tong, for the trouble they bring you, they always liked to joke around." He said politely.

"It's... It's okay..." It was a little shocking for her to hear him apologise. She was Tong Yue-Yan, who wouldn't want to marry her? She was pretty—had a compelling family background, and she graduated at the top of her class. Yet, everything does not seem to affect him, he was unmoved by her accomplishments.

Perhaps because Yang Tian-Xu was also an accomplished man with a strong background and education, he and Tong Yue-Yan would be a perfect match in the eyes of many. Many men in the world, none who wouldn't be interested in her, Tong Yue-Yan: she only had eyes for him, Yang Tian-Xu.

Tong Yue-Yan looked beautiful, sweet, and sitting like a proper lady, wearing a beautiful spring blue dress. Her hair tied up to the side, with beautiful, perfect curls. She dolled herself for him, yet his eyes seem uninterested, the only response she received from him was a simple greeting.

"Tian-Xu," His mother called his name, again. "You should show Yue-Yan around tomorrow, she hasn't visit City Y in a long time, our City Y differs greatly compared to City A, give her a fine tour."

"I'm sorry, but I have other plans tomorrow. I have to be at the company. There is the internship interview I have to attend." It was clear he prefers working instead of keeping a some-random rich girl company.

"Let Assistant Tseng handle the interviews, take the day off and show Yue-Yan around, it is rare for her to be in City Y." His mother demands him to take her out, and not giving him much of an option to opt-out.

Tong Yue-Yan sat there unable to believe his mother had to force him to take her out. How could she let her pride take it? She spoke up, "Mrs Yang, it's okay if he is too busy, we can re-schedule for another day."

"Oh please," she said, as she grabbed her hands gently. "Call me Auntie. Don't you worry, he needed time off from the company anyway, right Tian-Xu?" She glared at him, giving him no choice but to say. "Yes, mother. I shall come to pick Miss Tong up tomorrow and show her around the city."

Tong Yue-Yan stood up and gave a polite bow to him as she said, "Then, I will be in your guidance tomorrow?" She looked up at the antique clock that hangs in the living room and realised it was already 7:00 p.m. "It's getting late, I should re-turn home."

"Oh! Tian-Xu, why don't you take Yue-Yan home?" said Mrs Yang, smiling at him.

Yang Tian-Xu knew her mother's intention was to have him spend more time with Tong Yue-Yan. Even though he finds it a little annoying, he stills obey his mother's commands. His mother hopes that their relationships could improve into something more than just friends.

"Yes, mother." He replied, thinking of how short it would be to take her home, he couldn't care less about it if it makes his mother happy.

"Oh no, it's okay, President Yang just got home. I wouldn't want to bother him so much. I have my driver waiting outside."

"Oh please, both of you should stop being so polite to each other, Tian-Xu was only three years older than you. You can call him by his first name." Then she turned to look at her son, "You too Tian-Xu, stop being so polite and treat each other friendlier."

"Yes, mother." Tian-Xu obediently replied. "Yue-Yan,

shall I see you to your car then?"

"Oh, yes... Thank you." She lowers her head as she hides her embarrassed face away from them, she gave a slight bow as he walked to the front door, he opened it for her, and then they walked out together.

When the door closed, Mrs Yang smiled at Mr Yang and said, "Aren't they such a cute couple?" and Mr Yang would smile back at his wife and said, "Yes they are, in the future we'll have the cutest grandchildren."

Outside in the courtyard, they walked over to her car, parked at a pleasant two-minute walk away. The driver sat there waiting with patience. While Tong Yue-Yan takes her time, strolling with him slowly, in hoped to spend more time with him. Like a lady as she walked with Yang Tian-Xu beside her, she thought about how handsome he looked, while she sometimes glanced a peek at him now and then, her heart was racing at his presence.

Utter calmness, unlike the girl beside him. He never turns her way (not even once) and only walked beside her because he couldn't be improper and walk ahead of her.

In his mind, he thought, "Man, can't this girl walk any faster?"

He wasn't dense, he knew what his parents wanted, especially his mother—for a chance for them to get close to each other and perhaps start a political marriage.

However, towards Tong Yue-Yan—he harbours no emotions for her—to him she was just a random-rich girl his mother wanted him to marry. Tong Yue-Yan might be beautiful, smart, and elegant. But, she doesn't give him that *my heart just skip a beat* moment.

Again, he thought about *her*. The one stranger who made

his heart skipped a beat.

"Um, thank you for walking me to my car." Tong Yue-Yan said politely, as she smiled at him, she gave off a princess-like aura around her.

Yang Tian-Xu snapped back to reality and said, "It's okay, there's no need for the formalities. Shall I come by to pick you up? What time would it be more convenient for you?" he asked, the tone of his voice makes it sounds more like a business transaction than a date.

"Would 10:00 a.m. be okay? I have a lot of places I would like to see," she said trying to make excuses to see him earlier.

"Sure, I will meet with you then, I hope you have a safe trip home." He said as he watched her boarding inside her car from the back seat and like an exact way a gentleman should behave, he closed the door for her. He raised a hand up, gesturing a wave to see her drove off by the driver.

The moment he walked back in the front door, his parents stared at him. He could tell just from their looks what they wanted. "I will come to pick Miss Tong at 10:00 a.m. tomorrow now, I hope you're satisfied. Now please excuse me, I would need to finish up more work tonight, so I can free my schedule for tomorrow." He said as he walked up the stairs.

His parents looked at each other and thought—*did they pair them up?* Or was it unsuccessful? From the tone of his voice. He made it sound like a business report.

Yang Tian-Xu returned to his bedroom, well organised, clean, and being a precious child from an influential family, he need not clean anything. He took off his necktie, and threw them on his bed, and laid down for a moment. Before he bounced on to his computer desk, he sat down and turn on his laptop. He got documents after documents to look at and read through them. Then he gave his assistant a call ordering him, "Take over the interns interview tomorrow I have other business to attend."

His assistant agreed, "Okay boss!" and hung up the call.

Yang Tian-Xu's room was quiet, the only sounds he made was coming from his keyboard, typing out contracts, business plans, and future meetings proposals with other companies. In five hours, he completed everything he needed for work tomorrow. The time display on the clock was 12:20 a.m. Tired from the non-stop action, he got ready for bed.

He headed toward the shower and unbuttoned his shirts. Removing his clothing one by one, revealing his strong fit body, attractive, not a single tiny scar on him. A man with a perfect body, a perfect face, and the ideal family background.

After he came out from the shower, he dried his hair on a towel. He jumped onto the bed and fell fast asleep by 1:00 a.m.

That night, he had a dream: it's been a while since he dreamt about anything. Despite that, inside his dream, *she* was in it. The girl with that sweet smile as she patted the dog's head, that cheerful girl who helped an old lady pushed a cart up a steep road. Even if her hands became dirty, she didn't seem to care.

In the dream he saw *her* smile, smiling at him. It was a realistic and vivid dream. Almost like he could touch her, hold her, and kiss her.

Kiss her?

As he moved in closer, with his lips only inches away from touching *hers*. The alarmed clock rang, it was probably the most annoying sound he had ever heard, as he opened his eyes. The first time he had woken up later than usual. On a regular day, his usual routine includes waking up at 6:00 a.m. before the alarm rang, he would go out for a good morning jog. However, the clock rang at 8:30 a.m., he had no time to enjoy a run and rush to the shower, washing off his night sweat.

He dressed up like he would for work, just like he would attend a business meeting. Proper—in a blue suit that matches his body and skin tone.

It was already 9:15 a.m. when he left home. His parents were more excited than he was—they reminded him to be sure to treat her for brunch and so on. Yang Tian-Xu was always obedient, even though he felt like it was more of a business meeting than a romantic relationship, he still shows up on time at 9:55 a.m.

The Tong Family had a small villa in City Y. Their villa had a beautiful garden, in which Tong Yue-Yan's aunt had maintained. She took care of the businesses the Tong Family had in City Y while her brother; Tong Yue-Yan's father would take care of activities in City A.

By the time he rang the doorbell, she was ready. He said his greetings to Tong Yue-Yan's aunt when she opened the door to greet him. As he waited by the front door, by 10:00 a.m. sharp, she ascended down from the stairs and saw him by the door holding a beautiful bouquet of red roses in his hands.

His mother got the roses for him to give them to Tong Yue-Yan, hoping he would treat this as a date. However, he quickly clarified it to Tong Yue-Yan. "These are from my mother. She wanted to make sure you receive them."

She wasn't sure if she should laugh or cry. "Thanks..." She took the bouquet out of his hands and gave them to her aunt, "Can you please put these in a vase for me. Thank you, auntie."

Then she turned to him and said, "Shall we go?" He nodded, and they walked out to his car. While they were walking, it was quiet. Just like how it was last night when he walked her to her car. This time, perhaps she could spend more time with him? She was excited and extremely happy.

He opened the passenger's door to let her in, and he closed it once she got inside. He went to the driver's seat and started the engine without saying much.

It was like an awkward silence: she knew he had no feeling for her. Despite that, she doesn't want him to hate her. She wanted him to like her too. However, because of her shy personality. She could only make more small talk. "It's a beautiful day today, is it not?"

"Yes, it is." his simple three-sentence reply to her before going silent again.

She wanted to ask him, 'Is it that bad for you to spend the day with me?' But it wasn't possible for her to say it. Tong Yue-Yan tried to be as ladylike as possible. The way she walks, the way she smiles as he showed her around town. City Y was a big city, lots of beautiful sightings and locations. He asked if she had any special request, and places she would like to visit and then he would fulfil them.

She would name a few places, and he would keep her company; however, it all seems to her like he was treating her like a tourist, or a guest he must keep company. She asked him, "What about you? Is there a special location you like to visit?"

Just as she asked him, he thought about that coffee place where he had met *her*. He smiled to himself and said, "Yeah, I know a great coffee place I would like to visit."

He parked his car at the same place he parked last time. The two went together for a short walk to the coffee place he mentioned. They took an 18 minutes drive by car to reach the park-aid near the coffee place, then another two minutes walk to get to the area. They arrived and ordered two coffees. He paid in cash, they sat down at the same seat he was in last time and waited. Once the coffees came, a quick service he enjoyed here and they sat there while he enjoyed the silence atmosphere.

Tong Yue-Yan prefers tea over coffee, but she still agreed with Yang Tian-Xu, as she wanted him to acknowledge her. She watched him as he looked out the window. Her curiosity made her stared outside the window, yet not noticing anything unusual or entertaining about the busy street, she wondered about what made him fixate his gaze upon.

"What is so interesting outside?" She thought, as she kept looking at him, unnoticed.

It was around 12:00 p.m. The time for lunch, the street outside was busy with nearby office towers, people were at lunch. Even his employees were just out on their lunch break. There was also a University nearby. Yang Tian-Xu wondered, *maybe she was a University student instead?* He can't remember any high school nearby. He recalled she was young looking like she was 16 or 17 years old. Praying that her age would be older than her looks. If she were 23, it would be the perfect age for him.

A four years age difference should be his limit. On October 31st, Yang Tian-Xu would celebrate his 27th birthday. He doesn't know how he could take it. *Perhaps he would allow a seven years difference? No, eight years? No, he'll make it ten.* Ten years was the max he could tolerate their age difference.

Yang Tian-Xu kept wondering as he continued staring out the window. Then he thought—*Wait, what if she was older than him?* His mind was in a constant train of thoughts about her age. In silent—he kept wondering, "Will she come again today? Would I ever meet her again? Damn it all! Where are you?"

With Yang Tian-Xu looking out the window in silence, Tong Yue-Yan just stared outside with him. She was unsure about what he was looking at, and hope that she could see what he sees. But in her mind, she thought if she was that boring he had to entertain himself this way.

Yang Tian-Xu looked left and right outside, only the same homeless man still sitting in the same place, begging for a kind heart to give him something to eat, but *her*? No sight of *her*, he couldn't forget about *her*, the one who appeared in his dream last night.

The more Tong Yue-Yan speaks—the more Yang Tian-Xu *just* nodded as he paid his attention to the outside and not on her. She wasn't stupid, if anyone else does this to her—she would have thrown the drink in her hand in their faces and storm out. Also, no one had ever treated her this way before. His cold attitude towards her was something his mother had warned her about last night before Tian-Xu came home, she prepared herself for this.

CHAPTER 3
Where are you?

With his cold attitude towards her—Yang Tian-Xu's mother had already warned her last night, telling her how he could be such a workaholic. The thoughts of his seriousness made her felt like he would become a great husband.

She remained by his side without saying another word: she was in his presence silently watching him. Unaware he was thinking about another. Tong Yue-Yan thought perhaps she had taken a step closer to Yang Tian-Xu's heart. Enjoying the silence surrounding with him, being as patient as she could.

"Do you want another cup of coffee?" Tong Yue-Yan asked him politely. At 1:30 p.m., they were sitting around for over an hour. Yang Tian-Xu had finally turned to look at her and said, "Sorry, I must bore you. Would you like to go?"

"Oh, it's okay, we can stay if you like!" Nervous, not wanted him to think she was bored. "Are you—" Then her stomach growls a little. She had not eaten breakfast because she spent all day getting ready, undecided about what to dress herself in the entire morning. She blushes as she held her belly. "—sorry."

Yang Tian-Xu gave a gentle smile, "We should go for lunch. I wouldn't want you to starve."

They left the coffee shop and headed back to where Yang Tian-Xu had parked his car. The underground parking lot was at the opposite corner from the street, they had to cross the road, eventually. They could cross the road now at this street light, or they could go straight and stay on their current side of the street until they reach the other traffic lights, then pass.

Yang Tian-Xu had purposely walked across the street where the homeless man laid curled up—he passed by him and gave the man the change he'd received from paying for the coffees. Tong Yue-Yan was a wealthy lady, how could she have any change? She only had credit and debit cards in her wallet.

She wanted to look like a sweet and kind girl in front of Yang Tian-Xu, but she can't give the homeless man her credit cards, so she passed by the homeless man and said, "It's such a shame I don't have cash on me." Yang Tian-Xu didn't care what she had, not like it mattered to him. "It's okay, few people bring cash nowadays." A fact in this modern world, everything was digitised.

Yang Tian-Xu was just like Tong Yue-Yan yesterday—who only bring his credit and debit cards with him, if not he would use his apps on his smartphone. The thoughts of helping out the man only occur to him after he had met her. She had left an unforgettable impression in his mind that remains in his heart.

The time already displayed 1:45 p.m. They had reached the underground parking where Yang Tian-Xu parked his car. He stationed there twice now, in the same spot he parked yesterday. Perhaps doing so would allow him to meet *her* again?

They got into the car and he drove out—the traffic today wasn't as bad as it was yesterday. They got out into the street in less than 30 seconds, but still, he kept his eyes out for her.

Yang Tian-Xu took Tong Yue-Yan to an expensive restaurant nearby, it was already 2:15 p.m. when they got there. The fancy restaurant looked like a ballroom as they walked inside, and each table had its cubic seating area. This was a frequent place for him to conduct his business lunches.

The staff there recognised Yang Tian-Xu as he often came for business discussions. The crew showed them to his most frequented table. Tong Yue-Yan and Yang Tian-Xu looked good together as they walked towards the arranged table, sitting across from each other, face to face. The other staff member would often whisper about them behind their backs as they recognised the beauty to be the heir to the Tong Family's fortune.

Yang Tian-Xu was a tall, handsome man, who was over six feet tall. Perhaps six-foot-two or six-foot-three and Tong Yue-Yan had a height of five-foot-ten: tall enough to be a model, she had the looks and height to become one. However, with her family background, she had no desire to be a mere model. With the jealousy of many female staff, Tong Yue-Yan felt like she had it all. She had excellent table manners, once the crews gave them a menu and served them water, she didn't forget to thank them politely.

Tong Yue-Yan studied history and was a fan of Ancient Chinese history. She knew well of the Yang Family's heroic tales and admired them for it. Throughout the wait for their meals, she would tell him, just how fascinated she was about his family's history. Yang Tian-Xu heard his family tales from his father and grandfather many times before. It's not a surprise for him— he did not mind her talk about his family history. Nevertheless, he had no interest in it.

They ordered a western meal. Tong Yue-Yan had ordered a chicken salad, and he ordered the house pasta special. She would ask him questions about his life, and he would answer. Other than that, he seemed unwilling to engage in their conversation. Finally, the meals have arrived, and they would both eat their meals quietly.

During the entire meal, Yang Tian-Xu would often pull out his phone and text his assistant, Tseng Kuan-yin. He would ask about the interviews and demands he reported the current situations to him.

Tong Yue-Yan wasn't so happy about his scant attention towards her, but still, she endured it and was just satisfied to be enjoying a meal together. She takes her time slowly as Yang Tian-Xu had already finished his meal by the time the clock hit 2:45 p.m.

Assistant Tseng jokily texts him, "How's the future Mrs Yang?"

Yang Tian-Xu made it obvious in his replies, with no intention of marrying Tong Yue-Yan, his eyebrows frowned as he texts back, "What future Mrs Yang?" Assistant Tseng understood him well, so he stopped with his jokes, Yang Tian-Xu was a workaholic and only wanted to know about the current situation at the company.

"Stop joking around. How's this year interns looking? Any talents?" he quickly messaged back and enquired about the interviews.

Assistant Tseng text back, "Everything is doing great, boss. No need to worry, I can handle it, and I will keep you updated."

Yang Tian-Xu never worried about his assistant's work, he knew the guy was competent. It's just that he felt a little bored. How long does it take someone to finish a salad? As Tong Yue-Yan took her sweet time with her meal, Yang Tian-Xu didn't bother to rush her, he sat there quietly as he reads over the latest news in the business industry. Occasionally, he would pretend like he was having lunch with *her*, and let out a small gentle smile. He wondered about the girl again. *Where are you? If only you were here.*

A bright, beautiful Friday afternoon, the girl, with long shiny light-black hair, with light-brown eyes almost as if they were hazel. She appeared at Yang Corps' front entrance. With *her* name displayed on the visitor tag as Wang Yi-An. Comparing her and Tong Yue-Yan, she wasn't as pretty. However, she was the same girl that Yang Tian-Xu couldn't stop thinking about. Ever since the first day he met her. It was unfortunate that Yang Tian-Xu wasn't able to attend today's group of interviews, a missed opportunity for the both was like a cruel joke from the heavens.

Each year, the company would open opportunities to search for young talents to work for them. Yang Corps was one of the many big companies that does so. However, their internship program was hard to get in. Only a few got accepted each year. After the interns completed the program; it almost guaranteed them a job from Yang Corps. As a Yang Corps intern, it entitles them to great benefits and opportunities. However, all the interns' entitlement was incomparable to a real Full-Time employee.

The most important one for Wang Yi-An was the Educational Assistant program. The educational Assistant program was an exclusive benefit for their employees; Yang Corps would pay 100% of the employee's tuition fee, and book fees, supplies, equipment, etc. There was also a wage while you were in school! Yang Corps would pay an hourly wage for their employees to go to school, what other companies would do this? Only a big company like Yang Corps could afford it.

Wang Yi-An didn't had enough credentials to apply directly to Yang Corps employment. However, she had enough to apply for the internship program. If she got accepted, it would become the ticket to her better future. Desperate for the internship, Wang Yi-An hoped she could try her hardest with the opportunity given to her; the best she could as she worked towards success.

Wang Yi-An was working a part-time job at night, as she studied during the day. She lived a hard, strenuous life, but she still tried the hardest she can so that one day she could had the credentials to apply for the internship, and once she did, Wang Yi-An applied as soon as possible.

The Yang Corps internship program was three months long. Afterwards, Yang Corps would inform their interns with a letter of offer. Unless the student rejects it, or that the student had not reached their expectations during the three months; a rare case.

Anticipation kept Wang Yi-An nervous all week long since she first got the call to come in for the interview last Monday. She fidgets around with her small fingers, as she remains seated, quietly in the waiting room, along with twenty others. She had her eyes closed for a moment, so she could relax and calm herself down from the anxiety.

Wang Yi-An took a deep breath, each interviewee takes 15 to 30 minutes to complete their interview process. Wang Yi-An arrived an hour before her scheduled time. They scheduled her interview at 2:30 p.m., but she arrived before 1:30 p.m.

Once the clock reaches 2:30 p.m., a female employee of the faculty called out her name, "Wang Yi-An!"

"Here!" she answered as she got up from her seat and walked over to the female staff.

"Your interview is in room two," she said after informing Wang Yi-An the details, she showed her the directions to room two, and she smiled

"Good luck."

As the door opened for Wang Yi-An, she heard voices from a distant coming from inside the room as she entered. Assistant Tseng shout out "Next please!", The door opened as the previous interviewee walked out. Wang Yi-An walked in right after, with a bright smile on her face. She wasn't nervous anymore, she was just as excited as she was from the night before this interview. Working for the Yang Corporation was a big dream of hers, and with this interview, she would pave a path filled with hope for her and her family.

"Hello, my name is Wang Yi-An, many people call me Xiao-An or An-An. It's a pleasure to meet with everyone!" she said in an excited voice, as she lowered her head to greet them.

Three hiring managers, with Assistant Tseng Kuan-Yin in the middle. He had taken President Yang's spot in today's interviews. It wasn't rare for Yang Corps' president to do personal interviews. It often happens when the positions of the interns were essential for the company's development. Yang Tian-Xu would personally attend. However, today he couldn't make it, he was busy having a meal with Tong Yue-Yan.

The three hiring manager nodded their heads, and the hiring manager on the right side speak up. "It's a pleasure to meet you too, please take a seat."

As she sat down, she smiled at them. The first person to ask questions regarding her credentials was the manager on the right. He did most of the talking. Wang Yi-An had the credentials to become their intern. She took an Art program for two years, along with some managing courses. Wang Yi-An's dream was to become an Art Director; working for Yang Corps, Art Directors were responsible for developing promotions, commercials, and other events hosted by the company. Yang Corps offered the highest salary for the occupation, with plenty of hours, she looked forward to it. The entire interview went well, and she was confident in her arts because she had already submitted her portfolio, it was the reason they selected her for the interview. Even though they already saw her artwork and knew her abilities, they needed to know more about her, like her personalities or other talents, they still need to ask her some questions such as, "Why have you picked Yang Corps for your internship? There were many options."

"Yang Corps has the best benefits," She replied honestly.

"You know Pan Holding's Inc has good benefits too," said the manager on the left. Wang Yi-An didn't think before she said,

"But I like Yang Corps better."

They smiled, and Assistant Tseng asked, "Why do you like Yang Corps better?"

"Because Yang Corps cares deeply for their employees." This fact was that Yang Corps featured in an Employer of the year magazine. It highlighted them, and at the top 10 listed companies selected by employees in City Y, Yang Corps topped the list in first place. All the employees were proud to be part of Yang Corps compared to the other nine companies. In fifth place was Pan Holding Incorporated, although they had a higher paying salary than Yang Corps, and the other companies, their treatment for employees were not as good and fair.

Pan Holding Incorporated was a company of competition among each other. Where, if their monthly report wasn't as good, they would most likely be fired and replaced by a more capable employee. However, if the employees make lots of money for the company, they would receive better treatment, bonus and extra earnings. Most competitive people would prefer to work in that environment. However, Wang Yi-An was not a competitive person. She honestly told them, "Pan Holding Inc was a little too competitive for me, I don't think I can fit in with them, but I am sure that Yang Corps would be the better choice for me."

The three of them agreed with her analysis. After they heard her reasons for picking Yang Corps over the other companies, they asked her one last question. "Why should we pick you, compared to all the other applicants we have today?"

"Because I have a unique talent," she said with pride in her voice.

"What talent would that be?" he asked, as it raised his curiosity. He looked at the copies of Wang Yi-An's portfolio and noticed nothing much.

"I have a photographic memory, and I can draw at an immersive fast speed she said with a smile.

This amazed him, how could anyone claimed to have two talents so rare. "Really?" he seems to be a disbeliever as he asked her. "Can you prove it?"

"Of course I can." She said as she smiled brightly.

Because of her confident, Assistant Tseng wanted to test her. "Okay, I will show you two photos," and he did, flashing the photos to her, fast, one after the other. "Now tell me the details of both, in the same order I showed you." He places the two photos down backwards, hiding them from view. The other two managers thought he didn't show her the images long enough.

"Wasn't that too fast?" said the manager on the left, she was the only female manager on the panel, she didn't like how Assistant Tseng treated her, he only flashed her those photos for two seconds, who would remember all those details?

"Hey, she said she has a photographic memory."

"Maybe she meant she has a good memory." They wanted to give the girl a more reasonable chance, showing her two pictures in less than a minute, seems to be cruel.

"Show her the pictures longer just to be fair."

Assistant Tseng exchanged messages with President Yang at 2:45 p.m. He looked at Wang Yi-An as he typed, "Okay since she is young I might as well..."

"There's no need." She said as she interrupted him, and said, "Instead of going over the details in speech, would you like me to redraw it out?"

The three managers exchanged looks, they thought, Can she really do that? Is it even possible? and so they watched her took out a sketchbook from her mini-backpack. She drew them out, and sure enough, she took 15 minutes to draw out two pictures.

Amazed, the three of them became speechless, they saw how fast she could sketch out two images, as soon as she completed the sketch, she walked over and placed them both on the table. Assistant Tseng flipped over the two pictures he showed her and compared them with Wang Yi-An's rough sketch.

They were surprised, they looked (pretty much) identical, the pictures detailed and the colours all matched the originals, even for a rough sketch it was well done. "Wow, you sure are amazingly talented Miss Wang."

"Thank you!" she kept her smile at them, and put her sketchbook away in her small backpack, along with her colours markers and supplies she had used.

"Well, with a talent like that I want to hire you right away!" Assistant Tseng still couldn't believe his eyes. He started at the two drawings and compared them to the originals. Almost on point—every detail he reviewed side by side. "Well then, can you start work next week?"

"Already? I thought the internship starts in two weeks from now?" The sudden impulses surprised Wang Yi-An.

Assistant Tseng laughed, "Oh, right. I almost forgot." He was amazed, he had forgotten that! Wang Yi-An's talents amazed him so much he almost forgotten about the interview was only an interview for the internship. "Then you can start your internship in two weeks; you may go home and wait for your acceptance letter by email." Assistant Tseng's decision had surprised the other two managers.

The entire interview wasn't finish yet, and he had already decided on Wang Yi-An as one of the selected interns. No one would show their disapproval in front of him, and Wang Yi-An was indeed talented.
Wang Yi-An was glad to hear the news, she stood up to lowered

her head for a slight bow. "Thank you!" and she left the room.

One of the managers on the panel asked, "Mr Tseng, isn't it too soon? We haven't finished interviewing all the other students yet."

"Would it be necessary to wait on someone as talented as her? Her photographic memory is a rare talent! Don't worry about President Yang. I will inform him about my decision." Assistant Tseng made his intention to hire Wang Yi-An clear; the other two wouldn't question him anymore. Assistant Tseng position in the company was almost like he was a vice-president. Even their current Vice-President, Ma Wei wouldn't have as much authority as Assistant Tseng—who worked directly for President Yang.

Soon enough, Assistant Tseng quickly sent a message to his boss, Yang Tian-Xu. He had to tell President Yang the excellent news, photographic memory was rare, and she can draw so fast, he had to notify to President Yang:

'Boss, you would be so surprised about this student I recently interviewed...'

CHAPTER 4

If Only You Were Here

Just as Yang Tian-Xu waited for Tong Yue-Yan to finish the salad, Yang Tian-Xu was thinking about her, the girl he had a dream about and couldn't stop thinking of. He imagined the girl sitting across from him was her instead of Tong Yue-Yan. The corner of his lips curved up, and Tong Yue-Yan thought it was a smile meant for her. It made her happy and smiled back. Preoccupied with thoughts of another, Yang Tian-Xu completely ignored Tong Yue-Yan.

Yang Tian-Xu snapped out of his thoughts, back to reality as he heard a notification chime from his smartphone. He looked down to read the message.

'Boss, you would be in shock! This student I interviewed today, just wow! An amazing talent! A photographic memory, I tell ya! I already informed the student to start the internship in two weeks.

—Sent from Assistant Tseng at 2:50 p.m.'

Photographic memory? Yang Tian-Xu ponders, since it was his assistant that made the claim, Yang Tian-Xu was positive he had proof and backings for it. Yang Tian-Xu messaged back, 'Okay.' to his assistant. Showing the trust he had for him, after working together for five years—he placed high confidence in Assistant Tseng, and the guy never disappoints him.

After lunch, Yang Tian-Xu asked her if she had anywhere else she would like to see? All afternoon he had taken her to most of the attractions in City Y. Although she wanted more time with him, she can't visit all the places at once, she had to save those as an excuse to see him again another day. She told him, "It must tire you after all this walking, how about we wait for next time?"

"I don't think I'll have time next time." His reply was straightforward. He wanted this to be the last time he kept her company.

"Right, you must be busy with work." She lied to herself with a self-made reason for him to be so cold towards her, and then he replied, "Yes."

"Is there anywhere else you would recommend?" She asked him for his suggestion. However, Yang Tian-Xu was a busy workaholic, and he told her how busy he was, and he doesn't know a good tourism location. Then he thought about Jin Qi-Long, and he said, "I have a close friend named Jin Qi-Long, he likes to go to many places. If you like, I can recommend him to you."

Tong Yue-Yan didn't know if she should laugh or cry. *How can he push her to another?* She initiated and suggested a theme park. "How about visiting the theme park? I haven't been to the ones here in City Y."

"Sure," He nodded. Quickly paying for the meal they left the restaurant. Before moving, Tong Yue-Yan needed to use the lady's restroom. She excused herself and went to fix her makeup. She got out after she finished her business and apologised to Yang Tian-Xu and thanked him for his patience

The time was 3:00 p.m. They got into the car, and he drove to the nearest theme park, about a half hour drive from where they were.

At the same time at 3:00 p.m. Wang Yi-An had just exited Yang Corps' headquarter. She felt a sense of satisfaction and happiness with Assistant Tseng's offer of employment. So she headed home and didn't forget to drop by the supermarket to buy groceries to cook dinner for her and her mother.

Friday was a busy day at the market because it was already 3:20 p.m., even though it was a 24-hour store, the supermarket still had fresh produces every morning. In the afternoon, the prices for these fresh produces drops. Hence for Wang Yi-An who wanted to get the best prices possible, it was a godsend.

Meanwhile, Yang Tian-Xu and Tong Yue-Yan had reached the theme park at 3:25 p.m. and Yang Tian-Xu paid for the tickets, and they walked in through the gates. As they were walking throughout the theme park, Tong Yue-Yan felt like this was a date, she gets to be close to Yang Tian-Xu. To Yang Tian-Xu, he felt like this was a meaningless trip; he felt as if he was a babysitter.

Tong Yue-Yan didn't play on the rides or use any of the attractions. They strolled around the theme park, and she would watch the kids enjoy themselves. Tong Yue-Yan wanted to hint her love for children of her own. "The children are adorable, having lots of children would be wonderful, don't you think so?"

How could Yang Tian-Xu not understand what she meant? He ignores it. They walked around whenever she talks, and he'll pretend to listen, but he didn't care. He wondered if the girl he dreamt about would come back here with him one day.

Meanwhile, Wang Yi-An had a productive day. Strolling the supermarket for great deals and food that would last her and her family for three or four days. After a good 10 or 15 minutes of shopping for food. Wang Yi-An walked back home with hands filled with groceries while thinking about how happy her mother would be when she told her she had gotten the internship at Yang Corps.

Wang Yi-An had returned home after a 20-minutes walk from the supermarket. Her home was a small townhouse; he area had a lot of similar looking houses. With lots of townhouses confined together. The townhouse she lived at had two floors. The ground floor consist of the living room, kitchen, and upstairs were the three bedrooms.

For the interview, Wang Yi-An had scheduled herself off work today. Her mother, however, was still at work. She should be off early today. Wang Yi-An couldn't wait to tell her mother the good news.

Wang Yi-An cleaned the house, did the chores and prepared dinner for her and her mother. She put away the groceries and organised the fridge.

With only her mother left, her mother worked full-time,

and she goes to school and work, so it's best if she prepared all the food at home. Wang Yi-An prepared the meal first. She'd prepared them into ready-to-eat proportion; packaged in zip-lock bags. Placed them in the freezer so when they need to grab a bag for lunch, all they needed was to reheat it. The chores required time to accomplish, but Wang Yi-An had patience. After she cooked the meals, bagged them, and placed them in the freezers, she began her next chores.

Their home was small compared to the rich, but a perfect size for Wang Yi-an and her mother. The three bedrooms upstairs each labelled with a homemade sign, the largest room in the house had a sign that said, '*Mom*'. The second biggest room's homemade sign displayed, '*Yi-An*' and the last room at the end of the hallway, the handcrafted sign displayed, '*Yi-Xiu*' Wang Yi-An went to the bathroom and cleaned it up, then she went into each room to vacuum. She was a fast cleaner, and she finished in 20 minutes.

Then she vacuumed the entire home, she would often return to the kitchen to check on her stew for tonight's dinner. Today they were to have beef stew. Her mother's favourite dish. Wang Yi-An had spent the rest of her day, cleaning and preparing meals. The food should last Wang Yi-An and her mother for three or four days.

The time display 6:00 p.m. on Yang Tian-Xu's watch. Tired from all the walking, Tong Yue-Yan seems content, and Yang Tian-Xu had spent the entire day with her. He hoped it would satisfy his mother to hear he spent the whole day with Tong Yue-Yan, and she would leave him alone after this.

A hopeful thought he knew was too good to be true, he asked, "Anywhere else you want to visit?" hoping that this was the last time, and he doesn't have to be her tour guide anymore.

So that the next time his mother asked, he would had no reason to do so, because he had shown her all the places she said she wanted to visit.

"No," she shook her head as she smiled, thinking of how great it was to spend the entire day with Yang Tian-Xu, she hopes she had left him a good impression, and soon they could be something more.

He said, "We should head back." as he saw the time, "It's 6:00 p.m., I should take you home."

"Do you want to have dinner first before we return?" she asked.

He firmly rejected her, "After a long day, it's better if I take you home." Then they exited the theme park and his mother, Mrs Yang called him.

He answered the call, and his mother said. "Tian-Xu, my good son. You should invite Yue-Yan to our home for dinner. I have already invited her aunt to dinner."

Yang Tian-Xu sighed, but he obediently agrees, "Okay." Then he hung up and turned to Tong Yue-Yan and told her, "My mother called, she would like to have you over for dinner and had already invited your aunt. Would you like to come as well?"

Delighted when he offered her, so immediately she said, "Yes! I would love to."

On their way back to the parking lot, he was quiet the entire day, only spoke when she asked. He won't show his irritation, but to make his mother happy, he would do what she said and show her around in City Y, because he knew his mother couldn't force him into marrying someone he doesn't love.

Love, he thought about this word as they reached his car. For sure, he only kept Tong Yue-Yan company, but he felt nothing towards her the entire time.

A gentleman's gesture, as he let Tong Yue-Yan in the passenger's seat first, before he went inside the driver's seat. He buckled up, and he said, "It will be a long drive to Tian-Bo-Fu," he said as he started the engine.

"Tian-Bo-Fu?" she said with surprised, at first she thought they were going to the Yang's family manor in City Y.

The Yang Family called their family mansion, Tian-Bo-Fu, a *siheyuan* style home. *Siheyuan*—a traditional Chinese courtyard home. Built on 25 acres of land, located outside of the central city; it was a long drive there, but when they arrived, the enormous and beautiful traditional style home looked magnificent. It was akin to a palace in an ancient-costume drama or movie.

It was a well-styled courtyard home, modern yet traditional. This had been the Yang Family's main manor for over a hundred years. It wasn't the same Yang Family home as the one during the Song Dynasty where everyone knew it as Tian-Bo-Fu.

Documented in China's history literature, the Tian-Bo-Fu was a gift from the emperor of imperial China, to Yang Ye. Yang Ye was a hero who fought in wars for the emperor, he was the man that started the Yang Family's legend. The manor's name— Tian-Bo-Yang-Fu—was bestowed to them by the emperor. However, over time it named shorten to Tian-Bo-Fu; given to the strongest and bravest military family during the earlier years of the Song Dynasty, 960–1279.

The modern Tian-Bo-Fu was a remodel of the original. Designed and built by Yang Ming-Wa, a direct descendant of the Yang Family, who was Yang Tian-Xu's great-great-grandfather.

Yang Ming-Wa's dreamt of rebuilding the family's legacy and passing the teaching down to his descendants. Even as he accomplished the goals—teaching the ins and out of the business industry, but as the descendant of a military family; he felt something was missing.

Still a peaceful country was better compared to an outbreak of war. However, he wouldn't hesitate to join the army (and be like his ancestors), he longed to revive the Yang's Legacy even on his deathbed.

Over a hundred years, the Yang Family had regained their power and wealth, becoming more prestigious than they were back then. They became one of the wealthiest family households with plenty of reputation in City Y; perhaps the country.

The one who made it all possible was Yang Ming-Wa himself, when he built the home, he called it Tan-Tian-Bo Fu, meaning the new Yang Family's manor. However, over the years that pass, precisely people know the manor as Tian-Bo-Fu.

Yang Ming-Wa had three daughters and a son. His only son was Yang Wei-Bin, his only son. Yang Wei-Bin had two sons, and one of them had passed away at an early age, and his remaining son, Yang Bo-Ting was Yang Tian-Xu's grandfather. His grandfather had a son and a daughter. Yang Fei-Hung and Yang Fei-Fei. Yang Fei-Fei was Yang Tian-Xu's aunt, but she married the mayor in City X, far away from City Y. Rare for her to come to visit, but she tried her best come for the major family events, like great-grandfather's funeral.

Yang Tian-Xu was a newborn when great-grandfather, Yang Wei-Bin passed away. His grandfather, Yang Bo-Ting was still healthy and alive, for an 87-year-old man, he was a healthy man.

Yang Tian-Xu's parents always had dinner at Tian-Bo-Fu on Friday. When his parents got married, they lived in the Tian-Bo-Fu for a while, until they had to move closer to Yang Corps' headquarters. However, Yang Bo-Ting always wanted to see them and his grandson—Yang Tian-Xu, so they made it a tradition to come up visit on Friday and stay for the weekends.

Lately, Yang Tian-Xu had been busy and hadn't visited him for three entire weeks. Grandfather Yang wasn't so happy about that (he demanded to see him today.). Mrs Yang had no choice but to call her son up and tell him to bring Tong Yue-Yan with him. She didn't forget to use this opportunity to introduce her to Grandfather Yang.

From where Yang Tian-Xu and Tong Yue-Yan located, it would take a good hour drive to get to Tian-Bo-Fu. Tong Yue-Yan had always wanted to visit Grandfather Yang, but it wasn't like her, or her family was close to Grandfather Yang.

A long time ago, Yang Tian-Xu's father had a successful business deal with Tong Yue-Yan's parent that started their partnership in City A, they kept contact for future business opportunities ever since. Tonight would be a perfect time, for her to gain good points with Grandfather Yang—furthering the two families relationship.

When they arrived at Tian-Bo-Fu, Tong Yue-Yan was speechless. She never expected it to be so grand; it was like she had taken a step back into the past. Traditional, but had a modern twist to it. The front gate had electronic components that open with the push of a button, allowing them to drive inside. Cameras monitored by the 24-hour security company that always had two security guards.

An elderly lady rushes over to greet them, she was the head of the live-in maids, while they also employed ten to fifteen live-in maids, they were all full-time employees that worked at Tian-Bo-Fu, they also employed their own family chefs.

"Young master, you have come!" the lady smiled at them as she bows her head to Tong Yue-Yan, greeting her. "This way please."

"This is our guest, Miss Tong," he said as he introduces Tong Yue-Yan to the head-maid.

"Hello," the maid greeted her with a slight head-bow. "I am the head of the maids here, I have served the Yang Family for a long time. Please don't just stand there, the Madam and Master Fei-Hung are in the living room, with Grandmaster Yang."

The courtyard scenery was beautiful as a painting, the sight amazed Tong Yue-Yan. Like she had time travelled, venturing into the Emperor's palace.
The girl walking beside him may had been Tong Yue-Yan—but inside Yang Tian-Xu's mind, *If I had known her, perhaps I could bring you here one day?* He thought about all the possibilities. Silent as he smiled thinking about her expression when he shows her this place, *If only you were here.*

The manor shows off the extreme wealth and power of the Yang Family; not only do they own other estates and apartment buildings throughout the country. For sure, the most dominating family within City Y was their home turf.

No families could compare to them here in City Y, not even her Tong Family. However, her Tong Family was also wealthy. Her father was the current mayor of City A, making her family the most prominent in City A. If she were to marry Yang Tian-Xu, this political marriage would benefit both families. Determined herself become Yang Tian-Xu's bride; her purpose was to win Grandfather Yang's heart.

The time was 6:45 p.m., while Tong Yue-Yan attempt to gain favour points with Grandfather Yang. Tong Yue-Yan.

Wang Yi-An's mother had just got home. Happy to see her daughter had already prepared food for her. She saw the covered up dinner and saw her precious daughter, Wang Yi-An sleeping at the dinner table.

Mother Wang placed her hand on her head and patted her. "Oh, my sweet little girl. You shouldn't sleep out here. You'll catch a cold if you sleep like that."

Wang Yi-An made a small groan before she lifted her head up for a yawn. "Mommy? Welcome home!" she jumped in her mother's arm for a sweet hug.

Her mother smiled and laughed, "My baby girl, still acting like such a baby!"

"I will always be your little girl!" she smiled and babied to her mother. "Mom, I got the internship." She said as she laid her head on her mother's chest.

"Really? Already? Don't they wait for a while to announce their accepted interns?" her mother wonders as she pats Wang Yi-An's head.

"Well, the hiring managers today liked me, Mr Tseng said he wanted to hire me right away and asked if I could start work in two weeks. He said he'll send me an email soon." She said as she lifted her head up to see her mother's face.

"Wang Yi-An, you are just too innocent. Sometimes

they'll say that they probably say that to everyone!"

"Really?" she questioned herself, "Oh well, I'm sure I would get hired. Who do you think I am?"

"My daughter." She laughed and giggled at her as she pats her hair, "Of course, they'll hire you, my daughter is so talented! Come, let's reheat dinner and eat, Mommy is hungry."

"Yes!" she and her mother grabbed the plates and reheated the food. They had dinner at around 7:15 p.m., after dinner Wang Yi-An would help her mother do the dishes, and told her mother to go to bed earlier. She also had an early shift in the morning, so she washed-up and went to bed, nothing exciting.

CHAPTER 5
Someday, I'll bring you home

Wang Yi-An was already in bed by 9:00 p.m. sleeping like a baby, peacefully. Meanwhile, at Tian-Bo-Fu the heiress to the Tong Family came to visit Grandfather Yang. She regretted not being able to bring gifts with her to visit Grandfather Yang, this was because Yang Tian-Xu told her it wasn't necessary for gifts, so they didn't drop by a gift store. Still, Tong Yue-Yan felt ashamed to come empty-handed.

The moment the maids notified Grandfather Yang that his grandson had arrived, Grandfather Yang became too excited and cheerful. Gifts? He couldn't care less about them. He was just happy to see his grandson; Yang Tian-Xu, "Tian-Xu! My boy! Finally, you decide to visit this old man!" The 87-year-old man wore a male *hanfu*. A *hanfu*—an old traditional Chinese outfit. He genuinely likes the traditional styles, and it indeed suited him because it makes him feel comfortable.

"Ye-ye!" He called his grandfather, '*Ye-Ye*'. It means grandfather, and it was one of the most loving ways for a grandson to call his grandfather. Grandfather Yang came over, and Yang Tian-Xu got pulled into his grandfather's embrace. "You were supposed to be a filial child, yet, you take over three weeks to come to visit this old body of mine?"

"Ye-Ye, you might be old, but you are still very healthy! Work kept me busy, but I am here now, aren't I?"

"Work?" he lifted his eyebrows, then he looked over to Tong Yue-Yan. "She looks like she could be much work!"

Grandfather Yang laughed and smiled at the girl. Making her face glowing red. Yang Tian-Xu immediately explains and introduce her, "This is Miss Tong Yue-Yan, she is the daughter of Mayor Tong from City A, she just came to City Y, so I took her out to show her around the city as a host."

"Hello, Elder-Mr Yang." modest and polite as she lowers her head and bows at Grandfather Yang.

"Oh please, call me Grandfather Yang! No need for politeness, we lived in a new era! It's great to see you kids respect your elders, but that made me feel like a thousand years old!"

"Grandfather Yang, I am sorry I had not borne you any gifts today, for sure tomorrow I shall bring you some gifts as an apology."

"Nonsense, child! Your aunt came today bearing plenty of gifts! I'll feel ashamed to receive any more."

Tong Yue-Yan was happy to hear her aunt had brought gifts to Grandfather Yang. She thought, "Yes! Thank you, auntie, I won't forget to thank you later!"

"Come-come. Let's go enjoy a good dinner. Today's menu is your favourite dishes Tian-Xu! I had the chefs made them for you!" Grandfather Yang was a jolly old man. He loved to have guests over at his house, which had made Tong Yue-Yan less nervous.

They followed Grandfather Yang to the dining room, and

they sat down at their respected seating. The table was a round-table, Tong Yue-Yan sat next to her aunt, on the left side. Yang Tian-Xu's mother would have him take a seat next to Tong Yue-Yan, and she'd be in the seat next to him on his left hand, then her husband, Yang Fei-Hung. Grandfather Yang sat in the seat to the left of his son, it was a roundtable, so the middle would be undetermined from each person's point of view, but Grandfather Yang would undoubtedly be at the centre, in the Head-of-the-House seat.

The maids served them the dishes like they would be in a five-star Chinese restaurant. At the top of each seating area were public chopsticks and spoons. Used so they could pick their food into their plates. The table had a rotating centre in which the side dishes positioned.

Tong Yue-Yan felt like a new bride that just married into the Yang Family; she couldn't hide her smile. She would use her public chopstick to take food for Grandfather Yang's plate. The man was delighted, and he felt that this Miss Tong was indeed a wonderful girl. He would be more than glad to have her as his granddaughter-in-law.

Mrs Yang put all kinds of good words about Tong Yue-Yan, telling Grandfather Yang how great she be as her son's bride —all while they waited for them to arrive. Grandfather Yang had a perfect impression about Tong Yue-Yan, not only was she pretty, she was very knowledgeable about the Yang Family's history. As a man—so proud of his family heritage, he felt delighted to hear Tong Yue-Yan talk about how much she —admired the Yang Family.

Just like that Tong Yue-Yan had bonded into the Yang Family. Tong Yue-Yan had a fantastic talent to make other adores her. However, Yang Tian-Xu had remained unaffected by this. His heart and mind wandering off to a random stranger he knew nothing about! Yang Tian-Xu thought it would be impossible to tell his family that he had fallen in love at first sight, and the girl was undoubtedly not Tong Yue-Yan.

He doesn't think he could ever tell his families he fell for some random girl. Yang Tian-Xu remains quiet for a while. Until his grandfather jokily asked him, "If only I could see you married and have my great-grandchildren, I would be happy to pass then."

"Ye-Ye! Don't say that! Ye-Ye will live long enough to see your great-great-grandchildren."

"Oh, I could only wish so." Grandfather Yang hasn't seen his grandson in a while, so naturally, he would pull him over into the garden to enjoy the night scenery at Tian-Bo-Fu.

With just him and his grandfather, Grandfather Yang didn't push around the bush and straightforwardly asked, "You seem absent-minded, and uninterested in Miss Tong. Is there someone else you might have liked?"

Surprised at how sharp his grandfather was, his parents couldn't even tell that he had no interest in Tong Yue-Yan. However, Grandfather Yang certainly noticed it.

"Ye-Ye..." lost for words he didn't know what to say, but Grandfather Yang reassured him.

"My good grandson, listen to Ye-Ye's suggestion. Miss Tong Yue-Yan may seem to be the most compatible woman for you. However, if you have someone else you love deeply, don't be afraid to bring her home to meet Ye-Ye. Ye-Ye will give you his full support, no matter who you love."

Yang Tian-Xu and his grandfather had a good relationship. His grandfather always doted on him. After hearing his grandfather's words, he felt like he could tell his grandfather everything. Before Yang Tian-Xu could open his mouth, Mrs Yang interrupted him. His mother called out, "Tian-Xu! It's getting late; you should take Ms Tong and Yue-Yan home."

"Yes, mother." He replied and turned to his grandfather to face him. "Don't you worry, Ye-Ye. When I meet the girl of my dream; I definitely will bring her here to meet you!" he gave a slight head bow to his grandfather and left.

Yang Tian-Xu looked at the time; 9:30 p.m. as it shows on his watch. As he tried to remain quiet the entire trip towards the Tong Family's villa. He was driving so Tong Yue-Yan, and her aunt wouldn't want to disturb him. However, they mentioned delightful things about Grandfather Yang.

Yang Tian-Xu would merely nod his head, and occasionally he would thank them for their kind words. Tong Yue-Yan felt that today wasn't long enough, but to Yang Tian-Xu today so too long, he can't wait until it's all over. After he dropped them back to the Tong villa. Peace, at last, he can drive home alone without being pried at. His parents were to stay with Grandfather Yang for the weekend, so Yang Tian-Xu had the Yang Family's Estate to himself, by the time he reached home it was already 11:05 p.m.

The western architecture of the Yang Family's manor in the city differed completely from Tian-Bo-Fu. Instead of being traditional and grand, it was just a fancy modern mansion on top of a hill. With two live-in maids on the clock 24/7, one or two part-timers come in and out from the back door, cleaning, gardening and cooking for him and his parents. However, at night-time, the manor becomes a big empty house.

After a long day, Yang Tian-Xu headed for a quick shower to freshen up. Afterwards, he got out of his private washroom, and he was drying his hair with a towel around his neck. As he sat down at his desk, he opens his laptop and checks his emails. Assistant Tseng had sent him a detailed report about each student that was interview today. He even sent attached documents to his most recommended students. There was Wang Yi-An's name on his most recommended applicant lists.

It was a shame that there were no photos, however, unlike other companies, at Yang Corps, they do not need the applicator to attach their photo. Yang Corps wasn't about looking good, but talents. They need a capable employee, not a pretty ornament. However, that didn't mean they can't or would discourage those who want to attach a portrait to send in with their application. Some applicant had photos some didn't. The images did not appeal to Yang Tian-Xu, he first looked at the recommended ones by his assistant instead of reading through the entire reports. He messaged his Assistant on his smartphone and said, "Okay, send them an official letter."

It might be late, but his assistant was always on alert, as soon as he received the message. He messages back, "Yes, sir!" Then Assistant Tseng would jump out of his bed, accidentally waking his wife up, supposed to be asleep beside him, and confused she asked him. "What's wrong?" she was still half-awake.

Tseng Kuan-Yin patted her back and told her, "Nothing, it's work. Just go back to sleep, babe." after she heard his reply, she would return to her sleep. He looked over at this sleeping wife and gave her a kiss before he went over to his desk. He opened his laptop, and with his already drafted emails, he immediately clicks on the send button, he was fast and efficient. Then took his cell phone, and he sent another message to President Yang. "Okay boss! All sent!"

Yang Tian-Xu replied from his phone, "Okay. Have a good rest."

"You too boss!" Assistant Tseng breaths out, as he felt the burden lifted from his chest. He climbed back inside his bed and held his wife in his arms as he rubbed her big round belly.

With the last message sent to him from Assistant Tseng, he didn't bother replying. Yang Tian-Xu drops his entire body down on his bed, the silent gave him peace. It was already late, the day may make his body tired, but his mind was still awake. He thought, *If only my family would like you too*, with those thoughts he gradually fell asleep.

Wang Yi-An wakes up from the alarm that went off at 6:00 a.m. sharp. She got out of bed; hit the shower while she brushes her teeth under the hot running water, she got ready fast within 15 minutes.

Hair still wet as she rushed to dry them with a single towel. Regardless of how damp her hair was, she sped out of the house. On a usual school day, she would have grabbed two bags of the prepared food she made last night and place them in her lunch bag, but because it was a Saturday. No school and only work, her workplace was at a restaurant, and the owner provides her food; packing lunch became unnecessary. It was 6:20 a.m. her mother had already left the house at 5:30 a.m. for work.

Wang Yi-An's mother works at a walk-in clinic as a receptionist. The clinic opens every day, 24/7, and her mother would have to start her shifts at 6:00 a.m. every day. The clinic was only about a 15-minutes ride from their home, but they don't drive so taking the bus requires them to be early.

Wang Yi-An's shift starts at 7:30 a.m. The restaurant she works at was nearby, it's not like they needed a car, when buses in City Y runs 24/7; it was cheap and convenient as they lived closed by a bus station, just a block away from home. Paying for insurances every month would get expensive, and gas prices go up, and only a limited amount of parking spots for electric cars in their neighbourhood. It's better to take the bus instead of owning a car, with bus-stops at every corner it's just more affordable for them.

Living nearby her workplace, she had a bike she used to travel around with, every day she would stroll around her campus, work, and ride her bike home. The restaurant was so close by, she could walk if she wanted, but she loved her bike, so she used it every day.

Wang Yi-An and her mother had to save as much money as possible. Their little home was a recent purchase her mother invested in. They need to pay for mortgages and house bills. Wang Yi-An does not want to be a burden on her mother anymore. She worked hard for her allowance since she was old enough to wash dishes.

The restaurant Wang Yi-An worked at named, 'Happiness' and her mother used to work there at night-time as a dishwasher when she was still only a fetus. Now she was a lot older, she can help out; so her mother stopped during the night and focus at her job at the clinic. Wang Yi-An often comes here to work during her summer vacations since she was young.

Wang Yi-An had a close relationship with the owner, almost like she was a second mother to Wang Yi-An, the owner was a widower, with a son who was five years older than her. He used to watch over her and play with her a lot when she was younger. However, when children grew older, they changed, but they all treated each other like family. The owner, Madam Fung always wanted to have a daughter like Wang Yi-An. She hoped that her son would marry Wang Yi-An, but who could have thought their relationship was nothing more than a brother-sister feeling.

Wang Yi-An rode her bike and parked in her usual spot; she bent down to lock it in place. As she was locking her bike, someone ruffled her hair, "Hey!" she shouted, "stop that!" as she got up and shooed the man away, he was the owner's son, Fung Qi-Wei.

Fung Qi-Wei was average in looks, but like an older brother to Wang Yi-An, he loves ruffling her hair and annoys her. "You came early today." He said as he smiled at her.

"Why should I have come later?" she ridiculed him as she shooed his hands away. Yet, he still attempts to try again.

He laughed, "Okay, okay, thank you for coming so early! I need your help in the kitchen today!"

She replied "Okay!" to him happily like a little girl, and they would walk into the restaurant together, Fung Qi-Wei would place his hands on her shoulder and ruffled her hair again like she was a little girl. Of course, she would be mad and tried to fix her hair as they got in.

The restaurant was almost like a 24/7 restaurant, they closed shop for two hours from 4:00 a.m. to 6:00 a.m. Madam

Fung and her son, Fung Qi-Wei were the owners since it first opened, left to her by her late husband. The mother and son often work together, but they hire other staff members to cover their shifts when they aren't around. Wang Yi-An had worked for them for so long, they trusted her and gave her the managing position at the young age, and most of the time she'll help them deposited money in the bank for them. However, they want her to focus more on school, so she only managed on the weekends.

Happiness Restaurant was a bustling restaurant on the weekend as more people were reluctant to cook on their days off. Regularly, on the weekend the mother and son would take the days off and leave everything to Wang Yi-An. But, during good weather, they would come back and help host the busy crowd. It was a beautiful day outside; no one wants to stay cooped up inside. Spring was an excellent time for businesses to be promoted—specifically on the weekends. So Madam Fung and Fung Qi-Wei came in for work today.

After a long day of work, Wang Yi-An worked hard the entire day, and before she realised, it was already 10:00 p.m. On the weekends she would always get off this late, while on weekdays she had a shorter shift, depending on her school. Madam Fung sometimes worried about Wang Yi-An, because she worked too hard. Madam Fung paid her under-the-table and gave her cash every day, all the staff members shared the tips, once a week they would receive their tips. Wang Yi-An received her pay daily, and before she went home, Madam Fung paid her salary, they smile at each other before Wang Yi-An returned home.

The entire day, Wang Yi-An had been busy, but what about Yang Tian-Xu? The weekends were his days off, he didn't have to work hard while in school. Because his parents were wealthy, unlike Wang Yi-An, who had to work while attending school. He works a simple 9:00 a.m. to 5:00 p.m., Monday to Friday, as the President of Yang Corps. Such a tremendous difference between the two.

CHAPTER 6

I Like You!

The most anticipating *Day of her Life* had arrived for Wang Yi-An. Her official letter of acceptance—from Yang Corps' internship program—had been sent to her late at night; although it was an email, it was still official.

Jumping with joy as she received it in her 'Inbox', she told Madam Fung and Fung Qi-Wei, "Auntie! Brother Fung! I got the acceptance letter from Yang Corps!"

They both cheered with her and smiled because they were proud of her. They wanted her to take the day off tomorrow to rest; however, Wang Yi-An wanted to work and make extra cash. Rejecting the offer, she continued with her duties.

Two more weeks before she officially works for Yang Corps. During these two weeks, Wang Yi-An worked at the restaurant every day, until her school begins next term. She had an internship at Yang Corps for the entire summer. Still, she needed to make enough money so that she could help her mother pay off the mortgage as soon as possible. Wang Yi-An's long-term goal was to have her mother retire early and enjoy life. Wang Yi-An's mother was a single mother, and she worked so hard to raise her by herself. She wants to give all the best to her mother.

For two weeks, Yang Tian-Xu made excuses to his parents,

telling them how overwhelming it was at work. The business project with Jin Qi-Long and his company Faithful Gold Enterprise was very demanding, but he could handle it. Still, he told his friend, Jin Qi-Long to cover for him.

It was unusual for Yang Tian-Xu to make this request, so Jin Qi-Long accepted his request unquestionably. Often Mrs Yang would call Jin Qi-Long to ask him why he wouldn't answer her calls, curious about Yang Tian-Xu's whereabouts. Jin Qi-Long would tell her they were in meetings and Yang Tian-Xu was too focused to answer his phone.

Yang Tian-Xu wanted to avoid his parents, so he stayed at Yang Corps most of the time. He knew his parents would pressure him to date Tong Yue-Yan, but he was a man who knew exactly what he wanted.

Each day, he returned to the coffee shop, looking out at the same window, same seat, he would watch the street. Rather, he was on his way to or getting off work, even during his days off. He always paid attention to the roads, walking more often than he would usually. Yang Tian-Xu hoped that one day, he could meet *her* again.

His train of thought kept him spaced-out the entire day, with each passing day, he became irritated easier, his assistant noticed the change in his behaviour. Strange, but Assistant Tseng chose to remain silent. Until the end of the second week, Friday, the supposed last day of April.

Countless times he thought he could see *her* again, plenty of ways he would greet *her*. He replays the many possibilities of him meeting *her* again. When he does, perhaps he should ask for *her* phone number? *How could he ask her that?* He ruffled his hair as he sat in his desk, thinking. He would be a stranger to *her*—why would she give him her number? Probably, he would try to stalk *her* first? Find out where she lives, works, or go to school.

After that, he could pretend it was a coincidence to meet *her* one day. Wait... Wouldn't that make him suspicious and creepy?

Oh God, help me.

He had both his hands covering his forehead as a thought came to him. Maybe he could pretend he lost his phone and needed to make a call and ask *her* if he could borrow *her* phone? That way he can thank *her* for letting him use *her* phone, then he can get *her* number, and *her* name!

"Ah!" he let out a frustrated expression that startles Assistant Tseng. Yang Tian-Xu seems to be in his deep thoughts, he lost his mind, doesn't know what to do with himself. Those trains of thoughts in Yang Tian-Xu's mind kept going on endlessly. He ruffled his head in depression. He asked himself out loud, "Just how pitiful am I?"

"Ah? Boss?" His assistant finally brought out the courage to ask him, after two weeks. He noticed that President Yang had acted oddly ever since two weeks ago. "Is there something wrong?"

"No, it's nothing. I had a long night." He replied as he pushes the question off like it was nothing, the tone of his voice seems depressing, of course, Assistant Tseng didn't want to pry.

Yang Tian-Xu wanted to talk about it, but he didn't. Even when it was killing him inside, he wondered how he could go about asking a stranger out? He must be crazy; he had only met *her* once. It was not like he had a whole conversation with *her*, he laid eyes on *her* once. There wasn't even a single word of exchange between them. It had already been two weeks. Nevertheless, the images of her smiling at him remains fresh in his mind.

She wasn't really smiling at him, he wasn't sure of it. She was pushing the cart for the old-lady while laughing and smiling. At that time, Yang Tian-Xu was waiting for them to pass in his car. Did she see him? Did she smile as thanks for waiting? His reaction was silence for a minute before he screamed, "Ah!" He became frustrated with himself again, and this time he'd slammed his hands onto the desk hard, Assistant Tseng's eyes almost pop out of their socket from the shock.

"What's wrong? What's wrong?" His head sways back and forward, keeping a lookout for danger. He thought, "Something in the room?" Assistant Tseng questioned himself as he continued looking around. He noticed nothing odd in sight, he asked, "Are you feeling sick, boss?"

"I said it was a long night." an irritable tone in his voice, he wanted to be left alone as he replied to him.

Assistant Tseng felt awkward, "Well then, boss, I will go through the interns' schedule once more, and get that sorted out for you to view and sign for approval."

Supporting his head with one hand while the other shooed Assistant Tseng away. Tseng Kuan-Yin took it as a signal to leave him be.

Assistant Tseng returned to his office and finished up the schedule for the interns. This year Yang Corps selected only three interns, and he did the selecting himself personally on behalf of President Yang. Assistant Tseng took his job seriously, he double checked, and sometimes he would triple check for errors before he sends President Yang anything. Making sure for the third time.

Meetings after meetings, it packed Yang Tian-Xu's schedule. Need to meet with partner companies which hosted their products and events in Yang Corps Mall. The marketing and advertisement department of Yang Corps still need a Head-General manager, and with such a busy schedule—he was busy to the extreme. Unable to find a suitable candidate for the position, he worked twice as hard.

Yang Tian-Xu had a lot on his hands. Assistant Tseng could somehow understand President Yang's stress. "Boss seems stressed lately!" So he should help take some load off President Yang's shoulder. The new interns knew a manager from the M&A (Marketing and Advertising) department would mentor them throughout their internship. Assistant Tseng assigned them to an Art Director, Mr Han. Mr Han would be an outstanding mentor for them.

Mr Han loved teaching interns, and would never stop talking about passion. Assistant Tseng nodded his head in his third checks and sent out the schedule for the three interns, and a copy to the Art Director, HR Manager, Vice-President and President Yang.

Yang Tian-Xu opened the email and took a quick look at the documents. He signed to show his approval of the schedule. Send back to Assistant Tseng, and then he continued working on other contracts that needed his signature. A quick day passed by in a blink of an eye, day transcending into the night, and soon before he realised the weekend had arrived, repeating his everyday life, still wondering when he could meet *her* again.

The weekends were as busy as every other weekend in Happiness Restaurant; Wang Yi-An worked hard and returned late every day, but tonight she left work earlier, this was because she would have to start the internship tomorrow morning. Excited for her first day, Monday became her long-awaited day of the week. She waited for two weeks, waiting for tomorrow to come.

Wang Yi-An was too excited, she couldn't sleep. She got ready for bed, but she stayed awake in the living room as she waited for her mother to return home. Her mother said she would be home as soon as she could, so Wang Yi-An stayed up. The sounds of the doorknob twisted along with the keys rustling alerted Wang Yi-An. As the door opens, she rushed over to greet her mother.

"Mommy, you're home!" She said as she falls into her mother's arms. Her mother just returned from work, right when the time was 7:00 p.m. Wang Yi-An had eaten first already and saved her mother food in the refrigerator, easy to reheat in the microwave.

Wang Yi-An was a baby at heart, she wanted to see her

mother and made her cradle her before she goes to bed. So she waited, and a big warm hug as she held her, acting like she was still a little girl. When Wang Yi-An was little, she would hug her mother like this when she wanted something.

"Yes, yes! Why is my little An-An such a baby?"

"Mom! I love you!" she said and kissed her mother on her cheek, her mother smiled and patted her head.

"I love you too." as her mother let out a peaceful smile.

"After my job gets stable, I want you to retire early and enjoy life. I never want you to worry about money problems ever again!" Determined for her mother to have a better life, she felt like her mother deserved it, and she hated having to see her mother return home late at night.

Sure, tonight she came home at a regular hour, but there would be days her mother worked late and won't be home until morning! For the past two weeks, her mother came home late at night, sometimes even past midnight. Wang Yi-An worried about her mother to the point she couldn't even sleep.

Her mother sighed, "An-An." As she patted her daughter's back and said, "Mommy is thrilled to have you as my daughter."

"Hm!" she smiled and gripped her mother in her embrace, "I'm happy to be your daughter too."

"Okay," her mother said as she let go of her, "You should sleep early, don't you start your internship tomorrow?."

"Hm!" she nodded happily, "But I want you to tuck me in!" Her mother smiled, and told her, "You're 22 years old now! Stop being such a baby! Go now, go to sleep."

"Hm!" she nodded her head with a smile and head to her

bedroom. Wang Yi-An slept in peace that night.

Meanwhile, Yang Tian-Xu could not fall asleep. For the past two weeks, he had many sleepless nights like this. Only him in his room, he said out loud, "God, Dear Lord. If you want to torture me, please stop it and end my life right now! Stop making me suffer. If not, please just once more, please let me meet her! Just one more time!" Yang Tian-Xu covered the bedsheets over his head. He ruffled around, again and again, he turned right and left, he tried to count sheep. It all makes him seem restless, but the only thing that could keep him calm were the images of *her* smile again.

Sentimental thoughts emerged inside his mind, fast asleep, he dreamt about *her*. Every night, he had dreams of *her*.

Her smile, it looked so innocent when she smiled at the dog. He wished he was the dog, inside his dream, he transformed from the dog into himself. Together he would help her pushed that old lady cart, she would smile at him, laughing at him. In his dream, he could hold her tight. Wanting to give her a soft kiss, but as he leans in for the kiss. The goddamn alarm went off. *Again.* For the past two weeks, every time he'd be close enough to kiss *her*, he'd roll off his bed with the shrill sounds at 8:00 a.m.

Yang Corps was not only a business building but also a shopping mall. Although, every individual owner had their hours for their business. The Yang Corps entrances were open 24 hours a day, with a 24-hour security unit. However, their offices were open from 8:00 a.m. and closed at 5:00 p.m. Yang Tian-Xu always arrived at the office at 9:00 a.m and would stay until 5:30 p.m.

The day arrived, today Wang Yi-An came early to Yang Corps' headquarters. Her orientation was not until 9:00 a.m but being early kept her mind at peace. The other two interns, Kwon Li-Mei and Liang Shing, arrived early after they introduced each other they all went to enjoy a cup of coffee before they return for the orientation. When they returned, the receptionist told them to wait in the lobby. They sat there waiting, chit-chatting with one another.

They found out they were about the same age; however, Liang Shing was the oldest. Being two years older than Kwon Li-Mei, and three years older than Wang Yi-An, he was indeed the oldest. He wanted to be sure he could get in Yang Corps, and so he had completed his degree while Wang Yi-An and Kwon Li-Mei were in their third years. Kwon Li-Mei went to an expensive university, and Wang Yi-An went to a cheap third rate college. Not only does Kwon Li-Mei had a pretty face, but she also seems to be quite an intelligent beauty, but she sure loves to gossip, especially about President Yang.

"Did you know in the *Country's Top 10 Magazine*, they featured our President Yang! He's ranked as the hottest and most desirable bachelor!" with a copy in her hands as she waved, sure enough, Yang Tian-Xu's photograph as the magazine's front cover.

"It says here in the Fun-Facts section; Those who worked with President Yang Tian-Xu says he is strict at work, but fun when not. It also says in the Fun-Facts; If this country has an award for the most filial son, President Yang Tian-Xu would eventually win that award leaving others a milestone away! Oh my God! He is so—my dream guy!" Kwon Li-Mei pointed her finger at Yang Tian-Xu's face in the picture, like she was petting his face and what-not, but Wang Yi-An wasn't paying attention. She had a sketchbook out and was busy drawing the lobby area.

"*Whoa*, you are very talented." Liang Shing said as he was sitting in the middle between the two girls. He listens to Kwon Li-Mei gossips on his left side, but he would turn over and saw Wang Yi-An sketching on his right side.

Wang Yi-An smiled and said, "Thanks." The three of them waited until the clock turned to 8:45 p.m. Assistant Tseng arrived and saw them and said, "You youngsters sure are early today. Excited?"

"Yes," they said in unison. He smiled and said, "Okay, let's get you kids started." Assistant Tseng asked them to follow him, and he explained the overall structure of Yang Corps, as they walked into the elevator going to the seventh floor. He told them the history, and most important, he asked them.

"Anyone here watches the historical drama, Legend of the Yang Family?"

"Oh, I love that drama!" Kwon Li-Mei was excited about it, because of the drama, she had chosen Yang Corps and not Pan holdings Inc.

"That was my favourite drama of all time!" Liang Shing couldn't help it, but he also expressed his love for the drama. However, Wang Yi-An was simple as she said with little expression, "I don't have time to watch dramas."

They all looked at Wang Yi-An in silent, saying nothing else, they continued as they got off the elevator, the doors opened to reveal the busy office of Yang Corps. Each person was busy doing their job, most were on the computer typing, while somebody else was on a call line. The atmosphere was overall chaotic, and standing to the side chattering away was the Art Director Mr Han, and the President, Yang Tian-Xu. Yang Tian-Xu had his back faced towards them, face to face with Mr Han, they could see Mr Han, but can't see President Yang's face as they walked in, but Assistant Tseng knew it was President Yang from his back alone, he called out to him. "President Yang!"

Yang Tian-Xu was busy instructing Mr Hans, "I have high hopes for the new interns, I hope you can guide them towards success."

"Don't worry Pres, you know I might be old, but I'm still capable!" Mr Han laughs.

As President of Yang Corps, Yang Tian-Xu wanted to double check that the new interns could keep up with the quality of their productions and ensuring them as many hands-on experiences as possible.

"You have my complete trust, Mr Han. I thank you for your hard work."

Mr Han nodded his head, but when suddenly, Assistant Tseng called out to him. "President Yang!"

Yang Tian-Xu turned around, and as Assistant Tseng continued, "Here are our new interns."

When he turned his head, he saw *her*. Wang Yi-An—standing behind Assistant Tseng. His body became frozen, like time stopped, unable to comprehend his surrounding. His assistant's voice faded out, and his sight only focused on *her*. Assistant Tseng and the other two interns, along with Wang Yi-An approached closer and closer, Yang Tian-Xu couldn't see anyone else but *her*. Once they reach him, she was only an arm's length away. If he wanted to grab *her*, he could. Going mayhem with insanity, he pondered again, *This isn't a dream, is it?*

Lost within his own thoughts—he could not hear Assistant Tseng's voice as he explained to the interns their duties as interns—what the company's expectation should be and so on. Assistant Tseng introduced him and Mr Han and their respective position within Yang Corps.

"Mr Han is the best mentor you kids could only dream of," he said as he laughs, "He'll be your mentor for three months, and write an evaluation for every one of you. Trust me when I say you kids have the best luck ever!"

"Oh stop it, Assistant Tseng! You're making me blush!" While Mr Han and Assistant Tseng joked with one another. They laughed and talk about how many years they had worked at Yang Corps. Everyone was feeling chilled and casual.

Every one but Yang Tian-Xu. His heart raced, his mind went blank, unable to process the reality happening before his eyes. Their voices echoes, fading in and out, along with everyone else in the background, just as they greeted one another, shaking hands along the way. He could only see *her*, everyone else was a blur.

Although the interns didn't reach their hands out to shake with President Yang as they felt inferior to his status. They gave a simple head bow to greet him. Just when Assistant Tseng told them to follow Mr Han where he could assign them each a workstation.

They walked past President Yang one by one, Wang Yi-An was the last one, she was at the end of the line-up. She was the last person to pass by him. Like it was an instant reaction, he reached out a hand and grabbed her arm and pull her in towards him—he shouted aloud—loud enough for everyone in the office to hear him.

"I like you!"

CHAPTER 7

Dear Lord...

His large hand grabbed onto her tiny arm, pulled her in towards him. She lost balance for a short second, but as she was about to fall into his arms, she kept herself together and not slip. His tug had a slight force to it when he pulled her in, she let out a minor moan, "Ah!"

Everyone heard the loud shouts, turning their heads to watch as they became more curious, then as they all listened to the three words coming from their President Yang's mouth, "I like you!" they became startled by the catching rings attached to his masculine voice. Yang Tian-Xu stared deep into Wang Yi-An's eyes for a second longer. Still, he kept his grip onto her arm, tight.

Nobody could possibly understand his suffering, his long waits at the coffee shop. Two weeks he waited for a chance to meet her again. It felt like the first time he saw her, only this time his heart beats faster, almost like his heart could jump out of his chest. Dreams of her night after night, like an impulse remembered by his body after a constant repeat. He acted on his impulse.

At first, Yang Tian-Xu disregarded the crowd stares, and he looked straight into her eyes. Her eyes reflection stared back at him. Yang Tian-Xu thought how piercing her eyes appears to be (like it stared straight into his soul), mesmerised by them. It embarrassed him after he realised what he had done.

"I like you to operate under my supervision instead of Mr Han." A quick recovery from an embarrassing confession.

"Oh, its just works," The crowd heard his speech and return their focus and attention elsewhere.

He thought it was an excellent save. Not wanting to appear as a creep or like a pervert, he created this excuse. He would need to thank the Lord later, but now he needs to make sure she stays by his side.

"But, President Yang, we have already assigned her as my intern. Along with those other two." confused, Mr Han wasn't sure if he had received the correct schedule, so he rechecks it on his cell phone. He was always the one in charge of young interns why the change now? When had this regulation changed? Assistant Tseng was just as confused as Mr Han.

Assistant Tseng eyes widen, he opened his cell phone to check and recheck his schedule, "President Yang, you signed and approved to have Miss Wang as Mr Han's intern, your signature is right here." he pointed to the electronic signature on his phone screen.

"I know that, but having three interns under one supervisor might be stressful for Mr Han. It's better to have a one-on-one mentorship instead."

They stood there in silence as they listen to President Yang speak. Although, it's all bullshit—made upon an impulse to cover his sudden confusion. They stood still and nodded, "Oh, that makes sense." Mr Han nodded his head and agreed with the new arrangement.

"Okay, so who do I get as my intern? Now I can put all of my focus and teaching on this one special person." Mr Han was excited as he rubs his hands together. At first, he felt overwhelmed—because of him becoming older—but he still believed he could handle three interns. Now that a new arrangement in place, he no needs to worry about it as much.

Thanks to the new arrangement of the program, no longer would he worry about the heaps of work; or him being a sloppy teacher. Only one intern to guide and focus on, it's a much better arrangement for him, he prefers it that way.

A quick conclusion made at such short notice; with two Art Directors in the M&A department of the seventh floor. Mr Han, and Mrs Wong, he assigned them each a new intern. He appointed Liang Shing, the male intern to Mr Han. Afterwards, he assigned Kwon Li-Mei as Mrs Wong's intern.

He told Mr Han to bring the female intern to Mrs Wong in her office and tell her about his sudden change in the internship program, and as for Wang Yi-An—she would work under his supervision.

Well, not his exactly, but he said he would 'assign' her as Mr Gu's intern, once he returns from his vacation two months from now. However, Wang Yi-An's internship only lasted three months so she would be Yang Tian-Xu's intern for the first two months, and then he would have to hand her over to Mr Gu for her last month as an intern. *Only if he would be willing.*

"This way we can allow the interns to receive more hands-on experiences, and they can become more productive."

Yang Tian-Xu was truly fit to be the President. He wasn't the president because he was the chairman's grandson. No— Yang Tian-Xu was the company's president because of his natural endowments. A strong ability to have; being able to cook up a random excuse out of thin air. The most amazing part was that everyone buys it. The employees and interns all believed, he was paying attention to their demands and benefits.

"Thank you very much, President Yang!" Wang Yi-An said as she bowed her head low to him. For the first time, she smiled at him, as she raised her head upward, looking at him. "I will treasure this opportunity and do my best!"

Dear Lord, Yang Tian-Xu found himself thinking, *How can you be so wonderful, but cruel to me?* His heart ached again as she smiled at him. He turned about and said out loud. "Okay, follow me. I shall show you the office and explain to you my expectations."

Assistant Tseng was left speechless, "When did Boss thought of the idea? Just now? My God he is a genius!" filled with admiration as he questioned himself silently in his head. Assistant Tseng blinked his eyes and followed along behind them.

Yang Tian-Xu wanted to walk side by side with Wang Yi-An, during the walk, he asked her many questions. "What was your name?" He remembered her name. He saw the intern list and saw her name. But he wanted to ask so he could hear her answer and introduce herself to him.

"My name is Wang Yi-An, people like to call me An-An as my nickname." She responded to him as she walked on his left side.

Yang Tian-Xu thought she had an adorable name. *An-An...* He thought about how he could also call her by her nickname— so he could feel closer to her. "Miss Wang, may I call you An-An, would you mind?"

"Sure. I don't mind." What she replied was straightforward and down to earth. Her response made him feel happy deep down. Still, he should keep his emotion under control. He doesn't want to frighten her or make her uncomfortable.

A heart-aching expression appeared on Assistant Tseng's face, as he thought, "Boss, you never call me Kuan-Kuan and I'd known you for a long time! Years! Years!" It was usual for Assistant Tseng to feel that way.

The first time he met Yang Tian-Xu and worked for him as the assistant, he too mentioned that people like to call him by his nickname. Nevertheless, Yang Tian-Xu told him how un-professional it was for the president to call his assistant by a nickname.

Yet, it was all right for the president to call an intern by their nickname? But not him? 'Boss, how could you be playing favourites already?' Assistant Tseng screamed in his mind. Un-fortunately, he could never be able to show his enmity towards unfair treatment.

As Wang Yi-An, Assistant Tseng, and President Yang walked left Mr Han's department; Mr Han and the two interns stood still, caught by surprised as they watched them disap-pearing into another department.

Kwon Li-Mei said with jealousy in her tone, "An-An is so lucky, she gets President Yang as her mentor! Unbelievable! This is so unfair!"

Mr Han laughed "Or unlucky," he proceeded, "That guy became President because of his own ability, not because of his family background. Not only was he rigorous and exacting. If you could not give him perfection, then you might as well wish you were fermenting for the devil."

Kwon Li-Mei and Liang Shing break a sweat and thought, *Oh, An-An. You poor thing!*

"Anyway!" Mr Han said as he snaps them to reality, "I will conduct you to Mrs Wong. She is just as strict as President Yang. Thus, no need to be jealous." Mr Han gave out a subtle laugh, they turn the corner down the hallway, walking as he said, "Let's go, let's go."

At first, Kwon Li-Mei was relieved about how strict Presi-dent Yang was and was no longer jealous of Wang Yi-An. Now, she fell from being lucky, to unlucky in a short three second mo-ment. Mr Han words brought chills to her spine.

The lucky one today was Liang Shing, his mentor was one

of the best Art Director in the country—who had won countless awards. Mrs Wong was also really successful; in fact, she was one of Mr Han's student. Mr Han knew her so well, and everybody knew her to be just as strict as Yang Tian-Xu.

The three went to Mrs Wong's office, and Mr Han filled her in about the changes. Mrs Wong looked displeased, solely because President Yang created a sudden decision without notifying her, yet she couldn't do anything and had to suck-it-up as a mentor.

Mr Han and Liang Shing left, and before Liang Shing left, he smiled at Kwon Li-Mei and said mockingly, "Good luck!"

Meanwhile, Wang Yi-An walked down the hallway with Yang Tian-Xu beside her with Assistant Tseng trailing behind them. Yang Tian-Xu wanted to know more about Wang Yi-An, so he engaged her in a brief conversation. It was bare, he would call for questions, and she would respond, "I heard you have a photographic memory."

"Yes." a simple reply.

Straightforward, shy, and simple was her personality; this was who she was. Hates engaging in uncalled conversations, and she avoids meaningless conversations as much as possible. It always embarrassed her when she spoke to strangers. With the way she answered him, Yang Tian-Xu felt hopeless. If he didn't ask her, she wouldn't talk to him. But there was a question he wanted to ask her, bottled up inside him for two weeks, it took courage to ask her, "How Old Are You?"

"22." She answered him. She thought it was unnecessary for him to ask about her age.

There was a disappointment in his eyes when he heard her giving simple-straightforward answers. He felt like she did not desire to start a conversation with him. Hence he didn't follow up.

Yang Tian-Xu had a million questions to ask her. He wanted to know her better, but he doesn't want to make her feel overwhelmed, or uncomfortable. He stopped questioning her and felt gratified because he now knows one more thing about her—he did not before.

Yang Tian-Xu could have never guessed what Wang Yi-An was thinking, but his desires to give her the impression he was a decent and friendly man. It was a pity for him that her picture of him was nonexistent. "Why is he asking me so many obvious questions? Isn't all this information on my resume?" She kept silent, but if he knew what she was thinking—Yang Tian-Xu might feel heartbroken.

Assistant Tseng found himself pondering about President Yang's questions, Just how often do President Yang care so much about an intern, that he had asked her so many questions? Was it because he had missed out on the interview? Or perhaps because Wang Yi-An had such a rare talent it intrigued him?

Yang Tian-Xu told her what he expects from an intern, and it was uncomplicated. "Just do your best, and if there were questions, don't feel troubled coming to me for advice."

Wang Yi-An nodded her head as she stated, "Yes, thank you." They continued walking until they contacted the General Manager division.

The Yang Corps seventh floor had many office divisions. Each division works on a different project with different clients. This division; where he assigned Wang Yi-An to had about seven to eight workstations and three office rooms, and a modest meeting room. This division of floor seven looks very similar to the rest of the divisions on the same storey.

Their first day together was nerve-wracking for Yang Tian-Xu, after pulling a stunt like that. Grabbing onto her arms and telling her, "I like You." Although he quickly recovers from it. However, deep inside his heart—those words were his true feelings.

"This is your workstation." He stated as he pointed to the desk. The desk was simply outside of the General Manager office. If he glanced out, he could watch her with no vision obstruction.

"But isn't someone already sitting there?" She asked, as she looks at the desk and there were clear signs that this desk was in fact occupied. It seemed obvious who was sitting there— Assistant Tseng Kuan-Yin—he had a picture of him and his wife on the table. Although, it was only his temporary workstation.

It was both their temporary workstations. Their real offices were upstairs and twice the size. But, there were lots of projects and work to take care of on the seventh floor, they had to move into these offices and desks until President Yang can hire a new General Manager and secretary.

The secretary, Ms Mo was a victim of the missing plane. People named the plane, *Medaria* before it took off, hoping for a safe return. She boarded the plane with the General Manager, Jiang Fei as the secretary. Their objective was to attend a business meeting in a foreign country on behalf of Yang Corps. But, the plane disappeared, tragic because she was only 23 years old.

So, President Yang Tian-Xu had to used Manager Jiang's office temporary, while Assistant Tseng used Ms Mo's secretary desk.

"Assistant Tseng will move back up to the eighth floor, don't worry he has his own office there which is much bigger than a small secretary desk."

When Assistant Tseng heard he had to move all his documents and belonging back upstairs, he was not too happy about it.

'What has gotten into you? Boss? Are you going to kick me back upstairs? There are dozens of work here in this department! Boss, who will serve you?' He thought in silent as he wanted to cry while he packed up his belongings.

While Assistant Tseng was packing up, Yang Tian-Xu told him. "Assistant Tseng, once you're done. I would like you to help An-An settle in, help her out as much as possible." He twisted his body to face Wang Yi-An and told her, "If there is any question don't be afraid to come to ask me for help. I will be in my office." And so he quickly rushes off into his office.

They could witness him run into the office and getting on his computer as he typed away. Inconceivable for them to know what he was typing. It seemed like he was working, however, when he was on the computer to type out business contract proposal, a bunch of cases, that spelt, "WANG YI-AN" repeatedly appeared, obvious his heart was fluttered, he was in shock for a moment, then as he looked up he notices and stop. Quickly, he wiped out the words.

Subsequently, when he saw her two weeks ago, he had never stopped thinking about her. Now that he had known her, he wanted to see her every single day. He now and then looked out the window and watched her getting settled into her desk, and Assistant Tseng finishes his packing.

Without the boss in sight, Assistant Tseng felt the need to complain to Wang Yi-An. "This is all too sudden, sometimes he would make sudden decisions like this and expect me to be accomplished all the task!" He sighs and packed up as he was told.

"Has he always been very impulsive?"

"Not so much, but lately, yes. Yes, He has." He said as he sarcastically nodded.

"I see..." Wang Yi-An wasn't someone who likes to gossip, but she felt like she had taken over Assistant Tseng's desk. "I'm sorry I took your spot."

"Oh, no, no." He stated, "This wasn't my desk to begin. As

President Yang said, I have my office upstairs on the eighth floor. This desk used to be Ms Mo. It's a shame about what happened to her and the General Manager."

"What happened to them?" interested as she was about to take somebody's desk and make it hers.

"You know about the missing plane, *Medaria*. Right?" Assistant Tseng started, and then he explained what had happened to Manager Jiang and Secretary Mo who vanished mysteriously. Her eyes tear up, and a drop of tear falls down on her cheek.

"I'm sorry..." she uttered gently, as she attempted to repress her emotions.

Yang Tian-Xu saw Wang Yi-An sad face, and a tear dropped from her eyes. Immediately he bolted out of his seat. He believed his assistant was bullying her and came over to reprimand him, "She is new, how could you be so petty about a desk with a newcomer? Do you like the desk that much?"

"No, No, I wasn't!" assistant Tseng tries to explain himself, he waves his hands defensively.

Wang Yi-An wiped her tears and said, "No, Mr Tseng had been very nice. It's just... someone very important was also a passenger on *Medaria*."

"I'm... so sorry to hear that." Assistant Tseng felt ashamed, he speaks about the incident like it was zilch. He didn't stop to think about the friends and families of the victims, still mourning for their loss.

Yang Tian-Xu was angry at Assistant Tseng, "Go back upstairs and wait for me in my office!" He looked at Assistant Tseng and wanted to kick him in his rear end, but he did not.

Assistant Tseng had already felt the abuse emotionally. "Oh goddamn, I am in trouble now." He gulped as thought about what trouble he might be in—so he fled with a large box of his belongings.

Yang Tian-Xu had been gentle towards Wang Yi-An, and Assistant Tseng followed orders and went upstairs to wait for him to arrive. Yang Tian-Xu pulled out a hanky from his pouch and handed it to her. Wang Yi-An let out a laugh and smiled at him, "Who still uses a handkerchief nowadays?" Then she pulls out of her pocket a packet of biodegradable tissues. "Thank you very much, President Yang."

She left Yang Tian-Xu speechless for a second, he couldn't believe how fast she could bounce back, but he was glad. He prefers to see her smile, her smiles make his heart skips. Wang Yi-An sat down, and she was ready for anything. Unable to tell she had just cried, however, Yang Tian-Xu felt his heart was at ease, and so he instructed, "You settle in your station first. I will be back soon."

"OK," she asked as she seems surprised, he gave her no assignment, "But, is there a job I can do first?"

"No, not yet. Just sit there until I come back." He fed her a soft smile before he speeds out and he broke into the lift with an angry look on his face.

In the elevator, and the elevator-lady greeted him. Yang Tian-Xu didn't even bother with the woman and quickly reaches out his hand to push the button to the eighth floor. He got off immediately and saw Assistant Tseng's back. He was still making his way to the office with a large box of his belonging in his arms. "Tseng Kuan-yin!" He shouted aloud with anger.

Assistant Tseng heard his name being cried and twisted around. He saw President Yang, looking at him with a furious expression. Yang Tian-Xu went up to Assistant Tseng, with a solemn voice, he said, "I would like you to not make her cry from now on, if she does, you'll be in shit with me."

Assistant Tseng felt like he wanted to cry! He thought of

what he had done was innocent on his part. Yet, he kept it to himself as he thought, 'What have I done wrong?'

"I'm only warning you. Don't make Wang Yi-An cry again. If you make her cry once more, you are very much in trouble with me." After giving Assistant Tseng a warning, he twisted around and walked, then he paused and turned around again and tell him. "After you take your belonging back in the office, arrange for Wang Yi-An to have her new access card done quickly."

"Yes... Yes, sir!" Assistant Tseng didn't know what he'd done amiss, but the boss was showing favouritism towards Wang Yi-An. Then he thought again as he rocked his head. 'Ah, no way! Boss can't like her, they just met! Besides, she's not even pretty...' while he pondered, he became lost, unable to understand, yet he proceeded back towards his original office.

Meanwhile, Yang Tian-Xu rushed back to the seventh floor. And so he hurries towards the general manager's office, as he walked by Wang Yi-An, she smiled at him and stated, "Welcome back, President Yang."

He nodded and lowered his head as he steps back into the office, he shuts the door, and then his heart pounds quickly. Wang Yi-An was still outside, discombobulated as she recalled, "Shouldn't he assign me some work to do?" It was upsetting for her, and she sat there wondering to herself. "What do I do now?"

CHAPTER 8

Smile At Me Again?

After Yang Tian-Xu went back into the general manager's office, he messaged Assistant Tseng with his smartphone, "After you get the new admission card, bring them to me first."

"Yes, boss!" Assistant Tseng messaged him back. But he wondered, 'Why can't I deliver it over to Wang Yi-An directly? I had to walk by her first before I go see him in his office.' Assistant Tseng disregards his confusion. He puts down his belongings in his office, and he rushed to the HR department on level six.

In the Human Resource department; he placed a request for Wang Yi-An's new access card, and because everyone knew he was the president's assistant. They finished his application quickly; his wait time was only ten minutes while others would had to wait longer. When Assistant Tseng received the new access card, he went ahead to message Yang Tian-Xu. "Boss I just received the card. I am on my way back."

The messages appear on Yang Tian-Xu's smartphone, and he messages him back. "Remember to give it to me first!" Assistant Tseng saw the message and wanted to send a sweating emoji, but he did not. He sent him a simple, "Yes sir!"

Yang Tian-Xu put down his smartphone on the table and smiled, he desired to be the first to get her card, and he wanted to be the one to give it to her. Today he felt the happiest all week long! He looked out the small window from his seat. He looked at Wang Yi-An as she sat there at the desk.

Wang Yi-An was still outside waiting; as she sat in the secretary's desk. Sitting around doing nothing—wasn't how she was taught—she was raised to be active in her duties. And so she stood up, approached the door and knocked; the sign on the door displayed, '*General Manager*'. Just as Yang Tian-Xu saw her walking towards the door, he panics for a bit, but then he briskly regains his composure.

"Come in." He said, he sat like a king. Wang Yi-An opened the door and walked in, as she asked him as she closed the door behind her. "Would you like me to help you with anything, President Yang?"

Yang Tian-Xu tried to remain calm as he replied to her. "Not—at the moment. We need to provide you a new access card first."

The interns each received their own access card during orientation. Assistant Tseng explained the importance of these cards, and how to use them. A special coded magnetic stripe on the back of the card; Yang Corps high-end security machines at every door and equipment can only be accessible through the card usage.

With important information on the cards, containing their name, address, height, weight, and identification number; assigned by Human Resource and loaded into their cards. They must swipe or scan each time to use a machine, open a door, or sign-out supplies in the supply room. Each time they swipe or scan their card, it would appear in their record in Yang Corps headquarters.

Assistant Tseng had already told them how to use the access card, without it; entering the upper floor levels would be impossible. In the elevator, the elevator-lady only worked at certain hours, it would be impossible for her to be there 24/7. Sometimes the project would require employees to work overtime in the office.

The access card also functions as the employee's punchcard, because it recorded the time when they entered and exited the building. However, the most critical function of the access card was it double as a bank card, allowing employees to access their payroll.

Employees can use the card like a bank card; using with their fingerprint at any Yang Corps' Bank branches, they can access, and withdraw their pay, or use it directly through other merchant machines.

Wang Yi-An would need the card because of the specialised magnetic strip code. The magnetic strips had both digital coding and physical marking on the access card.

The physical trademark were small engraves that one cannot see with the naked eye; the code markings were encrypted, there had never been a single hacker that can penetrate Yang Corps securities. Both the physical and digital markings on the card made it near impossible to hack.

"A new card?" She questioned. She apparently had one hanging around her neck already.

"Yes." He explained to her the details. "Every floors' division has an access lock and needs a specified authorised key to open. We need to remake your access card so you can open the entrance door to this division."

"Okay, then would you like me to return you this one?" She said as she was about to remove the card from around her neck. Yang Tian-Xu quickly told her, "It's alright, you hold on to that until your replacement comes."

"Oh, then I will hold on to it until then, but what happens to it?" She looked at the card as she gripped it.

"The company has a manufacturer that can recycle old cards. Don't worry too much about it going to waste."

"Okay, anything you want me to do while we wait?"

"No, you may sit and wait until your new access card arrives, this is because you can't even access the computer until you have your new access key. Please just relax for a while until your new card comes." He smiled at her and hoped that she would give him a grin.

"Okay, thank you very much, President Yang, I will be back in my seat until then." Wang Yi-An gave him a slight bow, as she turned around and returned to her seat. Then she pulled out her sketchbook and drew. He felt disappointed as he watched her leave. He really wanted to see her smile at him again.

Yang Tian-Xu kept looking outside, he could watch her draw all day because she had such a peaceful expression on her face. He would sit in his chair and watch her with a smile on his face. He didn't forget to thank the Lord for letting them meet.

Perhaps this is destiny? He found himself thinking about it. A chance of a lifetime had arrived. Yang Tian-Xu become excited about it, he thought, *How do I make her like me?* Her name filled the computer screen, which he quickly noticed. Embarrassed, he selected it all and pressed delete.

He made a curriculum for her. As part of the Yang Corps promise to their interns. Hand-on experience was essential, and he made sure she would gain the most. So he started working out the schedule for her.

Mr Han made Wang Yi-An's previous work schedule. However, because he had practically stolen her from Mr Han. He decided to message Mr Han on his phone. "Can you send me the curriculum you planned for Wang Yi-An?"

Mr Han replied promptly, he worked for Yang Corps for years. He was more than happy to send the previous schedule he made before. In Yang Corp, every division had their own projects and clients. Once Yang Tian-Xu received the timetable, he changed the location and time to the ones his team was on.

Yang Tian-Xu's team comprise him as General Manager. With him, and his assistant, Tseng Kuan-Yin, there was also the art director; Gu Huan.

The first month would focus on Jin Qi-Long's company new product, called "Grace". However, Gu Huan was on a three-month vacation. He won't be back until late June. Yang Tian-Xu planned to have the other Art directors take over Jin Qi-Long's contract. Now he had an intern with no mentor for her. He had to be her supervisor. What does he knows about Art?

With limited knowledge about Art, he still had good taste in art. What others tell him, however, he was not an artist. Yang Tian-Xu looked at Wang Yi-An's art portfolio and thought she was very talented. Perhaps she could assume the responsibility by herself? He thought again, "This will definitely give her enough hands-on experiences."

Grace—the perfume that carries a sweet fragrance. The fragrance smells like a beautiful angel. When a person first inhales the aroma, the scent gives off a feeling; like an angel, ascending from above. The after effect of the smell seems to give those who believe; hope. The perfume truly deserves its name.

First, they must produce the logo design, package designs, and then shoot the promotional commercial. Second, the company; Faithful Gold Enterprise must email the request details to him. Jin Qi-Long wanted the packaging colour to be purple.

The rough draft of the logo was a single feather, and as for the bottle design of the perfume? A heart with two wings on each side, that was the shape he wanted, but the image looks like something very inappropriate, Yang Tian-Xu couldn't even look at it anymore.

Yang Tian-Xu stared at the documents, and he felt like it was off. Unsatisfied, he messages Jin Qi-Long. "Your designs look horrible for a product this elegant. Are you trying to make a condom brand or an energy drink?"

Jin Qi-Long messaged him back with a sweat-laugh emoji, "Is it that bad?"

"Not if your making a commercial for a condom or an energy drink!" Yang Tian-Xu looked back at the design, then he turned to look at Wang Yi-An's art portfolio, and soon decided. *"I have a new intern, perhaps she can design something better for you."*

"Okay sure, I trust your great wisdom, my friend!" Jin Qi-Long felt like he needed to tell Yang Tian-Xu the news, so he called him instead of a text message, "Hey! Also I told you who I wanted as the spokesmodel right?"

"Yes," he sighed at his friend, "had she agreed?"

"Her manager told me she would be interested only after she sees the product herself. Can we both come in on Monday next week? Because of her busy schedule this week I can only get her to come in on Monday next week."

"Yeah, that is fine." Then he ended the call conversation. Although Jin Qi-Long continued to message him back, he flooded his smartphone's mailbox with messages about Lee Yin-Yin and posted her pictures.

It would be natural for Yang Tian-Xu to disregard those messages, never opening them to read. Yang Tian-Xu looked over at Wang Yi-An's personal information on the computer, and added her name into the schedules, now he had her contact information. He saved it in his smartphone as, *'Future Mrs Yang.'* Yang Tian-Xu continues to look at the *'Future Mrs Yang'* on his phone and smiled. A sudden feeling as he realised, "No, too soon." Then he rushed to erased it, and type. *'My secret crush.'* Yang Tian-Xu looked at it for a moment and rocked his head. "No, no—What if she saw it?"!

While Yang Tian-Xu struggles on how to label Wang Yi-An's number in his smartphone, Tong Yue-Yan came by to give Yang Tian-Xu a surprise visit.

It would be unexpected for Yang Tian-Xu to have her visit him, and it would annoy him a little. Tong Yue-Yan had not seen Yang Tian-Xu in four days. She visits him at his home on regularly, and sometimes she would go over to Tian-Bo-Fu to visit his grandfather. Although Yang Tian-Xu tried to avoid her, however, Tong Yue-Yan was determined to maintain a relationship with him.

When Tong Yue-Yan walked in and saw him in the office. Tong Yue-Yan walked closer to the secretary's desk. She saw Wang Yi-An and thought, 'She must be the secretary.' And asked her, "Can you tell President Yang that he has a special guest?" Tong Yue-Yan emphasised the word, special as she smiled.

"Um," Wang Yi-An looked up her and asked her, "Who are you?" Wang Yi-An remain seated, clueless and thought, 'Why don't she go in there herself? Do I have to announce her arrival?' Wang Yi-An stared at Tong Yue-Yan with a confused look on her face.

Tong Yue-Yan felt like her jaw would drop as she thought, 'Who am I? Just who do you think I am? Don't you know I am Miss Tong? The heiress to the Tong Family?' She was pissed at Wang Yi-An, but still, she remained harmonious, and let out a fake smile.

Tong Yue-Yan had many people who would kiss her ass willingly! Plenty of magazines had featured her—and her father—the mayor of City A! She had the looks, the background, and the aura of a princess.

Tong Yue-Yan remains calm and friendly, even if she had to fake it through her teeth, she smiled. Just because Wang Yi-An disregarded her status, she must not show her despisement towards a regular secretary. "My name is Tong Yue-Yan, I'm a *friend* of President Yang," she emphasised on the word friend heavily and gave Wang Yi-An a gentle lady-like smile.

"President Yang is in the office." Wang Yi-An replied with a smile. "You should come in and tell him you're here. Girlfriends shouldn't need to be announcement when they come to visit."

Surprised at first, however, when Wang Yi-An told her those words, she began to thought, 'Oh my, has Tian-Xu told his secretary that I am his girlfriend? Does that mean I am the future Ms Yang?' She smiled to herself and said to Wang Yi-An. "Thank you very much. I will let myself in and see President Yang then."

Tong Yue-Yan was wearing these expensive heels, the height wasn't too extreme, but it made her look very elegant as she glided by Wang Yi-An. Then, without warning, she opened the door. "Tian-Xu! I came to visit you!" She said happily as let herself in, and with a big smile, she closed the door behind her.

As the sudden door closed, it made a loud sound, Yang Tian-Xu jumped from the loud door as it shuts. "Shit!" he shouted as he saw Tong Yue-Yan letting herself in. "Don't you know how to knock?

Startled because his focus was not on work, but Wang Yi-An. He was battling with himself how he should, 'label' her in his phone contact.

Yang Tian-Xu had been struggling for about ten minutes! He had a bunch of epithets for her. For examples; Lover, My love, An-An, My (heart-emoji), Yi-An baby, and My Future Wife. Too much on his list, but he soon decided on, *'An-An'*, with a heart emoji beside it.

With the door closed behind Tong Yue-Yan, it made a loud sound, and Yang Tian-Xu was not happy to see her. Of course, Yang Tian-Xu was not pleased. Not only he yelled at her, in a cold voice he interrogated her, "Who said you can come in here without notice?"

No one had ever raised their voice at Tong Yue-Yan before, never the way he did. Her eyes began to teared up, and the rims of her eyes became moist.

"But, your secretary... She said I should come in." She said with a sad face.

"What secretary?" he questioned her again, his emotion was unaffected by her tears. In fact, it was puzzling him. Clear to him, his secretary was still working on the eighth floor. Yang Tian-Xu had a male secretary working for him named Geng Yijun.

Geng Yijun share similarity to Assistant Tseng and had worked for him for five years. Secretary Geng would invite no one into his office without getting his permission first.

However, how could Tong Yue-Yan know this? She remains with a sad expression on her face as she pointed out the window. "Her... The girl outside."

Yang Tian-Xu looked out and saw Wang Yi-An from the window. Then he asked her ruthlessly. "Are you stupid?" He left Tong Yue-Yan speechless, unable to talk back to him as he continued, "How can you mistake her for Secretary Geng? Can't you see the access card around her neck? It clearly says she's an intern?"

Yang Tian-Xu thought, "How can someone be this dumb?"

Meanwhile, Assistant Tseng came back to the division; he held the card in his hand and walked by Wang Yi-An. She greeted him as he went by, and Assistant Tseng would welcome back. Assistant Tseng knocked on the door once, and then open it, he opened his mouth to let out a "Pres—" and immediately he could feel the intensity in the room.

"Miss Tong," he greeted her as soon as he saw her. Still, as Tong Yue-Yan stood by the door, her eyes tinted with a little redness. Perhaps they had a fight? He wonders but didn't ask. Instead, he said, "Hello Miss Tong, it is so nice to meet you. You look prettier in person!"

CHAPTER 9
Speak to Me

Assistant Tseng hoped that he could break the ice, and calm the intensity in the air. But, Tong Yue-Yan remained the same. She looked sad and seemed as if she could break out crying. Tong Yue-Yan felt sad, and as she compressed her lips together, she looked away from them. Tong Yue-Yan was trying to control her emotions. Yang Tian-Xu was unaffected by Tong Yue-Yan's expression, and shot a look at Assistant Tseng and demands, "You brought the card?"

Assistant Tseng nodded his head. "Yes, sir!" Then he rushed over to the desk and gave the card to him. Assistant Tseng looked over at Tong Yue-Yan and saw her wiping her tears. He thought, 'Oh, how could anyone still look this pretty when they cry?'

Assistant Tseng had worked for Yang Tian-Xu for so long, that he recognised the guy would make countless girls cry. Nevertheless, Assistant Tseng thought, "Why did Miss Tong cry? I'm sure he had said something mean to her..." Although he separated his thoughts from his movement--he could never pry into their business.

Tong Yue-Yan was apparently trying to contain her tears, but how could an heiress like her take the verbal abuse? She determined not to utter a sound, and she knew Yang Tian-Xu wasn't even paying attention to her. Was she that worthless to him? Does he hate her so much that he refused to look at her?

"You may leave now." With insensitivity, he told Assistant Tseng, "Also show Miss Tong her way out," Tong Yue-Yan was depressed, how could he treat her so poorly? Then just as they were about to leave, he called out, "Wait!"

Assistant Tseng first thought he must want to apologise to Miss Tong. "Yes, boss?" He asked as he stopped himself from opening the door.

Tong Yue-Yan had thought perhaps Yang Tian-Xu had changed his mind and wanted her to stay with him. Nevertheless, he demanded. "Tell An-An I need a short talk with her."

Assistant Tseng was furious, 'Can't you see Miss Tong's eyes? It's bright red. She still had tears lingering in her eyes!' However, he could only obediently nod and said, "Yes sir, I will pass along the message." Forcing out a smile as he opened the doorway for Tong Yue-Yan.

Tong Yue-Yan heard the conversation between them, 'That girl must be in trouble now! How dare she send me in so I can make a fool of myself in front of Yang Tian-Xu?' as she wished she could stick around to see him yell at her! That would made her feel a lot better after being called, '*stupid*' by Yang Tian-Xu. She wanted him to like her, but now she angered him—now—this possibility seems distant.

Assistant Tseng opened the door for Tong Yue-Yan. The two of them walked out of the office, and he called Wang Yi-An, "Little An, President Yang would like to speak to you."

"Okay!" She said and got up from her seat. Just as Tong Yue-Yan and Wang Yi-An passed by each other, Tong Yue-Yan looked at her with contempt.

Wang Yi-An could sense the arrogance in her expression; she saw Tong Yue-Yan's eyes, red and swollen, Wang Yi-An knew she had cried. Yet, Wang Yi-An remained silent, as she wasn't someone who likes to pry, and so she tried to let out an encouraging and gentle smile.

However, Tong Yue-Yan thought Wang Yi-An was mocking her, and she did not see the concern and care that Wang Yi-An was trying to express through her smile. Assistant Tseng walked passed her and whispered into her ears, "Boss seems to be in a bad mood so be careful okay? He might be spiteful, but don't mind him. He had been a little irritating lately."

Tseng Kuan-Yin s a decent man, and he likes to take care of newbies as much as he could. Often, when he felt something odd with President Yang, he would warn others about it.

Wang Yi-An nodded and persisted in silence. She knocked on the door lightly. "Come in," he called out from inside.

Wang Yi-An opens the door, and as she walked in Yang Tian-Xu gave her a gentle smile. Wang Yi-An did not say a word and headed towards the desk. Yang Tian-Xu got up from his seat and went over to move a chair back for her. "Here, take a seat."

Meanwhile, Assistant Tseng would turn his head to Tong Yue-Yan and told her, "I'm sorry for the trouble. The workload has made him irritable lately. I hope you can understand his reasons."

Tong Yue-Yan was an understandable girl after she heard him defend Yang Tian-Xu. She no longer felt the agony and smiled at Assistant Tseng, "Thank you for letting me know."

Outside the office, Tong Yue-Yan had her front facing toward Assistant, as they engaged in their conversations about Yang Tian-Xu's and his busy schedule. Tong Yue-Yan had her back towards the office, but Assistant Tseng, however, could look inside from the window.

Confused as he witnesses the entire event, he thought, 'Did I just saw that right? The boss pulled a chair for an intern?' He was dumbfounded as he continued to pondered, 'Wasn't he in an angry-mood just now?'

How could Assistant Tseng know it was Wang Yi-An, who had caused his President; Yang Tian-Xu to be aggravated for the past two weeks? Tong Yue-Yan was busy listening to Assistant Tseng, also with her back facing the window, she could not see that Yang Tian-Xu had moved a chair back for Wang Yi-An. Perhaps it would be a good thing she didn't see him expressing his smile and concern towards Wang Yi-An. Tong Yue-Yan just assumed that Wang Yi-An would receive a good berating session.

There was no way Yang Tian-Xu could berate her. Wang Yi-An saw his smiles, and she thought, "What is he smiling about? He probably had a good time with his girlfriend, right? But, why was she crying so much? Maybe she didn't want to part with him?" She was uninterested and disconcerted and thought, *Oh well, not my problem!*

Wang Yi-An went over to sit down and ask him. "You needed me for something?" She asked as she placed her focus on her obligation.

"Yes, here is your new card." He said as he handed it to her. Yang Tian-Xu didn't return to his desk and stood by her as she sits in the chair. He wanted to be as close to her as possible.

"Thanks," she reached out her hand to accept it.

"Did anyone told you how to use it?" He asked, showing his concern for her.

"Yes." She nodded and inquired. "Can I start work now?" Wang Yi-An had been feeling unproductive since the change in her schedule.

The agenda she had set up in her email was a schedule sent by Mr Han. If Mr Han were still her supervisor, she would attend and work on a photo-shoot right about now. However, she sat at a desk doing nothing, and out of boredom; she drew sketches of her environment.

Yang Tian-Xu smiled at her, and said, "Yes, I had printed out a copy of your schedule. I will also email it to you later today."

"Thank you." She replied as she received the single piece of the document. "But, I don't need a copy." Wang Yi-An's photographic memory allowed her to remember anything with just one glance—she could remember it forever. Never have to look at it again.

"Ah, right... I forgot you have a photographic memory." Yang Tian-Xu paused for a minute and soon continued, "I guess I could explain to you the abbreviations on the schedule."

Yang Tian-Xu made it clear how much he wanted to interact with her. Yang Tian-Xu felt like she had spoken a few more words to him compared to earlier.

"It's alright, Mr Tseng had already told me how to read the abbreviations." She rejected his offer to help. Yang Tian-Xu could only curse in his mind, 'Damn-it Assistant Tseng! Why are you so capable?'

Assistant Tseng felt Yang Tian-Xu's execrated thoughts from inside the elevator, and so he let out a sneeze. "Ah-Achoo!" He sniffed his nose and apologised to Tong Yue-Yan as she was behind him in the elevator. They were heading their way back down to ground level.

Meanwhile, Yang Tian-Xu was feeling down, wanted to interact with her more. Much more. So he could only do a brief explanation about the client's company and review the schedule for May.

Faithful God Enterprise—a famous merchandise brand for women, and they carry a large selection of clothing, accessories, and cosmetics aimed for luxurious women of all ages;

even though they were an expensive brand name. 30% of the women in City Y became their clients. 40% were consumers of *Colerida Enterprise*, and 5% were Yang Corps consumers, and the other local brand takes up the last remaining 1%.

Yang Corps may be an immense business tycoon in City Y. However, women's merchandise was not their forte. Yang Tian-Xu and Wang Yi-An were together in his office—alone. Yang Tian-Xu could feel the pulsing of his own heart, as he leaned in closer.

"These are the current designs and planning for their new product. The release date would be somewhere in August. The product is a fragrance, called *Grace*." He speaks to her as he reaches over across to take samples from his desk.

Wang Yi-An leaned backwards on the chair to make way for him. She ponders why he couldn't have just gone around. 'He's too close.' She thought as she became uncomfortable, but she remained still in her seat. After he takes two packs of the sample from a small shipping box—he gave Wang Yi-An a package then he distanced himself a little to give space.

Jin Qi-Long has sent Yang Tian-Xu plenty of samples. Jin Qi-Long told him that every time he smells this fragrance he had thoughts of Lee Yin-Yin. However, as for Yang Tian-Xu; he had thoughts of Wang Yi-An all the time, no matter what he smells.

Wang Yi-An was right there. This close to him, more so than he ever imagined. He told her, "Here try it and tell me your opinion."

Wang Yi-An opened the small little package to smell it. A gentle and sweet smell, it was refreshing, and she let out a smile. "Smells wonderful! I like it!" She said happily.

Yang Tian-Xu watches her inhaling the fragrance. Her expression squeezed Yang Tian-Xu's heart. *It's like when you see something so cute and innocent it makes you feel tight inside*—then he became speechless, lost for words for a moment. He tried to keep himself calm and cursed in his mind. 'Ah, damn it!'

He sighed, "Anyway, here is more information about Faithful Gold Enterprise. You can see that the design looks incorrect. I would like you to redo the logo, packaging, and the container designs."

Then he gave Wang Yi-An a ten-inch tablet and showed her the documents regarding Faithful Gold Enterprise. Wang Yi-An viewed the designs on the tablet and when she saw the container design; she giggled.

To her it looked like a man jewel so she couldn't help but let out a laugh, "That looks terrible! It reminds me of my brother's Willy."

"… Wil—" Yang Tian-Xu shunted to the side. He wanted to remain his cool, but. "Will—Willy?"

Should he cry or laugh? He wanted to laugh when those words came out from her mouth. However, he couldn't. He wanted to show her his maturity.

How could he though? She just said '*willy*'! Out of all the words she could have used to describe a male genital. She used the word '*willy*' he let out a small chuckle. However, he tried not to laugh out loud. He thought, "Why are you so cute?"

Yang Tian-Xu could not face her any longer, he turned around and held his stomach as he tried to keep the laughter. After Wang Yi-An finished viewing the designs, she turns over and saw his back. He looked like he was in pain, so she asked, "Are you feeling alright, President Yang?"

He cleared his throat and calmed himself down, and he turned around as he curled the corners of his lips up and said, "Yes. I am feeling great, thank you for your concern."

"Sure thing." She said as she smiled at him. "Okay, I will get myself busy with the new designs now. May I ask when the deadline is?"

"Monday we will meet with Faithful Gold Enterprise and their spokesperson, it's better to have the new design approved by the end of this week. But if you can, send me the draft today."

She smiled at him and said, "I will get it done—ASAP!" Then she got up and lowers her head, "I will email you the drafts as soon as I can!" she said as she lifted her head and smile, before leaving.

Yang Tian-Xu placed a hand on his chest. He felt the rapid beating of his heart, perhaps because he never been in love before in his life. Yang Tian-Xu had finally known what it felt like for the first time.

Wang Yi-An was not only simple, dull, and average looking. Consider being short, at five-foot-nothing, and she would reach his chest when they stand side by side. Yang Tian-Xu would be in awed as he thought, 'Gosh, she's so cute.'

Wang Yi-An had plain taste in fashion, a simple pair of black dress pants and a white top—a plain business attire. Instead of styling her hair, she let it open. However, when she gets serious with her work, she would tie it up into a bun.

Yang Tian-Xu watched her as she went back to her new desk. The desk was emptied by Assistant Tseng, with a clear table she pulled out the chair. Happy to receive her first workload, and she sat down with a smile on her face as she tied up her long hair into a bun.

Yang Tian-Xu stares from inside his office, and in his view; he can see the back of her nape. He watched her power on the computer to begin her work. From where he stood, his eyes never left her. With a pure thought in his mind as he watched her, *Why are you so cute?*

CHAPTER 10
You Satisfied Me

Wang Yi-An was ready to begin work; she was (in fact) excited. She returned to the desk, for the first time she took the new card she had received from Yang Tian-Xu, and inserted the card into the computer card slot.

Yang Corps invented these super intelligent computers called, 'Ultra-Plus'. With the advanced technology; employees can turn on the computers when they insert their cards in the reader, to turn off, employees must eject the card. The machines record the users' activities, one that takes place on the specific machine. If someone with a high authority wants to view the logs they can check by logging in to the company server mainframe.

Making sure no hackers could get into the system, the IT employees would monitor 24/7 on these server networks. Yang Corps hired specially trained units of cyber-security personnel to monitor all IT-related activities. Employees could not bring their work home unless they were given special permission to sign out an Ultra-Plus machine. Yang Corps offered these Ultra-Plus-laptops for their employees; used the same way as the desktop computers in the office, everything was accessible through the company network.

Yang Corps developed a similar technology to be sold to

other companies; similar to the Ultra-Plus, but the coding was tailored to each company. However, the price was so high that only the government could afford it. Mayor Cheung was first to purchase the system. With his relationship with the Yang family, he decided to purchase the security systems for City Hall in City Y, and to his surprise, it was a wonderful system.

Mayor Tong was the second to purchase the system, and it happened many years ago when he came to visit City Y after he won his election. He visited the City Hall and saw how great the system worked and wanted one for City A. It was such a great system that even till this day Ultra-Plus remained bulletproof, word spread out, and Yang Corps become the number one security system in the Country.

Wang Yi-An had been working on sketches non-stop for three hours. She loses track of time when she was focused on working. The time was 12:45 p.m. and Yang Tian-Xu saw the time. He looked over at Wang Yi-An and knew she hasn't gone for her lunch break yet.

Yang Tian-Xu ratified a document he had looked over and put it back into the folder. He placed it on his finished pile and stood up from his seat and went outside his office. Like a stalker, he stood there to look at her for a while, before he built up his courage to ask her. "An-An. Did you have lunch yet?"

Absorbed in her work, Wang Yi-An forgot about time, she took a quick look at the time displayed on her screen, and articulated, "Oh..." She smiled and laughed, "I completely forgot about eating."

Yang Tian-Xu took out his courage to ask her, "Would you like to have lunch together?"

"No thank you. I have already packed my lunch." She replied, she reached into her bag and pulled out her lunch box, then she asked. "Can I eat here?"

In the past, Yang Tian-Xu would have said no. He hates it when people eat their food right where they work! He would frequently lose his appetite. However, he didn't know why, but he jokingly urged her, "Only if you would share some with me then I will grant it."

She pondered about it for a little while. She thinks, did she need to eat all of it or could she share some? Wang Yi-An didn't feel hungry when she was focused on work. So sharing half of her food would be better than wasting it. Food loses flavours when reheated for too many times, and so she decided sharing would be the best choice.

"Hmm..." after she buzzed, she instantly replied, "Okay!" Then she smiled at him briefly, approvingly. "But, can you heat it up? I'm too lazy to go." She stated as she opened her lunch box and gave it to him.

Yang Tian-Xu froze for a second and thought, "For real?" *Is he about to share a homemade lunch with her? This is a dream, isn't it?*

Anyway, he took the lunch box and went into the break room to reheat it. The lunch was made by Wang Yi-An last night. Stewed chicken meat with rice. It turned cold, however, after he re-heated it. The food looks delicious and smells even better. He arrived back with the lunch box in his hands, "Here," he places it on her desk.

"Thank you!" She said to him, then she took her lead and split the meal in half, she places her half on the lid, and handed Yang Tian-Xu the rest. "Let's dig in!" She brings a spoonful to her mouth and chomps down.

For a minute he stood there thinking, "This is seriously happening." He smiled and pulled a nearby chair over and sat down across from her. The table was in between them, but he could still see her face as he eats. He couldn't help but smile.

"The food looks delicious. Did you make it?" He asked, about to have his first bite, as he smelled the food. While she concentrated on her work and responded with "uh-huh."

Yang Tian-Xu was a fussy eater, considering he was born rich. He took a bite of her homemade food and fall in love with her all over again, and said, "Wow. It's delicious!"

Wang Yi-An didn't answer him, and she immersed herself in her work. Yang Tian-Xu didn't mind she ignored him. Somehow he felt contented this way, as he sat there across from her, watching her, and enjoying her home cook meal!

With every bite he takes, it filled him with happiness, contentment with what he had. Her homemade lunch suited his taste very much. Although, even if her food tastes awful, he will continue to eat every bite! Perhaps his love for her had made his taste buds crass?

At times, Wang Yi-An would take a spoonful from her meal, and then she would divert all her attention back into the computer, continuing drawing sketches with her drawing tablet. Yang Tian-Xu told her, "You don't have to work so hard. Finish your meal first." She would say one word to him. "Later." Wang Yi-An's focus remains on the computer screen.

Yang Tian-Xu felt like crying as he thought, "How can you treat me like this? I'm your boss! I am the Yang Corps President!" However, he could only remain his cool, and just smile back and said, "Don't overwork yourself. You should take better care of your health."

Wang Yi-An nodded, "Hm!" And then she stops for two minutes and swallows her whole lunch. Yang Tian-Xu could not believe how fast this girl can eat! She gobbled her entire meal within seconds.

"Done!" She said as she bolted back to the computer, continuing her job. If Yang Tian-Xu can use an emoji to express his feeling, a sweating-grin face emoji would be the best one.

Able to enjoy a meal with her, he felt content. He enjoyed every bite he took as he sneaked glances at her from time to time.

The new designs she made was a total makeover. Because the previous container design seems unacceptable to her view, no matter how many times she tried to change it, she can't seem to be satisfied. She thought of having the design remade utterly. She gave it a heart-shaped teardrop, with a hollow centre. Inside the centre would be a sparkling rhinestone. Allowing the beautiful glass to shine, with elegance. The clear glass allows the transparent pink liquid to stand out.

Then, she wasn't sure if the client would like to have their idea redesigned. So she made another design. By using the old one, she had the wings resized, enlarging them as she gave it more life, and feathers. She drew on definition to the crease, to make them pop-up, looking like actual wings, this time the wings on the bottle seems much better.

The rounded bottle-shape container looks terrible to Wang Yi-An, and so Wang Yi-An had changed it into a cylinder instead, still keeping the pattern. With just that, she spent most of her time working; she wouldn't notice that Yang Tian-Xu would look at her the entire time as she drew each sketch one by one.

Wang Yi-An had another talent, and perhaps it was with the aid of her photographic memory. However, she could reach out her hand and take her water bottle and guzzle it down with her eyes still glued to the screen.

"That's some talent," he thought as he watched her guzzled down the bottle of water, without looking at it once, her eyes still glued to her screen. He thought, "Girl, you need a break." However, everything he wanted to say, it wasn't possible for him to say. He doesn't want to make her hate him. Yang Tian-Xu wanted her to like him, so he stood there in silence by her side.

If Yang Tian-Xu believed in karma, this was perhaps his punishment. He used to be the one to ignore others, to be the one who never pays attention to anybody else. Yang Tian-Xu was the only child and used to having everything given to him on a silver platter. His good looks were a bonus; he would receive attention everywhere he goes. This cold treatment he received from Wang Yi-An; felt like a punishment or a test of his patience.

A quiet time in their division with everyone gone out for lunch, it was just them. Another blissful reason Yang Corps got voted as one of the best company to work for; because employees have a paid two-hour lunch break. The entire division went out for lunch together; leaving only them, however, Assistant Tseng returned as he saw a view that shocked him.

After spending three hours trying to console Tong Yue-Yan, he returned. For the entire three hours, he defended Yang Tian-Xu's cold attitude towards her, saying, "He's like that to everyone." Assistant Tseng continued to reassured Tong Yue-Yan, "President Yang has always been a very strict and serious President. He had a lot of stress lately because he took both the job of a CEO and a GM (General Manager). Please don't take everything he says to heart!"

It was the Vice-President's job to find a replacement for the position. However, Vice-President Ma had been a good friend of Yang Tian-Xu's father; he was picky to the extreme about who he wants to promote into the GM position. They could only rely on Yang Tian-Xu's help until they find one, and so Assistant Tseng complains about how much work he had, and so Tong Yue-Yan understands his reasoning, she felt better and left the moment her driver came to pick her up. Assistant Tseng bid her farewell as he sent her home, making sure she got inside her car safely.

When Assistant Tseng returned, he stepped in and could smell the food. He walked further down and saw Yang Tian-Xu sitting across from Wang Yi-An as they shared a lunch box. His face dropped. He couldn't believe his eyes. "What in the world is going on?" he froze, unable to process the scene he witnesses. He couldn't even take another step closer! He stood still, and it was like he was having a stroke!

Yang Tian-Xu was actually having his lunch at work, at a workstation, with an intern. Assistant Tseng knew just how much President Yang hated when people eat at their desk and always tell them how unhealthy it was for their health. Yet, right at this moment as he witnesses the entire scene with his own eyes, he felt his jaw dropping to the ground.

After he pulls himself together, he called out "President Yang!" and so he came and reported to him, "I have successfully sent Miss Tong home."

Yang Tian-Xu heard Assistant Tseng's voice and turned to look. "Hey, you're back early."

"Early?" He widens his eyes, almost as his eyes could pop outside of their socket because of the shock. In silent, as he thought, "Boss I have been away for over three hours..."

Yang Tian-Xu still doesn't seem to care about how long Assistant Tseng had been away. "Okay, you can go into my office and take the documents I had already sign and sent them off to their department." He demands.

"Yes, sir!" An instantaneous replied as Assistant Tseng understood President Yang's cold attitude because that's just how he was. Assistant Tseng passes by them and into the office, but before he went inside, he twisted around to sneak a peek at them and saw the empty lunch box.

There was one last bite before Yang Tian-Xu finished it up. However, he was reluctant to finish it. Wang Yi-An had already completed her share long ago. She was about to put the empty lunch box away, but saw Yang Tian-Xu still unfinished she said, "It's okay if you can't finish it."

"Oh, I will! Your cooking is very delicious." He said as he takes the last bite in his mouth. His reaction was like a child that doesn't want his favourite toy taken from him. He smiled as he chewed and swallowed. "Thanks for the meal." He said as he smiled at her again.

She smiled back and cleaned up the table as she puts away the empty containers. And so she went back to business. Working, typing, drawing, all while Yang Tian-Xu sat there looking at her.

"President Yang, I drew a few different designs, would you like to look?" She said as she stared him in his eyes.

"Yes, please." He responded to her with a smile; he couldn't lock stares with her. When their eyes met, he felt an electric impulse shocking him from inside out, he turns away and got up and went around the table so he could look at the computer screen from over her shoulders.

Yang Tian-Xu was tall hence he did not need to get too

close to her to see her screen, but he still did so. He bent his back down, and his head would float over the shoulder. He was so close if he wanted he could kiss her nape. However, raised as a gentleman, he would never be able to manage something so outrageous like that!

She shows him the drafts she completed. He nodded with satisfaction, "They all looked better than the original. Send the files to me, and I will email Faithful Gold Enterprise CEO."

The CEO of Faithful Gold Enterprise was Jin Qi-Long. She had about four different revisions of the original and the one she had redesigned entirely. As told, Wang Yi-An sent all the designs to Jin Qi-Long.

Out on a date with a random girl he met at a nightclub, he took out his cell phone to peek at it as it rang once for a notification pop-up. Jin Qi-Long was busy enjoying his time with a hot lady beside him as he opened the message to see who it was. He liked the new designs Wang Yi-An made for him, so he messaged Yang Tian-Xu. "Your artist is outstanding! I like the fifth one!"

A prompt notification appeared on Yang Tian-Xu's phone, he opened it and replied to Jin Qi-Long with a thumbs-up image. Then, Yang Tian-Xu turned to look at her as he told her, "He likes your design. The fifth one you sent him."

"Okay, cool." She said, then she added, "Wouldn't it be easier if I have direct contact with Mr Jin?"

"Ah right... Maybe you should." Yang Tian-Xu was reluctant to give her Jin Qi-Long's contact information. A secret dislike, a hatred for the fact he had shared her contacts with another man, worst, the guy was a well-known playboy.

Yang Tian-Xu sent another private message to Jin Qi-Long, "I just gave you the artist contacts, don't you dare try anything on her. You know what I mean."

"Try what?" Jin Qi-Long messaged him back, and he was

both curious and confused as he asked, "Why is she hot?"

Yang Tian-Xu hated Jin Qi-Long's playboy personality, and would message back, "..."

Jin Qi-Long messaged him a happy, smiling emoji with the text, "Alright, I'm just joking. I wouldn't lay a hand on your employees! I am so madly in love with Lee Yin-Yin." And so he went on.

Yang Tian-Xu ignored Jin Qi-Long's message after that. He trusted that Jin Qi-Long would keep his word and not make a move on her. However, he wanted her all to himself!

Wang Yi-An added colours and life into the design and spent more time perfecting them. However, She got uncomfortable with Yang Tian-Xu hovering over her shoulders. She couldn't focus, it was a weird feeling for her. "Um... President Yang, can you not stare over my shoulder like that? You're too close..."

Yang Tian-Xu hadn't noticed how close he had gotten; he jumped back up as he straightened out his back. "Sorry," he said as his face heated, it felt hot.

Assistant Tseng saw his reaction from inside the office. He was watching them the entire time. Thinking, "Holy Mother of Hell... Is... Is he...?" Assistant Tseng's face blushes. He covered his mouth with both his hands. "Oh dear Lord, the boss looks hot when he blushes!"

Assistant Tseng had never seen this side of Yang Tian-Xu ever. It amazed him so much, he couldn't look anymore. He rushed to grab the signed documents on Yang Tian-Xu's desk. He knew the completed files were on the piles to the right and so he took them all, placing them in a box as he carried them out the office. Without a word, Assistant Tseng just rushed out.

Wang Yi-An could not work with Yang Tian-Xu standing behind her; then she turned to look at him. "President Yang, I can't focus with you standing behind me like that!"

"Right, sorry! I'll be back in my office, come and let me know once you're done. Please come find me, okay? Anything." Yang Tian-Xu said, as he drifted backwards approaching the office, as he stares at her for a while longer.

Without saying another word, Wang Yi-An returned to face the computer; she worked at a fast pace. However, Jin Qi-Long wasn't. He liked the design, however, for colour this guy was fussy. Wang Yi-An had the patience and adjust the colouring to his taste and re-send it back to him. However, he would change his mind and messaged her, "I want to see it in another colour."

Annoyed as she thought, "Just how indecisive is Mr Jin?" However, as part of her job description, she must complete every request the client might have, at this point she cannot complain as an intern. It took Wang Yi-An a while to satisfy Jin Qi-Long's demands with the final product, but once he replied, "Yes, that is the design I wanted." She felt relieved and stretches out her arms as she checked the time.

"Oh, God!"

The time she saw was 7:23 p.m. The office hours at Yang Corp was already over at 5:00 p.m. During all those times, Yang Tian-Xu was also in a daze as he watches her, and imagine what it would be like for her to come to ask him for help.

Disappointed when she didn't come to him for any help, he sighed a little. What made his mood worst was when he had received a message from Jin Qi-Long, "Whoa, your intern is amazing! She got so much done already. Now I can't decide!" Filled with jealousy as Yang Tian-Xu wanted her to message him, back and forward, just like that.

CHAPTER 11

I'll Do Anything For You!

Jealousy filled up Yang Tian-Xu's heart, as he received Jin Qi-Long message. Even though Yang Tian-Xu knew just how awesome and talented Wang Yi-An was, he felt like he wants to keep her entirely to himself.

Yang Tian-Xu kicked his table and scream, "Ah, fuck!" He also wanted to message her back and forth like how Jin Qi-Long and Wang Yi-An were. Even when the contents of their message were work-related, he could at least interact with her.

Since the final design got Jin Qi-Long's approval. Wang Yi-An completed her job. "She won't need to contact Qi-Long anymore now would she?" Yang Tian-Xu drowned himself with thoughts. A sudden knock sounded on the door as Wang Yi-An stood behind the door. Startled because his focus was out of place, he exclaimed, "What is it?"

"Um—" She hesitated, Wang Yi-An thought she must have disturbed him as she said. "—Sorry, it's me. Wang Yi-An."

At 7:23 p.m. Yang Tian-Xu knew it had to be her. Nervous as he told her, "Come in!"

Yang Tian-Xu pretended he still had a lot of documents, looking and flipping each paper on hand. He acts, but he wasn't looking at them. Busy at staring her for most of his time, he barely works much today. Usually, he would have completed most of his work on schedule. Still, he had only finished 2/3 of his workload today.

Everyone in the office had already left. Even Assistant Tseng had disappeared when the clock hit 5:00 p.m. Yang Tian-Xu messaged Assistant Tseng that he need not work over-time with him, and so he may leave. Only Wang Yi-An, who was so absorbed in her work, she hasn't noticed the surrounding people left one by one. The people still on the seventh floor with her was Yang Tian-Xu.

Wang Yi-An opened and alleged "President Yang I am sorry it was already so late. I came to report that I have received the final approval of the designs from Mr Jin."

"Yes, I had already received his message. He told me you did an amazing job!" Yang Tian-Xu smiled, as he asked her, "Is there anything you need my help with?"

"I would need you to sign my overtime sheet for the school, is that alright?" She enquired gently. Wang Yi-An's school was just a third-rate school, where they offered the cheapest course—ones she could afford—and the total hours of internship count towards her graduation was crucial, she needed the hours.

Yang Corps pays well for over-time every week. But she also desired to gain acknowledgement from her school by logging in work hours as an intern. It was like killing two birds with one stone.

"Of course," he pronounced, and she would smile as she brings over a sheet of paper with details of her overtime hours. Yang Tian-Xu filled out what he needed to fill out, sign it, and return her the document.

"Thank you!" She chirped as she lowers her head in gratitude.

"I'll do anything for you!" He stated as he smiled back at her.

"You are too kind President Yang!" She smiled sweetly at him. Although his speech was what he exactly felt inside, Wang Yi-An thought, "Oh Yang Corps takes good care of their employees! Even interns get such good treatment!" How could Wang Yi-An know the only person who receives such proper treatment from Yang Tian-Xu was just her?

"It is late now; I will take my leave, thank you again!" She said and just as she was about to turn around and leave, but she stopped as she heard him speak up.

"Oh, right? It's already 7:30 p.m." He said as he looked at his phone. Secretly, his heart was throbbing. It was only him and her left in the office. Then he asked her, "Would you like a ride home?" He volunteered, hoping she would say yes.

She said the cruelest two-letter word to him. "No—It's okay! I don't need a ride; I will be fine getting home on my own." Wang Yi-An said one more thing to him, "Thank you for the concern, and I will see you tomorrow!" as she lowered her head slightly, she shows her respect towards him as the President. Just like that, she left, gone from his sight again.

Depressed as Yang Tian-Xu held on to a mere hopeful wish for tomorrow to come earlier so he could see her again! So he could spend his entire day watching her. Those were the feelings Yang Tian-Xu would carry home with him. The endless longing for her kept springing up within him, and he would be capable of performing anything for her smile.

The clock was 8:00 p.m. by the time Yang Tian-Xu had gotten home. His mother and father were sitting in the living room with his aunt, Cheung Yun-Er. Yang Tian-Xu saw her as he came in from the entrance, he nodded at her with respect and greeted her, "Good afternoon Auntie."

"Oh my, my little nephew! Tian-Xu! Come here and let auntie look at you!" She sounded out with a smile on her expression, as she opened her arms.

"Big-Sis, stop teasing Tian-Xu! He's a grown man now; he's 26!" Mother Yang wasn't so happy to watch her older sister teasing her son.

However, Yang Tian-Xu would accept an elder request and came over to sit by her side. "Auntie, have you been doing well lately?" He asked her softly.

Then suddenly her expression saddened. She turned away for a moment as she wiped her tears.

Worried for his aunt, he asked, "Auntie, what's wrong?" Although, she doesn't visit them often, however, she was still the aunt that had shown him as much love as his mother. He sat there and listens to her tell him, "Tian-Xu, you must always remember to stay a good man as you are now, alright?" His auntie cried as she faces away.

"Auntie, did something happen?" He followed with a worried expression on his face.

"This is all that Pan Rong's fault!" Mother Yang shouted as she blamed her brother-in-law who had caused her older sister heartbroken.

Cheung Yun-Er married Pan Rong, and people call her

Madam Pan. Married for over twenty years now, but Madam Pan had no child of her own, so she dotes on Yang Tian-Xu. Madam Pan felt devastated when he asked her. "What did uncle do?"

"Pan Rong is cheating on me." She cried with tears bursting out from her eyes. She couldn't face them with her shame at all. However, the only person she can come for emotional support was her younger sister—Cheung Lan-Er.

Although sometimes the two sisters would compete against each other for things when they were younger—they grew up together like twins as they were only two years apart. Mother Yang bolt over to hold her sister as she cried in her arms.

Madam Pan calmed down and told them that her husband, Pan Rong had not returned home for two weeks, and when she called him. He would say to her, "I am busy with work." And so he would hang up and ignore her calls and messages.

The history between the Yang and Pan families took place many years ago during the Song Dynasty period. Still, there may be a lingering grudge between the two families. However, now they were related through marriage by the Cheung Family. They must pretend to get along, like families. But, if Pan Rong and Yang Tian-Xu's aunt were to divorce, it would make Grandfather Yang incredibly happy. However, it would still be wrong for them to ask Madam Pan to divorce her husband.

Mother Yang was incredibly angry that she made looks at both her husband and son, "You two better not copy that cheater Pan Rong!"

"My dear, how can you say that! Who do you think I am, I am Yang Fei-Hung!"? Father Yang stated. "I could never become someone like Pan Rong, That cheating bastard! Also, he is our

Yang Family mortal enemy!"

The Yang Family and the Pan Family both carried a similar family history. The Pan Family was a high-ranking military general and a statesman of the Song Dynasty, their ancestor at the time named, Pan Mei. Yang Family ancestor at the time named, Yang Chonggui, also known as Yang Ye. He was a man that had a great passion for his country and his people.

Yang Ye had seven sons and two daughters, and he had a wife whom he loves dearly, his wife had to send her husband and her seven sons off to war without leaving a single man behind, and the woman and children stay back at home. With his loyalty to the imperial family, he and his seven sons fight against the threat of the Liao Dynasty.

The Song Dynasty spans from 960 to 1279. While the Yang Family was the first to help the Song dynasty establish and spans from 950 to 1050.

In 986, it was a time of war against the Liao Dynasty, and it was that year that Yang Ye had died. Pan Mei's force was under attack by enemy forces, he was a man without integrity.

Pan Mei forced Yang Ye's and his troops to resist, the more massive armies of the Liao Dynasty. Pan Mei told Yang Ye that he should fight the enemy first, and he would send reinforcement after.

Without a word of complaint, he led his armies to a bloody battle at *Chenjiagu*. However, the promised reinforcements never arrive. The Liao armies captured Yang Ye, and he starved himself to death because he doesn't want to betray his country. The emperor later relegated Pan Mei and demoted him by three ranks. Pan Mei hated the Yang Family because of how the emperor favours them. So he kept plotting against them.

When the war with the Liao Dynasty finally ended, and the Liao armies retreated. Many soldiers had returned home safely. However, only one of Yang Ye's seven sons had returned home. Still, they blamed no one and remained true to their post in the imperial palace.

The history between these two had been many generations ago. Yet still, they hated and despised each other. Perhaps it's because both families were in direct competition in the business world. More than ever before—they carried unexplainable hate for each. Yang Tian-Xu does not hate Pan Rong. However, his father hated Pan Rong. Yang Tian-Xu's father and Pan Rong were the same age, and they would often compete against each other while they were in their school days. His father cannot wait for his sister-in-law to cut off ties with the man. However, Madam Pan loves him sincerely, and so Father Yang could only dislike the man more and more.

The time was 11:00 p.m., and after Madam Pan had vented out her anger and cooled down her emotions; she returned home—alone. Tired, Mother and Father Yang went to bed. Yang Tian-Xu's parent never stays up late anymore; tonight they stay up late because they want to console Madam Pan.

Yang Tian-Xu went to take a hot shower before he got out and changed into a comfortable shirt and sweatpants. He went on to his computer and stared at Wang Yi-An's profile. Yang Tian-Xu smiled to himself and thought, "What if she was my wife?" He would never cheat on her. How can he be certain of his feelings? Never in his life, someone could hold this much power over him, since the first time he met her, she was always on his mind.

"Wang Yi-An," he smiled and said out loud to himself in his room. "I can only love you." Believing for his entire life, with her in his mind, he went to bed and quickly he fell asleep. Hoping so he could see her again when tomorrow comes, he never expected to see her in his dream again.

The fantasy he had was a vivid one, Yang Tian-Xu cannot tell if he was dreaming or was it real? A vivid dream he had that night, where it was just him and her, late at the office at 8:00 p.m. It was after hours and with minimal lightings. The dream felt so real, and he could not believe he was dreaming. Wang Yi-An came in and smiled at him, "President Yang, I'm done with the illustrations!"

Her bright, beautiful smile, as he thought, "This is a dream, right?" No—she stood there in front of him. A déjà vu? Her first day at work, as she wore a simple dress suit, her hair up in a bun. Yang Tian-Xu questioned himself: a dream so substantial, *perhaps real and not a dream?* She worked for hours trying to satisfy the client's requests. The clients were quite demanding and required her to work over-time. He was her boss, so he stayed behind with her.

With a satisfied client—she had completed her task. She came into his office to notify him of the good news. However, after he longed for her days, weeks. This time, he couldn't hold it in any longer and pulled her into his embrace. The countless times when he wanted to kiss her; keep her in his arms forever.

Was he even able to?

However, this time in his dream. He could hold Wang Yi-An in his arms. Yang Tian-Xu places his hands around her waist, and slowly with one hand; Yang Tian-Xu holds on to her chin and leans in for his kiss.

Wanted to be as passionate as possible. He rolled his tongue around and suckled Wang Yi-An's tongue. He wanted to bite down hard on her lips, marking her his; but no. Gentle, sweet, yet passionate at once he held her as their tongue rolled around.

Her breathing was heavy. Wang Yi-An tried to push Yang Tian-Xu away as she told him, "No president, we can't." She tries to catch her breath as he continued to move his kisses down her neck. She had a sensitive body, so she moaned every time he touches her. He whispered in her ears and said, "I want you."

Her knees became weak as her face flushed and she could no longer stand anymore. They slid down to the floor, and Yang Tian-Xu lies on top of her, kissing every inch of her body as he feels her up. As he crept his hands, lurking down into her pants, slow; and just as when his hand almost reach inside her pants. She held onto his hand, "No! Don't President, and we shouldn't be doing this!" She cried.

However, Yang Tian-Xu wanted her. He wants her now—he forced her hands down—untied his tie and used it to tie her hands down. She struggles as she tries to break free. But how could he let her go? He pinned her down beneath him. He kissed her lips, and fondles her breast, then slowly reaching into her surfaces. Yang Tian-Xu messed up her clothing and exposed her smooth, soft skins.

Wang Yi-An could only struggle, but she could never break free from her imprisonment. She cries for him to stop, but he ignores it. He could not control his body. His obsession with her had reached to this point. He could no longer stop himself.

He scrambles to get his pants undone with one hand. Wang Yi-An cry out, "President Yang, please!" She struggles again and again, but his strength suppressed hers. His eyes were looking at her body as he removes bits of her clothes off. Then finally, he pulls off her panties.

Disregarding her endless cries for help. Yang Tian-Xu was ready to insert himself inside her, and his roughness towards her made her cried out, "President Yang, don't!" She cried as she continues her useless struggles to break free.

But he still did it, anyway! Yang Tian-Xu ram himself hard and deep inside her when he entered. He thrust inside her for the first time. He penetrated her deeply; his movement was quick. He moved inside her continuously, and he was extremely rough. As Yang Tian-Xu trusted her from the inside, he kissed her lips violently, biting down on her lips, as he continues to thrust her deep. The room filled with their moans.

When he stops his kisses for a breath of air, she cried out, "President Yang! Please don't! It hurts!" For once, Yang Tian-Xu looked at Wang Yi-An's face and not her body. He can see the tears in her eyes and as his body froze. Wang Yi-An's tears had made his heart aches painfully; it was like an awakening to his dream. Awoken by the sudden feeling of pain in his aching heart, he exclaimed, "Shit!"

Yang Tian-Xu woke up, and he couldn't believe himself, "How could I have made her cry in my dream!!!" He hated himself, as he shouted. Frustrated and angry at himself "Fuck! I am pathetic!" Yang Tian-Xu hated how he had raped her in his dream. Even though it was an illusion, however; Dreams are your hidden desires is it not?

Yang Tian-Xu's beautiful fit body covered with sweat, and sure enough, he was still erect. He needed to cool himself down. He took off his sweat-soaked T-shirt, and glance over at the clock and saw the time; 8:32 a.m.

The Yang Family's housemaids all start work at 6:00 a.m., so he picked up the intercom phone near his bed and made a call to the on-duty-housemaid. "Can you bring me a bucket of ice water?" He requested.

"Yes, I will be right up now." A minute later the housemaid knocked on his door.

"Come in." He told the maid. Then the maid opened the door and walked in with a bucket filled with ice water. It was heavy, so she carried it with both hands. The housemaid saw him, and thought he looked dazzlingly good-looking, she blushes at the sight of Yang Tian-Xu's naked top body.

"Just leave it there, and you may go." He commands, he was still erect from under the sheets, so he waited until the maid leaves. The maid replied, "Yes young master," and closed the door from behind her as she left.

Yang Tian-Xu got up with the sheets wrapped around his waist and went to grasp the bucket. He was strong, so he only needed one hand to hold the bucket. He rushed to the washroom in his room, and removed the sheets off, and hopped in the shower.

Once he got into the shower, he gave himself a moment. He held the bucket up above his head. He breathed out slowly, and he counted. "1, 2—3!" And on three he dumped the entire bucket over his head.

"Ah! Fuck! AH FUCK!" He screamed. The cold ice-water made his body trembles, but it sure helped with his erection.

CHAPTER 12

I am in Love

In the morning at 8:35 a.m. Yang Tian-Xu was ready for work. Not having a good night's sleep shows on his handsome face. After an ice-cold-shower, Yang Tian-Xu head to work, arriving at Yang Corps at 9:00 a.m. His expression made him look gloomy and down, he looked as if he had no soul.

His usual walk shows confidence, like a general leading an army to a battlefield. However, today he walked like a gloomy cloud hovering over his body, he looked like hell! The sight of him, lowering his shoulders as he looks down at the ground can show his depression.

Assistant Tseng saw Yang Tian-Xu's back by the entrance and greeted him. "Good Morning, boss!"

Yang Tian-Xu's body turned around slowly like a ghost and stared at him.

"What's wrong boss? You... Look..." Assistant Tseng wanted to say, "You look like shit." But how could he say it? Instead, he asked "President Yang. You look horrible today, did you not get enough sleep?" Concerned, never have Assistant Tseng saw President Yang looked like that, ever.

Yang Tian-Xu sighed, he was like an undead corpse as he turned around to continue walking into the Yang Corps' entrance. The rest of the staff saw his depressed state as he walked in, and could only wonder to themselves secretly, "What on earth is wrong with our President?"

Yang Tian-Xu and Assistant Tseng, both walked into the elevator. The elevator-girl saw and greeted them, and press the close-door button, and the switch triggers for the elevator door to close. Yang Tian-Xu was unresponsive until he heard a voice shouting out, "Please wait for me!" Sure enough, he could recognise this voice already. This sweet, cute, and beautiful voice belongs to his Wang Yi-An, most definitely.

Just as the elevator door was about to close and she shouted for someone inside to stop the closing door. A hand reaches out fast, preventing the doors from closing all the way, they retracted and reopened as Wang Yi-An stood from the outside, while Yang Tian-Xu stood inside. Their eyes met, and he stood there as he blocked the doors from closing, with his arms rested on the metal frame.

Wang Yi-An looked at him with a gentle smile, and she greets them all with a "Good morning!"

Wang Yi-An wanted to get inside. However, Yang Tian-Xu blocked the door; his right arm remains rested on the rim of the frame; preventing the doors from closing in on her.

"Um... President Yang, I need to get in—" Wang Yi-An said with a confused tone, and she wonders why he would keep the door from closing still, perhaps someone else is coming in as well? She turned her head around, behind her was nobody. She turned her head back and again, stared deep into his eyes. "President?" she called for his attention.

Yang Tian-Xu looked into Wang Yi-An's eyes for a second and suddenly his face flushes. Yang Tian-Xu suddenly remembers something as he turns to face away from her, and then he let her in.

For a minute, she slightly touches him as she walked in. Yang Tian-Xu was too close to the opening she had no other choice but to jog her way inside. Yang Tian-Xu dropped his arm from the door and went to stand by her side; the door closes.

The elevator-lady and Assistant Tseng, both greeted Wang Yi-An and so she would do the same. Yang Tian-Xu continued to look away from her. His heart throbbed. She was so close to her he wanted to grab her and kiss her, however, he won't; he promised himself he would never hurt her and hates to see her cry. Even in his dream, he hates it.

After the short ride up to their destination. The elevator-lady bows down at the president as they all went off to their division. Assistant Tseng asks Wang Yi-An, "Little An, how are you enjoying your time so far. Good?"

"Yes! I really like my job! Yang Corps is an excellent employer!" She smiled as she fixed the sliding backpack she always carried with her. As she walked along with Assistant Tseng beside her, they face each other and chit chatted happily.

Assistant Tseng was a friendly guy, Wang Yi-An naturally felt comfortable around him, so she grins at his jokes and humour, and then Assistant Tseng finally felt a chill down his spine.

Yang Tian-Xu had long legs. However, he tried to lower himself down to listen in on them. Yang Tian-Xu could not stand the laughter between them. Jealous, as he forces his way in between them, he faced Assistant Tseng and said. "Can you report my schedule for today?"

The sudden tap Assistant Tseng felt on his back, where Yang Tian-Xu touched—felt like ice. "I'm gonna be murdered now... Won't I?" Assistant Tseng thought about death once he caught President Yang's eyes. His body shivers with fear and thought, "President Yang, please don't kill me..."

Assistant Tseng kept quiet and did as told. Reporting every detail of President Yang's schedule like a soldier reporting to a superior officer. "Today you have a board meeting at 4:00 p.m..." They continued to walk down the hallway. However, Yang Tian-Xu made sure that the person next to him was Wang Yi-An and made sure she was further separated from Assistant Tseng.

Once they reach into the office, Wang Yi-An continued her assignment—to complete the logo—and packaging designs for Faithful Gold Enterprise. Jin Qi-Long likes Wang Yi-An's art. So he messaged her earlier this morning to redo his logo designs and the packaging designs for Grace.

Meanwhile, Yang Tian-Xu and Assistant Tseng walk into the office while Assistant Tseng finished his report about Yang Tian-Xu's busy schedule. Yang Tian-Xu was not paying attention, however, as soon as Assistant Tseng closed the door behind him, Yang Tian-Xu turned around and looked at Assistant Tseng in the eyes as he told him. "I'm jealous."

"Eh?" Assistant Tseng paused for a while, confused. And so Yang Tian-Xu placed his hands on his shoulder and told him in the face. "I am jealous of you. How can you easily talk to her like that?" He asked as he frowns, his expression was sombre.

"Ah... President... What's gotten into you...?" His response baffled Assistant Tseng, as he asked in a soft-spoken tone, "Are you feeling sick, boss?"

Indeed... He thought, he felt lovesick. Yang Tian-Xu looked out the window and can see Wang Yi-An powering on the computer to continue her next work. He looked back at Assistant Tseng and told him straight on. "I am in love."

"Boss, don't tell me you're..." Assistant Tseng had worked for Yang Tian-Xu for a long time. He notices the changes in President Yang's mood. Assistant Tseng thought, "Maybe I am wrong... Maybe it's someone else."

And so Assistant Tseng just had to ask, even when he

thinks he knew the answer. "President Yang, just... Who are you in love with?" He enquired.

Yang Tian-Xu looked outside the window for a brief second and looked straight into Assistant Tseng's eyes, and with a voice loud enough for him to hear, he said. "Wang Yi-An."

Assistant Tseng's eyes pop out wide open, his mouth dropped, and he thought. "Did I hear that right..."? Then he shouted, "Wang Yi-An!?" Yang Tian-Xu jumped, and he hurried to cover up Assistant Tseng's mouth as he hushes him.

"Shh... You are too loud!" He whispered, he looked outside to make sure that the people outside heard nothing, as he slowly removed his hand from Assistant Tseng's mouth. And so Assistant Tseng lowered his voice and whispered back, "Wang... Wang Yi-An?"

Yang Tian-Xu nodded, he sighed and looked back outside to watch Wang Yi-An as her focus glued to the screen. Then he sighed again, and turned back and asked Assistant Tseng, "Tell me how can I get her to fall in love with me?"

Shocked to the point of no return, Assistant asked, "Boss... Why are you asking that?" Assistant Tseng couldn't believe what he had heard from his President.

Yang Tian-Xu was the company's president! How could he have such low self-esteem to fall for an intern? What was so great about Wang Yi-An that makes our President Yang Tian-Xu become such a... Girl?

Yang Corps is a busy company, and Assistant Tseng had no time to wonder about his boss love's affair. Yang Tian-Xu was also working, and he had to prepare his documents for the board meeting today. Everyone in the office was busy.

However, it doesn't mean that Assistant Tseng can't take a glance at Wang Yi-An and wonder, "What is so great about her?" He thought, "Miss Tong is so much prettier. Not only that, but she's also the Mayor's daughter from city A..." Assistant Tseng may have a million reasons why Tong Yue-Yan would be a better choice to be the President's bride. However, Yang Tian-Xu was dead set on Wang Yi-An.

No matter how busy Yang Tian-Xu maybe, he made sure that every day at 12:00 p.m. he would ask Wang Yi-An "Would you like to go for lunch?" She rejected him and told him she had already brought lunch. And again, every day at 5:00 p.m. he would ask Wang Yi-An "Would you like a ride home?" Again, she would reject him, saying she can get home herself.

Assistant Tseng could not believe what he had witnessed and could only shake his head to pity his president. Assistant Tseng ponders about Yang Tian-Xu's taste in women, everyday Assistant Tseng would see the look on Yang Tian-Xu's face as she rejects him for lunch, a ride home, and if anyone in the building finds out. They would be so jealous and would think she was crazy. Heck, even Assistant Tseng himself was jealous.

Meanwhile, Tong Yue-Yan was feeling in a new low after Yang Tian-Xu mistreated her. His cold attitude towards her made her sad, and Tong Yue-Yan had liked him ever since she was nine years old. She remembered that he had given her a classical music box. She would always bring it with her on her travels.

Yang Tian-Xu was only three years older than her, so she felt like she matches with him well. Tong Yue-Yan believed no one could look as good as she could when she stood side by side with Yang Tian-Xu. However, he was angry with her that day, and it was all of Wang Yi-An's fault!

Tong Yue-Yan was so angry about it she had even asked Assistant Tseng for her name. Tong Yue-Yan would remember it for sure, and the next time. She won't be too kind to her! Tong Yue-Yan lays in bed all day feeling depressed about the incident with Yang Tian-Xu.

However, Tong Yue-Yan's aunt told her, "You don't need to win his heart. Yang Tian-Xu was a filial man; if you get Grandfather Yang to like you, and make Grandfather Yang want you as his granddaughter-in-law, he won't have a say in it!" Tong Yue-Yan listened to her aunt's advice and nodded in agreement.

And so every single day, she and her driver went to visit Grandfather Yang for about an hour or two, and she would tell him how much she admired Grandfather Yang and wanted to hear more of the Yang family heroic stories. Few people visit an old man like himself, so he was grateful to receive the company. Grandfather Yang welcomed her with open arms, she visited him regularly, even on the weekends; when Yang Tian-Xu came to visit his grandfather, he would see her there.

Friday was when Yang Tian-Xu and his parents would come to visit Grandfather Yang, and so they could stay for the weekends. Yang Tian-Xu was not happy to see Tong Yue-Yan. However, his parents were delighted to found out how she would visit Grandfather Yang every day.

At 7:30 p.m., Grandfather Yang requested for her to stay for dinner, and after they had their meals, Yang Tian-Xu and his grandfather went to have a chat together in their family garden. This time he mentions his thoughts to Yang Tian-Xu.

"Tian-Xu, Ye-Ye is getting older now. If you cannot find a woman suitable enough to be your bride, you should consider Yue-Yan." He said while they were sitting under a traditional Chinese gazebo. Surrounding them was a beautiful scenery like that of an imperial palace.

Yang Tian-Xu might be a filial child, and however, for who he should marry, he was dead-set on Wang Yi-An. However, how could he tell his grandfather it was still only a crush? He wanted to tell his grandfather he already had someone he likes, however, he was rudely interrupted by Tong Yue-Yan as she brings them over some fruits.

Tong Yue-Yan walked over with a tray of cut up fruits for the two to nosh. She carried the plate with both her hands and when she bends down to place the dish on the table in front. Grandfather Yang joked, "My! Yue-Yan was already behaving like a good granddaughter-in-law already."

A shy blushed face appeared on Tong Yue-Yan as she faced away from them, "Grandfather Yang, you are embarrassing me." As she let out a secret smile—A sweet secret smile like she had already become his wife. However, the look on Yang Tian-Xu's face shows he felt annoyed.

With a serious look on his face as he told his grandfather, "Ye-Ye, it is getting late. Miss Tong should be on her way home now." Yang Tian-Xu wanted her to leave Tian-Bo-Fu, he doesn't want his family to like her any more than they already were, because once he introduces Wang Yi-An to his family. How would they be treating her?

"What? She can stay and have a longer chat with our family. Yue-Yan is such a sweet child." Grandfather Yang said as he smiled at Tong Yue-Yan, Grandfather Yang wanted Tong Yue-Yan to stay longer, she had been visiting him so much that he felt like she should be a part of the family.

Saddened by Yang Tian-Xu's suggestion, she could only think he wanted her to leave already. Tong Yue-Yan didn't argue, or beg to stay; she wanted Yang Tian-Xu to like her, so she slightly bows to Grandfather Yang and told him, "Tian-Xu is right, it is very late already I shall take my leave and return home, I wouldn't want my auntie to worry." She said as she makes an excuse to leave.

Grandfather Yang was very understanding; Tong Yue-Yan was still the young lady of the Tong Family. She must not stay too late at the Yang Family without her elders there. And so Grandfather Yang told Yang Tian-Xu, "Tian-Xu, you should go sent her to her ride safely."

"Yes, Ye-Ye." Yang Tian-Xu replied obediently and got up, as he looked at Tong Yue-Yan, he said, "We should get going before it gets too late." Tong Yue-Yan nodded and bid her farewell to Grandfather Yang before she left with Yang Tian-Xu.

Yang Tian-Xu and Tong Yue-Yan had to walk through the Garden before they headed out towards the main gates of the Tian-Bo-Fu. The Tian-Bo-Fu had a beautiful large garden. As much as Yang Tian-Xu hated that he had to be the one to send her off, he still did as he told, only because he wanted her to leave. Meanwhile, Grandfather Yang thought perhaps Yang Tian-Xu and Tong Yue-Yan could have the time to understand each other better.

The scenery surrounding them was a field of beautiful roses and flowers. It smells refreshing in the first week of May. The flowers were all blooming beautifully, as they walked through, he thought about how great it would be if the person next to him would be Wang Yi-An.

Yang Tian-Xu knew the woman his parents wanted him to marry was Tong Yue-Yan, they couldn't have made it more visible. Now, even his grandfather had taken a liking towards Tong Yue-Yan. A sudden thought occurred to him, "What if my family objects us from being together? What would she do?"

There was a sweet smile on Tong Yue-Yan's face as she walked side-by-side with Yang Tian-Xu, at this moment she was sure she had his entire family on her side. He surprised her with a sudden question, "Can I ask you a question, Miss Tong?"

She answered, "Yes, of course, you can." But, in her mind, she thought, *Is he gonna propose already? That is so fast!* She smiled at him as she waited for his question. They stopped and stood in place for a few seconds, he asked her without hesitation. "What if the family of the person you love object you two from being together, what would you do?"

Yang Tian-Xu had a severe look on his face. However, Tong Yue-Yan giggled at the question and asked him, "How can that ever happen? Your family loves me." She couldn't stop the grin on her face. However, Yang Tian-Xu knew it was a fact, and it wasn't just only his parents who love her.

Now that Grandfather Yang had taken a liking to her, it annoys him so. He was most annoyed by her overconfidence. "You sure have extreme confidence, don't you?" He asked, "Can you just answer it as an if-factor."

"If...?" She looked puzzled as she thinks for a moment. Then, with her overconfident attitude, she replied to him with a smile, "I'm sure I can make anyone like me." She felt confident why shouldn't she be?

Who wouldn't want to fall in love with such a beautiful and educated girl like herself? Her background and education were so remarkable, and with her looks, every man on earth would drool over her, they can only dream of having her as their wife.

Yet, Yang Tian-Xu, the only man to break down that confidence of hers; he looked at her for a brief second before he told her, "It's a shame that my family likes you, but I don't. I hope you can tell them you don't really like me. That way it will shield you from embarrassment." After he made his statement, he turned around to walk away.

Shocked from his words, Tong Yue-Yan stood there, baffled, "You—Yang Tian-Xu!" She shouted his name, and he turned to look at her as she came up to him. "What do you mean by saying that?" She demanded an answer from him. How could he treat him so cold and cruel?

Yang Tian-Xu said it out loud and clear to her, "I thought I was very clear." Yang Tian-Xu pushes a button to trigger the main gate to open wide, and he said word per word, slow enough to get his point across, "I—Don't—Like—You—!" then he signals for her to leave with his right thumb pointing at the gates.

Tong Yue-Yan's face was flushing red from anger as she walked out the gates. Never had she got treated this way! *Never! Ever!* She was like a princess born with a silver spoon in her mouth. How could she take this emotional abuse? She tried to calm herself down, but when she saw Yang Tian-Xu calls over her driver to bring the vehicle over, the anger boils up inside her blood.

She rushed inside the vehicle, without another word. Her blood boils with anger as she couldn't believe it, unable to say anything to him, she wasn't able to look at him. *How could he say something like that?* Tong Yue-Yan thought it was a sure thing that Yang Tian-Xu would become her husband. However, it was a sudden shot down, and she left the Tian-Bo-Fu feeling all furious inside.

CHAPTER 13

She is My Crush

Monday morning was the scheduled day to meet with Faithful God Enterprise; the time had just reached 9:00 a.m. when Yang Tian-Xu had arrived at Yang Corps. Standing inside the lobby was a handsome man, five-foot-eleven inches tall, and he carried a grin on his face as he saw Yang Tian-Xu walked in from the entrance.

The man was Jin Qi-Long—he wore a dark blue suit with his hair gelled up into a stylish Korean-model hair-style. It was spiked and flashy, and it matches his personality.

"Tian-Xu! You are late!" he shouted with excitement, Jin Qi-Long had been at Yang Corps since 8:00 a.m. this morning, he had been too excited he couldn't wait to meet his idol—Lee Yin-Yin.

"Late? Buddy, it's 9:00 a.m... The meeting doesn't start until 10:00 a.m. How am I late?"

"You are late for me! You hear me! Late!" Jin Qi-Long acts like a child when he couldn't compress his excitement.

Yang Tian-Xu couldn't deal with his friend's childish attitude and look around. Assistant Tseng realised the reason for Yang Tian-Xu to be on a lookout for, Wang Yi-An. She usually shows up early around 8:45 a.m. every day. However, today it was already 9:01 a.m. and she was still nowhere to be seen. Yang Tian-Xu felt nervous, and his worried expression showed, all the worries made his heart felt like it could stop at any moment.

Assistant Tseng knew why Wang Yi-An was late. She had already messaged him on his phone at 8:00 a.m. that she would be about two hours late today, and so Assistant Tseng had already told her it was all right for her to show up late.

However, Assistant Tseng hasn't reported to Yang Tian-Xu that Wang Yi-An won't be coming in until 10:00 a.m. Assistant Tseng just wanted to see how Yang Tian-Xu would react if Wang Yi-An were to be late.

Would he yell at her, like he usually does to him when he was late? Even though Assistant Tseng had messaged President Yang about being late—hours in advance.

Yang Tian-Xu was restless, and he looks around the front entrance as he stood there in the lobby for 20 minutes with Jin Qi-Long. The guy kept rambling on about nonsense, and Yang Tian-Xu would keep scanning his surroundings.

"Tian-Xu!" Jin Qi-Long cried out for attention. "What are you looking for?" he said as he tried to follow and see where Yang Tian-Xu focus was on.

Then he suddenly had an idea and asked Yang Tian-Xu, "Tian-Xu! Are you perhaps seeking my Lee Yin-Yin? Are you that excited to meet her too? You know she's my idol right!..." and so he continues again.

Jin Qi-Long was hovering around Yang Tian-Xu like he was an annoying fly. Yang Tian-Xu tried to brush him off as if he was one. Yang Tian-Xu was already restless all weekend. He couldn't eat, he couldn't sleep properly for two days. Yet, he still looks as handsome and dazzling as ever.

Yang Tian-Xu could not wait to see her any longer. However, why was she so late? He kept thinking and worrying if an emergency might have had happened to her. Still, Assistant

Tseng remained silent and waited until Wang Yi-An shows up late.

After all the suffering he has endured over the years as Yang Tian-Xu's assistant. He now felt like perhaps this was how the heavens thanked him for his hard work. The expression on Yang Tian-Xu's face was his reward!

The three of them went upstairs to prepare the meeting room for Lee Yin-Yin's arrival. Jin Qi-Long had brought over a lot of snacks and drinks for the meeting. He wanted to show how much he values having Lee Yin-Yin over.

The staff that came with Jin Qi-Long today was hired by him to set-up the meeting room. Yang Tian-Xu was too restless; he was pacing back and forward. The President, Yang Tian-Xu doesn't seem like himself. Even Jin Qi-Long knew the usual calm friend of his—would sit still and not give a damn about anything.

However, today he seems different. Yang Tian-Xu would often glance at his watch, and he would look outside the ceiling-high window to see if he can see Wang Yi-An. The meeting room they were in was on the top seventh floor, and if he sought the surrounding carefully, he hoped he might see her.

After a while, he pulled out his smartphone. Yang Tian-Xu was so worried he wanted to call or message her and ask if she needed his help, but it worried him he might have interrupted her.

"What if I called her now and caused her to have an accident?" He thought about the endless possibility as he struggled with his inner thoughts. "No! Her safety is more important! But! What if she needed my help now? And I'm not there to support her?"

Like Assistant Tseng could read President Yang's thought, he let out a chuckle, and finally—he reported to him. "President

Yang, Wang Yi-An had already messaged me she would come in late today, I forgot to tell you. My apologies, sir."

He felt calmer after Assistant Tseng told him the truth. However, he felt agitated for one and a half hour! "Assistant Tseng, if An-An will be late again, please tell me ASAP!"

"Yes, sir!" He said as he straightens his back and salutes him like a soldier.

"An-An?" A confused expression appeared on Jin Qi-Long's face as he asked, "Who's An-An? Is she pretty?"

Assistant Tseng's expression showed like he wanted to say, "An-An was the artist for the designs." But, Yang Tian-Xu beat him to it, and with said, "She's my crush." with a straight face. Then Yang Tian-Xu continued to stare at his phone and continued to act as if what he said was only natural.

"What!?" Jin Qi-Long shouted from the shocked, "For Real!? For the first time in your life, you have a crush!? Seriously?" Jin Qi-Long had known Yang Tian-Xu ever since they were four years old.

Jin Qi-Long had heard nothing about his friend being in love, he always thought perhaps Yang Tian-Xu wasn't interested in women. He was worried, however, now Yang Tian-Xu told him about a girl he had a crush on. It made him curious!

Does this An-An have the beauty of a Goddess, even Lee Yin-Yin couldn't compare? Jin Qi-Long felt dead-set on meeting this girl!

However, Assistant Tseng patted on Jin Qi-Long's shoulder and said, "Mr Jin, you shouldn't have your hopes up too high. You might be very disappointed."

"Eh?" said Jin Qi-Long with a baffled expression on his face.

Yang Tian-Xu had a smile on his face, and he could not

hear what Assistant Tseng and Jin Qi-Long was talking about. However, he calls him out. "Assistant Tseng!"

Assistant Tseng heart almost dropped out of his chest, and jump up, "YES SIR!" he shouted at the top of his lungs.

"Could you print out the contracts?" Yang Tian-Xu demands. Assistant Tseng wonders, "Did boss heard that? If he did, I am so dead..." as he went to get copies of the contract and help set up the table.

Dressed and set-up in a few minutes the table was about ready, they only needed to wait for the star to appear—Lee Yin-Yin. Curious about who Wang Yi-An was like, Jin Qi-Long kept thinking about it. However, just as Assistant Tseng told him not to place high hopes on her looks. Jin Qi-Long thought, perhaps it's something else about her that makes Yang Tian-Xu likes her so.

Jin Qi-Long was a curious man, and he too loves to gossip. His thoughts were killing him inside, he had to open his mouth and asked, "What do you like about this An-An?"

Curious to know the answer himself, Assistant Tseng eavesdropped in their conversation as he distributed the contract copies. Yang Tian-Xu can see the curiosity on their faces, he let out a grin. Assistant Tseng's body froze as he became absorbed, as he listened in on President Yang's answer.

Yang Tian-Xu sat down in his chair, relax as he waited for the spokesperson to arrive. After Yang Tian-Xu heard Jin Qi-Long's question, he hummed for a second, and as he was thinking about his reasons. He let off a handsome smirk. "I can't tell you guys yet, I want to tell her first."

Jin Qi-Long and Assistant Tseng wanted to spit out blood. Jin Qi-Long became even more curious than before. "Tell me already! God damn it!"

And so Yang Tian-Xu replied, "Never." As he smiled and

teased Jin Qi-Long.

"You asshole! I thought we were friends!" Jin Qi-Long cursed at him for his mysteriousness, he wanted to know so badly.

"Are we really? Could just be because of our families." Yang Tian-Xu continues to joke and mock Jin Qi-Long. Jin Qi-Long was a grown man—He hated how cruel and cold Yang Tian-Xu could be. He never understood why when they were in high school Yang Tian-Xu was so popular. Jin Qi-Long himself believed he too had good looks and the family background.

Sometimes Jin Qi-Long would be jealous; he remembered that he was so insecure about a popularity poll in high school one time, and he was placed second. Second! He was furious whenever a girl asks him to pass a love letter to Yang Tian-Xu he would rip them apart. He would treat the girl who had a crush on Yang Tian-Xu like she was a princess and slowly makes her fall for him instead.

Perhaps his jealousy towards Yang Tian-Xu had made him become such a horrible playboy? No, he can only blame himself for being such a womaniser, he couldn't help, but admiring Yang Tian-Xu because surrounding him were the beautiful women. If Yang Tian-Xu wants to, he could have any woman he wants. Everywhere Yang Tian-Xu goes there would be countless women who would throw themselves at him.

Yet, Yang Tian-Xu had dated no one, the guy was indeed a workaholic, and so it was impossible not to think Yang Tian-Xu wasn't interested in women! However, now that Yang Tian-Xu had finally told him he has a girl he likes, and he won't even tell him the reason.

Perhaps he felt the need to steal her from him. However they had been friends for so long, he won't do something like that for Yang Tian-Xu. There were a thousand thoughts in his mind when Yang Tian-Xu refused to tell him his reason. However, he could only reply, "Fine! Don't tell me! I'll find out on my own, I'll know once I meet her!" as he sat down on his chair.

Yang Tian-Xu got up from his chair and went over to the sitting Jin Qi-Long. He slams his hands on the armrest, and leans in and stared at Jin Qi-Long in the eyes. "You better not tell her anything when you see her." Yang Tian-Xu demanded, his expression was humourless and stern.

Jin Qi-Long was sweating with anxiety. "What are you talking about?" With Yang Tian-Xu's face closing in on him, he tried to look at another direction. "Bro, you're too close to my face!"

"Right... You better not tell her I like her." Yang Tian-Xu said as he pulled his body away and looked outside the ceiling-high windows.

"Why not?" Jin Qi-Long asked as if he was the professional about the subject of love and he asked Yang Tian-Xu, "I'll be helping you, man! Don't you want my help?"

"No thanks. I want to tell her myself!" He said as he blushes at the thought of her. One day he would tell her how much he loves her. But, they only met for about a week. How could Yang Tian-Xu bring himself to tell her he likes her?

Yang Tian-Xu felt timid. His fear of rejection made him cowardly useless. He could only sigh out aloud and said, "I want to make her love me for who I am, having outside help means nothing. I want her to love me as much as how I have fallen for her."

Jin Qi-Long felt embarrassed at the sight of Yang Tian-Xu professing his love. Will he one day able to experience it? Have no one make him feel the way Yang Tian-Xu felt about someone. Love... Jin Qi-Long questioned himself, "Just who is this girl?" The feelings... Would one day he'll be able to feel the same way for someone? Lee Yin-Yin? He only likes her for her looks and her singing voice.

He couldn't say he had loved anyone like how Yang Tian-Xu has. Easy for Yang Tian-Xu to proclaim his love aloud, Wang Yi-An: a girl Yang Tian-Xu loved so much, she means a lot to him.

Jin Qi-Long let out a smirk and told him. "Don't worry I won't say anything, but when you confess to her, I want to know all the details!"

Yang Tian-Xu let out a handsome smile to his friend and said, "You are my best friend if I don't tell you, who else am I supposed to tell these things to? But for now, it's my secret."

In the second week of May, and May was the month where the temperature rose. It might still be spring, but the summer's heat was getting to the citizens in the Country. It was also the time when hot supermodels would dress in shorts or summer dresses. Perhaps a reason for all the men at Yang Corps to become excited, today was the day when the famous singer, Lee Yin-Yin appear to sign the contract as the spokesperson for Faithful Gold Enterprise's new perfume, Grace.

Faithful Gold Enterprise was owned by Yang Tian-Xu's friend, Jin Qi-Long. An extreme fan of Lee Yin-Yin. It's like he devoted his entire life to her. His company had offered her a lot of money, but she had a second request: it was to visit Yang Corps and sign the contract there. She said she wanted to see the design for the packaging for the perfume herself before she signs the contract.

In the second week of Wang Yi-An's internship, she couldn't be more excited. Finally, getting her hands on a big project, she can do anything art related. From designing a logo and packaging designs to animating the entire rough draft of the commercial. Her work requires a lot of time, with a deadline. She needs to work closely with her supervisor, Yang Tian-Xu. And the client, Jin Qi-Long and the model: Lee Yin-Yin.

Today they had to meet up, making plans and ideas for the commercial, the most important person who decide the commercial would be Jin Qi-Long, however, Lee Yin-Yin want to hear out the plans. Having everyone in agreements would be today's goal. Wang Yi-An task for the day was to take notes for Yang Tian-Xu to review later and make the rough drafts.

Lee Yin-Yin was not only famous, but she also had a semi-wealthy family background, thanks to her hard work. She walked like a proud princess. She was wearing a beautiful long summer dress—Lee Yin-Yin had gorgeous and long slender legs.

The bottom of part of the skirt was a little see-through where you can glimpse her beautiful legs. It had a floral design with light pink and yellow flowers that match well with the spring or summer. With confidence and beauty as she walked, every man that sees her would take a second look, or stares at her like the abyss (like a dark hole that had sucked their soul away).

The receptionist greeted her, and the elevator girl felt ashamed to be standing next to her. She refrains herself from asking for her autograph. As soon as she got off, Jin Qi-Long greeted her. He got there early in the morning just to welcome her. The contract signing and discussion were at 10:00 a.m., yet this guy got here at 8:00 a.m.

"Miss Lee!" He happily greeted her. The time was 9:58 a.m. "It is such a pleasure to be meeting you. I am looking forward to working with you." He said as he reaches out a hand to shake with hers.

"And you are?" she said as she reluctantly reaches out her hand to shake his.

"Oh, I am the owner of Faithful Gold Enterprise. Jin Qi-Long." He said.

"Oh... I heard you are Yang Tian-Xu's best friend."

He laughed and replied, "Yes, I am his best friend. We are also partners."

"Hmm..." She nodded her head, she didn't seem impressed by Jin Qi-Long. She only cared about his relationship with Yang Tian-Xu. Of course, she heard about their good-friendship, and how well they partner up in the business industry.

The second best young entrepreneur would be Jin Qi-Long, but Yang Tian-Xu would be number one. Why settle for the second best when you can aim for first? Featured in the World's hottest and talented Young Entrepreneur of the country magazine was Yang Tian-Xu.

It's not like Jin Qi-Long wasn't an attractive man, however, if you were to compare the two. Yang Tian-Xu was a little taller and had a more distinctive facial feature. An equal footing in their family background, however, Yang Tian-Xu had always been more successful, regarding business matters. Fifty years ago, the Jin Family had just as much power as the Yang, but the Jin family were declining, compared to the Yang family now. The Yang Family had a better connection in the business industry.

It was more obvious what the differences between them were when Yang Tian-Xu walked over to greet them, and you could see the difference in their looks, heights and persona. As the two stood side by side. Lee Yin-Yin seems to be only looking at Yang Tian-Xu.

The clear-one-sided treatment she gave to Yang Tian-Xu compared to how she treated Jin Qi-Long was like Heaven and Earth. Everyone in the office could tell. This famous singer, actress, and model had a thing for their President Yang. Then again who wouldn't?

Just as a staff was leading them into the meeting room, the elevator door opened with a chime, and Wang Yi-An rushed out with heavy breathing. "I'm so sorry I'm late!" She said as she rushes over and bows down.

"It's okay. You're not that late, it's only 9:58 a.m.," he said. "I would wait for you no matter how long you need."

The entire office was in shock to hear their President Yang said that. Generally, if they aren't in time for at least 10 minutes earlier. It would have irritated him, yet he said in a calm and caring tone, "It's okay." Wang Yi-An was almost two hours late for work.

The thoughts that ran through everyone's mind was, "Is this even our President?"

When Jin Qi-Long met Wang Yi-An, he couldn't believe his eyes. he thought, "This is the An-An...?"

He stared at her from top to bottom—and still, he thought. "What the hell...?" he turned to look at Assistant Tseng and pointed as he'd mouth-out the words without a sound. "Is that her?" Then, Assistant Tseng nodded.

Wang Yi-An was a little sweaty from the panic and running. She saw Jin Qi-Long and Lee Yin-Yin—she wiped the sweat off her hands and offered it out to shake theirs. But none of them reciprocates and completely ignored her.

Her hands remain still in the air, she wondered as she looked at the palms of her hands, "Is my hand still sweaty?" Then, a sudden pull from Yang Tian-Xu as he pulled her towards him, he said. "Come on! Let's start the meeting, we can't waste any more time."

He places his hands on her shoulders and led her into the meeting room. They closed the door and sat down in their respective seat.

CHAPTER 14
You Can't Call Him That!

They started the meeting; it was at 10:00 a.m. sharp. There Yang Tian-Xu introduced Wang Yi-An as his intern. "This is Wang Yi-An. She is my intern and will act as the Art Director on this Project."

Yang Tian-Xu said as he kept his hands on her shoulders. Never wanting to take them off of her, Wang Yi-An stood out with a smile, "It is my pleasure to be meeting with you." Wang Yi-An took a bow as she greeted everyone. Wang Yi-An went to take her seat on the right side next to Assistant Tseng and then she takes out her sketchbook from her backpack she was carrying around her.

Yang Tian-Xu could only clutch his own hands and thought. "I don't think I can wash these hands today..." Then he snapped out of his fantasy and took a seat down in the president's chair, even though he honestly wanted to sit next to Wang Yi-An. While Jin Qi-Long, Lee Yin-Yin and her manager sat in the chairs to Yang Tian-Xu's left side.

Wang Yi-An might have just average looks, and perhaps a little short, Jin Qi-Long stares at Wang Yi-An and still, he cannot believe this is the girl they were talking about just now. Jin Qi-Long let out a smirk on his face and shook his head.

"What?" Yang Tian-Xu said after he saw Jin Qi-Long shook his head.

"Nothing..." he replied and just kept smiling and then he focused his attention towards Lee Yin-Yin and engaged in a conversation with her.

Not looking like a supermodel or amazing; normal people would consider Wang Yi-An's looks to be average. However, she had a talent that was so rare, perhaps only she possessed such talent within City Y, or maybe the entire Country. Photographic memory and speed drawing. Speed drawing was when someone could draw just as fast as someone could speak. If she wanted to, within an hour, Wang Yi-An could draw up the entire conversations they had, but that would be unnecessary. These two talents of her were why Assistant Tseng was so impressed with her during the interview. However, that was not the reason Yang Tian-Xu was so into her.

No, Yang Tian-Xu had fallen in love with her at first sight. He wanted to keep the reason he loves Wang Yi-An so much a secret, all to himself, only until he can finally tell her one day.

At the meeting, they discussed the commercial story. The story was straightforward, as Lee Yin-Yin had such an angelic and graceful look, Jin Qi-Long wanted the story to be about an angel that had ascended from the heaven. The angel's scent carried an irresistibility that no man can resist.

Lee Yin-Yin liked that idea. They sat there and talked about what the colours of her custom outfits would look like. Meanwhile, Wang Yi-An quickly drew sample sketches of the entire story, while they speak.

Of course, Jin Qi-Long loves to throw compliments at Lee Yin-Yin. Lee Yin-yin's manager would just sit there laughing along with him was doing chit chats. All while, Yang Tian-Xu would ignore them as he glances over at Wang Yi-An's work.

He smiled at her as she continues to draw without even noticing his, or anyone's present. She was always absorbed in her work, a great focus appeared on Wang Yi-An's expression, she never complains about it, she loves her job.

Jin Qi-Long curiosity continues, as he wonders why. Why would Yang Tian-Xu love such a dull and average girl? However, he cannot stop his stares at the beautiful woman sitting beside him—Lee Yin-Yin. Jin Qi-Long's current thoughts were how he could get Lee Yin-Yin to fall for him, perhaps sleep with him.

Jin Qi-Long was a typical wealthy playboy. Yang Tian-Xu was someone different, He was serious about his work and always had been. However, because of Wang Yi-An, he had become someone who desires such a fantasy.

Yang Tian-Xu couldn't stand sitting far away from Wang Yi-An, so he made an excuse, he got up and went over the other side of Wang Yi-An and pretend to tell her what colours to use. It would take Wang Yi-An 20 minutes to finish the rough drafts, however, with Yang Tian-Xu kept changing his demands she took a whole hour to complete. After completing the sketches, Yang Tian-Xu would present out for Jin Qi-Long and Lee Yin-Yin.

The well-done sketches won't be used during the real filming of the commercial which was a little sad, because the drawings looked terrific. Everyone thought they could just use it. However, Faithful Gold Enterprise wanted to have Lee Yin-Yin act in this commercial. They could also feature her new hit song, "I long for you."

After Yang Tian-Xu went over the script, it impressed everyone. Satisfied with the plan, they went with the idea. However, the only changes needed was the packaging design. Lee Yin-Yin suggested having it in a cuter style: so Wang Yi-An drew a new design, and later after about 20-minutes of back and forth discussion, the final sketch had satisfied Lee Yin-Yin's demand. What's left was for Wang Yi-An to make a digital printable-template design for the packaging, for that she'll be able to complete it within three to four hours. However, she would need to use the computer to create the printable templates for the manufacturer.

The time was almost 12:00 p.m., and finally after Lee Yin-Yin was happy with her contract with Faithful Gold Enterprise, and the third party organisation as the production company, which was Yang Corps. She signed the contract as Faithful Gold Enterprise's Spokesperson for the perfume Grace. Jin Qi-Long was so delighted that he had to offered to treat everyone to lunch. It was now finally the time for Yang Tian-Xu and Wang Yi-An to have a meal together! Yang Tian-Xu couldn't be any happier and asked her, "Do you want to come?"

"Sure." Wang Yi-An said as she smiled and thought, "Free food, why not? I didn't bring my lunch today." Wang Yi-An had been rejecting his offer to lunch for the first week. And now she had finally agreed to go out for lunch with him—but yet they won't be alone—he wished they could have just gone alone together.

It had been two days since Yang Tian-Xu had rejected her firmly. However, that did not stop her from coming to visit the Yang Family. Tong Yue-Yan was taking her aunt's advice and even though she knew Yang Tian-Xu does not like her.

She won't give up! Tong Yue-Yan felt destined to become Yang Tian-Xu's wife, and so what if he had no feelings for her, for now? Determined to become his wife, Tong Yue-Yan let out a courageous smile. And so this morning Tong Yue-Yan had gone over to visit Grandfather Yang and had taken a morning walk with him. She would make sure that Grandfather Yang would favour her as Yang Tian-Xu's number one bride candidate.

Grandfather Yang sees how much Tong Yue-Yan likes Yang Tian-Xu, and so he wanted to give her a chance to get closer to Yang Tian-Xu. Grandfather Yang told her to bring Yang Tian-Xu's favourite snack and say it was from Grandfather Yang.

With such a great opportunity given to her by Grandfather Yang, Tong Yue-Yan walked into the Yang Corps main entrance with a bright smile as she carried a box filled with Yang Tian-Xu's favourite snacks.

Father and Mother Yang had already given her a VIP guest pass they had created just for Tong Yue-Yan, which was how she had gotten in the last time she was here. She still remembered that day when he yelled at her. However, she was still thick-skinned enough to come by to see him after he had already rejected her.

Tong Yue-Yan's confidence had not wavered. In fact, it made her more confident, she wanted Yang Tian-Xu even more, perhaps because he seemed unobtainable for her? She will make him bend his knees down to beg for her forgiveness and beg her to marry him. Just the thoughts of that make her feel happy and excited inside. This time for sure she contacted Yang Tian-Xu's secretary.

Nevertheless, Secretary Geng Yi-Jun would tell her. "I'm sorry, I am not obligated to tell you the where-about of our President. You can book an appointment with our President Yang, and the earliest time slot is in August of next year."

"However, if you must meet with our President immediately: I will relay the message. May I please have your name and number?" Secretary Geng is a serious, and professional man, the tone of his voice was like a recording. He takes his work seriously, and he was the one responsible for keeping President Yang's schedule active and organised.

Tong Yue-Yan was furious at the treatment she was receiving from a mere secretary! She was Miss Tong Yue-Yan, and she had to make an appointment to see Yang Tian-Xu? She doesn't know if she should laugh about it, or cry about it.

Still, however, she waited for Yang Tian-Xu outside. This time she would remain there until he comes out! He had to go on his lunch break eventually, so if she waited here in the lobby. For sure he has to come out!

Tong Yue-Yan's timing was impeccable. The moment she walked right into the entrance, she saw the group of people getting ready to leave for their lunch.

Walking side by side with Yang Tian-Xu was Lee Yin-Yin, she wanted to use her role as an excuse to spend more time with him. She would take out the contract and go over it again with him once more, as they walked, Jin Qi-Long was jealous, however, now he knows the girl Yang Tian-Xu liked was Wang Yi-An he wanted to see the look on his friend's face when he was walking beside her. Jin Qi-Long would chat with her and ask questions about the designs. He pretended to be satisfied with the drawings, he used them as an excuse to get closer to Wang Yi-An, they walk and talk about her designs. Jin Qi-Long just wanted to make Yang Tian-Xu jealous.

Did it work? Yes! It did!

Yang Tian-Xu couldn't focus on Lee Yin-Yin even though she kept asking questions. Yang Tian-Xu was so annoyed he had to tell her, "If you have any more questions about the contract you can contact your manager or a lawyer. I don't have the patience to go over it with you again, now please excuse me." And so he brushes her off, and went to walk over to Wang Yi-An's side, and push in between him and Jin Qi-Long. Lee Yin-Yin was not so happy to be brushed off like that, as for Jin Qi-Long? The guy thought it was entertaining, and smiled as he thought, "Oh god our Tian-Xu is such a child!" But the real child is himself.

Yang Tian-Xu walked side by side with Wang Yi-An and asked her with a handsome smile, "What do you want to eat?"

"Anything." She replied, of course—Wang Yi-An wasn't a picky eater. If it fills her stomach, she'll eat anything. Assistant Tseng was a little jealous of Wang Yi-An and sighed as he thought, "Boss, you never ask me what I wanted to eat. Ever!"

When Tong Yue-Yan saw Yang Tian-Xu, she went over to greet him. "Tian-Xu! Ye-Ye told me to come to bring you your favourite snacks." She said happily, and lifts the basket in her hands, and continued, "Ye-Ye said he wants you to eat it all or else he would be mad." And she smiled at him.

Wang Yi-An gave a slight head bow to greet Tong Yue-Yan as she saw her approached them. However, Tong Yue-Yan had completely ignored her, and also the rest of the world as she stood close to Yang Tian-Xu.

Nevertheless, Yang Tian-Xu had thought he was clear about his feelings toward Tong Yue-Yan. Yang Tian-Xu couldn't believe how thick-skinned this girl can be. And so he told her, "Sorry, I'll have it later, I'm about to go on a business meal with my partners."

Tong Yue-Yan had only eyes for Yang Tian-Xu, and then she finally looks around and sees Lee Yin-Yin. As a woman of equal beauty, she felt that Lee Yin-Yin's presences were a threat to her. And so she thought, "I can't let them go out for lunch together."

Tong Yue-Yan gave out a big smile and said, "How about I come along too? I'll even pay for the meal."

Tong Yue-Yan's beauty astonished Jin Qi-Long, how could Yang Tian-Xu refuse such a beautiful lady, so he speaks up, "Oh no, I could never let such a beautiful lady such as yourself pay. You should join us, the more, the merrier. Right, An-An?" He said, as he looked at Wang Yi-An and smiled, and glance over at Yang Tian-Xu.

Wang Yi-An nodded, "Mr Jin, you are a very kind man!"

"Oh please! Call me Qi-Long, or better yet, call me brother!" Jin Qi-Long said as happily, as he gave her a warm smile, Wang Yi-An didn't know what to say, and so she thought about it for a second.

Yang Tian-Xu's mind filled with jealousy, he glared back at Jin Qi-Long enviously, and said, "You can't call him that. Mr Jin is the most appropriate way to address our business partner, An-An. Otherwise, it would be unprofessional."

"Yes, President Yang. It is better for me to address you as Mr Jin." Wang Yi-An agreed and gave a slight nod.

Yang Tian-Xu could never allow her to call Jin Qi-Long by his first name. No, how would he ever like her calling anyone else by their first name, while she was calling him President Yang? Yang Tian-Xu felt ashamed at his own jealousy, and he thought, "When did I become so pitiful?"

Even though Yang Tian-Xu was frustrated about it, however, it only made sense for Wang Yi-An because she was an employee at Yang Corps, and her status was below Jin Qi-Long. Wang Yi-An still prefers to address Jin Qi-Long as Mr Jin. Yang Tian-Xu gave Jin Qi-Long a stare, and Jin Qi-Long would give out a smirk.

"Okay, how about we go to a nice restaurant?" said Jin Qi-Long as he finally leads them out to his mini-van. The van was tremendous and can fit everyone. Lee Yin-Yin tried to stick close to Yang Tian-Xu. Meanwhile, Tong Yue-Yan attempted to do the same. They can sense each other threat and stared at each other in the eyes vigorously, Assistant Tseng must have been the only one that can feel the intensity, as he offered his seat in the back to sit in the front role with the driver! And then so the two girls fought over who can sit next to Yang Tian-Xu.

"It's only right for me to sit next to Tian-Xu. After all," Tong Yue-Yan smiled as she made her excuse, "Ye-Ye told me to tell him a lot of things today when I visited Ye-Ye."

"I signed the contract with both Yang Corps and Faithful Gold Enterprise," Lee Yin-Yin made her excuse and, she got her manager to show Tong Yue-Yan the recent contracts they signed. After her manager showed Tong Yue-Yan the contract,

Lee Yin-Yin said, "So, it's only right for me to sit with them."

Jin Qi-Long could only sigh and thought, "Oh Lord, why is it that everyone is always after Yang Tian-Xu? Am I that bad compared to him?" and so he went ahead, changed his seat, and instead of sitting with Yang Tian-Xu he went to the backseat to sit with Wang Yi-An.

No way, could Yang Tian-Xu ever allow Wang Yi-An and Jin Qi-Long to sit next to each other in the back seat. Annoyed and irritated, Yang Tian-Xu shouted, "You two can sit in the first row yourselves!"

Yang Tian-Xu stood up from his seat and made his way in the back seats. He wanted to have a seat next to Wang Yi-An. But she was already inside the back row seats, with Jin Qi-Long sitting there right beside her. Yang Tian-Xu looked at Jin Qi-Long and said, "Move it!" he demands it as he pushed out Jin Qi-Long over to the side, to make himself enough room to for a seat beside Wang Yi-An.

"What? I was getting comfortable!" he cried, even though he knew Yang Tian-Xu was jealous. He smiled and couldn't believe how childish Yang Tian-Xu can be. Baffled as Jin Qi-Long thought, "When have Tian-Xu ever been this cute?"

"I don't want you to harass her sexually." He said aloud. Assistant Tseng thought it would be better if he covered for his President Yang, he let out an awkward laugh, yet he felt his sweat gland secreting, "President Yang really likes to protect his employees!" Assistant Tseng prefers not to have to deal with Tong Yue-Yan's or Lee Yin-Yin's jealousy, at all. It was only better for Wang Yi-An if they don't find out that President Yang had a crush on his intern.

The entire ride to the restaurant was overall awkward, with Tong Yue-Yan and Lee Yin-Yin and her manager sitting in the first row. It can feel like they were glaring at each other. While Wang Yi-An, Yang Tian-Xu and Jin Qi-Long were in the back row seats, a heated, intense look on Yang Tian-Xu's face every time Jin Qi-Long asked Wang Yi-An a question.

Yet, Wang Yi-An doesn't like to engage in conversations with anyone. She answers a simple, yes or no. And then Wang Yi-An would say, "Excuse me." And so she would pull out her sketchbooks again as she draws the scenery that passed by.

They sat in silence while she drew, he watched her as she was drawing. Amazed at her incredible talents, he let out a handsome smile the entire ride as he thought, "If I can hold you now, that would be the best thing that ever happens." Yet, how could he? Yang Tian-Xu's heart pound, and it was like he couldn't breathe, however, without her, he felt like he cannot live without her, unable to go on.

After a short 10-minute ride to the restaurant. They all stepped out of the mini-van. Jin Qi-Long had taken them to a famous and expensive restaurant call, Seasons. Yang Tian-Xu and Jin Qi-Long were both VIP members of this restaurant, and they frequently hold parties and events at this fancy place. As they walked in, the staffs welcomed them.

The place looked grand and enormous, as it often used as a wedding banquet hall, for the rich and famous. A staff member led them into a private room, big enough to fit everyone. Equipped with a mahjong table, a karaoke machine, and a large twelfth-seaters dining table in the private room. Tong Yue-Yan and Lee Yin-Yin both wanted to sit next to Yang Tian-Xu, so they told him to come to take a seat beside them, each sitting on the opposite end of the table. With Lee Yin-Yin on the left, she sat down first and asked Yang Tian-Xu to have a seat beside her so they could, "discussed" their work.

Tong Yue-Yan stood as she waited for Yang Tian-Xu to find a seat. Hoping that he won't sit next to Lee Yin-Yin. Just as annoyance had struck Yang Tian-Xu's nerves, Wang Yi-An took a seat. Yang Tian-Xu rushed over to take a seat beside her. His actions were quick like he was afraid someone might take his spot.

"It's better if all of Yang Corps members stay together," said Assistant Tseng as he made his excuse. He sat beside Yang Tian-Xu. Making Yang Tian-Xu in the middle of Assistant Tseng and Wang Yi-An. Assistant Tseng said, "It's better if we Yang Corps members stay together."

The table was round, and it did not matter where anyone sits however Tong Yue-Yan was mad that she could not sit next to Yang Tian-Xu and so she asked Wang Yi-An to switch seats with her. However, how could Yang Tian-Xu let her leave? As Wang Yi-An got up, he held on to her hand. "Don't go."

CHAPTER 15

Stay With Me

Willing to offer her seat to Tong Yue-Yan, Wang Yi-An got up from her seat, however, Yang Tian-Xu grabbed onto her wrist —he pulls her down on her chair—as he held on to her hand he said, "Don't go." he said aloud, as he gripped harder onto her wrist, "Why do you have to go?" He made it clear he wanted her to sit beside him, "I want to sit next to you." Yang Tian-Xu never cared about how anyone thinks of him.

If Yang Tian-Xu had enough courage, he wanted to confess to Wang Yi-An right now at this moment. He wanted to tell her he loves her so much: he can't seem to be apart from her. Hesitance about his confession—he can't fight a battle he was unsure of winning. He doesn't want to make her hate him. Rejections were the result he feared the most, he won't be able to handle it.

Needed to be sure he was more than just her boss, so for now, he told her, "Stay with me."

Nonetheless, Assistant Tseng knew his President's intent was, so he helped make an excuse, "Right! Wang Yi-An is our employee, it's better if she stays with us. Miss Tong, our president, likes to make sure our intern is being watched over our with the greatest care. Also, it's easier for us to discuss our workload if needed. There are plenty of places you can sit if you don't mind you can sit next to our intern."

Yang Tian-Xu still holds onto her hand from under the table. No idea what was going on, Wang Yi-An remained silent, as she thought, "Perhaps President Yang wants to discuss the project during lunch together?" She wanted to release her hand from his grip, and so she wiggles her hand out, hurting Yang Tian-Xu's feeling in the progress. He tried to hold on to her hands forever, but he can't, and so when she wiggled, he let go of her hand.

Tong Yue-Yan doesn't want to make a scene just because she can't sit next to Yang Tian-Xu, so she sat next to Wang Yi-An. Tong Yue-Yan looked over at Lee Yin-Yin, and they glared at each other. It's like in their mind they can talk to one another. "Stay away from Yang Tian-Xu."

Meanwhile, Lee Yin-Yin would glare back from her eyes, and it was like they said, "Why? He's not yours, he doesn't even want to sit next to you, and he would rather sit next to his employees." Lee Yin-Yin had a smirk on her face that reveals her intentions.

Now as the official spokesperson for Faithful Gold Enterprise, she would have lots of opportunities to spend time with Yang Tian-Xu. Not feeling the rush to become close to Yang Tian-Xu she let out a smirk. As the spokesperson for the perfume, Grace, Lee Yin-Yin need to visits Yang Corps building multiple times. Each time she had promotional shootings, photo-shoots, and voice recordings for the promotional videos: she would need to go see Yang Tian-Xu. Friday was the scheduled day for her photo shoot at Yang Corps so Lee Yin-Yin would have some alone time with him.

Lee Yin-Yin sat in between her manager and Jin Qi-Long. Jin Qi-Long notices the cold shoulders. However, it doesn't stop him from trying. A sheer fact that Lee Yin-Yin likes Yang Tian-Xu; Jin Qi-Long knew the man wasn't blind. Uncaring about who Lee Yin-Yin likes now, he was sure: confident he could make her fall for him. "Miss Lee, you have such a beautiful singing voice, we would love to hear you sing, may I ask if you can sing a song for us?" Jin Qi-Long was sincere with his request.

"Of course, Mr Jin. I'll be more than happy to." Lee Yin-Yin got up from her seat and went over to the mini-karaoke bar. The private room had a high-tech entertainment system. Everyone paid attention to Lee Yin-Yin as she got up on stage. Tong Yue-Yan felt like she too can sing just as good as Lee Yin-Yin, however, in her mind, she looked down on Lee Yin-Yin's profession and smirk as she rolled her eyes at Lee Yin-Yin.

Everyone's eyes were on Lee Yin-Yin. However the only one who didn't seem to care was Yang Tian-Xu, his eyes were on Wang Yi-An only. Assistant Tseng took a glance back and noticed, and he whispered in Yang Tian-Xu's ear. "President, could you be more obvious?"

In a calmed voice, Yang Tian-Xu whispered back, "Am I?" he never cared if anyone else knew about his feelings towards Wang Yi-An, he wanted to make it obvious to everyone else. However, until he heard Assistant Tseng's reasoning.

"Yes! Yes, you are! Boss, you want to make Wang Yi-An a victim of these two furious girls?" Assistant Tseng worried, he wanted to protect this innocent girl himself, as he knew how anyone would react once they find out about President Yang's feelings.

"No..." Yang Tian-Xu thought, and then in a low voice, close to a whisper, but loud enough for Assistant Tseng to hear loud and clear, he said: "If these two girls try to touch her I'll make their life a living hell!"

With excellent hearing, Wang Yi-An asked, "Whose life a living hell?" She only paid attention to some part of the conversation and was unsure of what the discussion might have been, she assumed it was work related.

"Nothing!" Yang Tian-Xu freaked out, and his heart felt like it would pop out of his chest. "Don't worry too much about it and enjoy the show."

"Hm!" she nodded as let out a happy smile.

Her memories of when she was little came back to her as she watched Lee Yin-Yin's live performance. She had a bright smile as she remembered about her days as a little girl. Her mother never had the chance to take her out because her mother had to work two different jobs just to sustain the family. Wang Yi-An and her mother lived a rough life, but overall they were a happy family.

Jin Qi-Long had already pre-ordered all the meals on their way to the restaurant as they got there the table was ready within five minutes of their arrival. Once the food comes, it was at the perfect temperature they should be at: there were a lot of dishes, each one makes Wang Yi-An's mouth watered. Happy to eat, she had a first taste of the rich person's meal, Wang Yi-An hoped to take some of these excellent food homes with her if she could.

Yang Tian-Xu smiled as he watches her dug in as soon as the food arrived. Yang Tian-Xu took out his chopstick and took some beef and place it into her bowl, "Here, try some of these stir-fry beef, it's pretty good, but your cooking is much better." As he let out his handsome and charming smile at her.

It might be a good performance by Lee Yin-Yin—but wasn't enough to impress Tong Yue-Yan. Inside Tong Yue-Yan's eyes: Lee Yin-Yin was nothing more than a mere singer. Often, Tong Yue-Yan would look over to Yang Tian-Xu side and notices he had been placing food on Wang Yi-An's plate. Tong Yue-Yan never thought anything more to it and only believed Yang Tian-Xu was nice towards his employee. As a matter of fact; the best employer of the year title belonged to Yang Corps.

Tong Yue-Yan thought perhaps he was trying to show this new intern, why, Yang Corp ranked first place as best employers. Tong Yue-Yan didn't want to miss this chance to show her

"Future Mrs Yang" semblance. And so she had used her public chopstick to take a piece of the fried chicken dish and place it in Wang Yi-An's bowl. "Here, try this as well; the flavours here are delicious."

"Thank you very much, Miss Tong." Sincere gratitude from Wang Yi-An as she placed the food in her mouth. Yang Tian-Xu would frown his brows, he wanted her to eat only the food he picked for her. "Here, try these," he said, as he placed more food on Wang Yi-An's plate.

Wang Yi-An said with a bright smile on her face, "Thank you, President Yang! You are all such kind people! Here, have some too!" she then picked a piece of the food from the serving plates with her private chopsticks for both Yang Tian-Xu and Tong Yue-Yan.

Born from a poor family, they only used one type of chopstick to eat and server their food with, however, wealthy families were different. The two different chopsticks have different purposes. Chinese dinner comprised many side dishes of food. Like stir-fried, sweet and sour pork, or BBQ meat; laid out on the dining table. To select a piece of food on those side dishes, people have to use the public chopstick and place it into their own side bowl or plates. To transfer foods from their plates into their mouths they would use private chopsticks. This way, there won't be any cross-contamination of germs or saliva among them, a more sanitary table manner.

However, Wang Yi-An never had to deal with public or private chopsticks, she wasn't aware of it. Born in a single family home. Her mother wasn't wealthy, so how could Wang Yi-An know about the differences? At home, Wang Yi-An and her mother used one kind of chopstick; the same one to pick food off the serving plates of foods, and place them inside their mouths. She never had to use a public chopstick; there was no such thing as family etiquettes when she was with her mother. Sometimes, they'll take food off the serving plates and feed them directly into each other's mouths. At home, Wang Yi-An raised without family etiquette, and it shows in her table manners.

The rest of these people who were present there at the dining table were all from wealthy families, except Assistant Tseng; he was born in a middle-class family like Lee Yin-Yin was until she became rich and famous as a singer. However, even the middle-class family knew about dining etiquettes. Everyone stared at her as she places food on both Tong Yue-Yan's plate and Yang Tian-Xu's plate. Tong Yue-Yan wasn't so happy and found it disgusting, and so she wouldn't even touch the food given by Wang Yi-An and push the plate away.

However, as for Yang Tian-Xu, he smiled as he took the food and placed it in his mouth. "This one tasted delicious." He chewed and smiled as he continued to eat and wanted her to take more food for him. "Can you give me some more?"

"Ah, sure. You want these?" She asked, and he nodded, and then she continued to use her own private chopsticks to take another piece of food and places it in Yang Tian-Xu's bowl. Tong Yue-Yan felt disgusted by it, and could only shake her head and told her, "Don't you know how to use a public chopstick? You're feeding everyone your saliva."

Wang Yi-An looked at everyone and finally notices that people were taking food with another pair of chopsticks. "Oh, sorry, I didn't know we have to use a separate pair of chopsticks." Wang Yi-An felt embarrassed. However, Yang Tian-Xu didn't mind. In fact, he was happy to eat her saliva.

Yang Tian-Xu felt like he had an indirect kiss with her, so he speaks up, "It's okay, you don't have to be so formal with me. I don't mind if you used your private chopstick. Just eat comfortably."

How can anyone else complain after hearing Yang Tian-Xu said those words? Yang Tian-Xu was a man of high-class, born and raised in a wealthy powerhouse. The Yang family was all about table manners and etiquettes.

Yang Tian-Xu continues to use his public chopsticks to take some food and place it on a separate plate for Wang Yi-An to take from.

Yang Tian-Xu acted like he was helping her take food from far away places and placing it closer to Wang Yi-An. However, Yang Tian-Xu was personally afraid that she would share her saliva with the rest of them and wanted her all to himself.

"However, it's better for these guys if you use a public chopstick, or better I'll take a few foods for you. How about it? Here, let me place the food closer to you here, so you don't have to worry about public chopstick or private chopstick with the rest." he said as he placed more food on her plate.

"Thank you, President Yang! You are indeed a kind boss!" Wang Yi-An smiled at him and continues to use her own private chopstick to pick the food off the separator plate.

Yang Tian-Xu had taken a lot of food, she couldn't possibly finish it herself, so she grabbed some food and places it in his bowl. "President Yang, you have given me too much food, I can't finish them all!"

"Oh?" Yang Tian-Xu let out a smirk, and said, "How about we share them together."

Jin Qi-Long and Assistant Tseng could both feel the goosebumps on their skins as they watch the expression on Yang Tian-Xu's face. Yang Tian-Xu was happy, and he couldn't be any more delighted that he was sharing food with Wang Yi-An.

Yang Tian-Xu and Wang Yi-An would exchange food into each other's bowl. However, this did not make Tong Yue-Yan or Lee Yin-Yin jealous.

All they thought was that perhaps Wang Yi-An was very

closed to Yang Tian-Xu, or because she was his intern he acted nice towards her? And so they thought perhaps Wang Yi-An was their key to get closer to Yang Tian-Xu.

At 1:24 p.m., everyone filled their stomachs with a fancy meal. Wang Yi-An needed to use the washroom to wash her hands, as she had always been a messy eater. Yang Tian-Xu stood and waited for her, without moving away from the entrance. Yang Tian-Xu refused to leave without Wang Yi-An. So, who else would dare to leave without them? So they stood in front of the hallway with him, waiting for Wang Yi-An.

Yang Tian-Xu smiled as he watched her walked into the lady's restroom. He watched Wang Yi-An's back, as he thought occurred to him, "This has got to be my happiest day!" A big grin appeared on his expression as he continued to daydream. Assistant Tseng notices the glaze in Yang Tian-Xu's eyes, and coughed, "Boss, you're out in the open..." he whispered, his voice was low, and it was loud enough for Yang Tian-Xu to hear.

Meanwhile, Wang Yi-An was at the sink, washing her hands, Tong Yue-Yan walked in. Tong Yue-Yan stood next to Wang Yi-An. And she said, "Wang Yi-An." The way Tong Yue-Yan called her name, startled Wang Yi-An. Wang Yi-An turned to see who it was, and as she saw Tong Yue-Yan she smiled as she asked in a refined manner, "Yes, Miss Tong?"

"You seem to get along well with Tian-Xu." Tong Yue-Yan was standing beside her with her arm crossed, and she looked all high and mighty when she speaks to Wang Yi-An.

A sweet and polite voice as Wang Yi-An smiled and said, "Yes, President Yang had been a very kind boss."

"Of course; he's a kind boss." Tong Yue-Yan looked at her with disdain, and her arrogance showed in her attitude when she spoke, "I want you to become my messenger, and every time you relay a message about Tian-Xu, I will pay you handsomely. What do you think about this arrangement?" Tong Yue-Yan smirked at she believed to be capable of anything, with her family's wealth and power. If money can solve the problem, then it's not a problem.

"Messenger?" Wang Yi-An was a little confused, "I don't understand what you mean by that."

"Look, I am Tong Yue-Yan. I don't know if you know my father is City A's Mayor or not, however, let me tell you this; when I become Yang Tian-Xu's wife; I won't forget to reward you." The smirk on her face remains as she felt she could use her money for anything.

Yet, how could Tong Yue-Yan knew, Lee Yin-Yin followed into the washroom right after her. Lee Yin-Yin laughed as she said, "Why should she help you? When she can help me instead?" Lee Yin-Yin stood behind them when she spoke; she startled Tong Yue-Yan. Wang Yi-An and Tong Yue-Yan turned and saw Lee Yin-Yin as she stood with her back straight, and her arms crossed, leading with her right shoulder on the wall. Lee Yin-Yin's height was a little taller than Tong Yue-Yan, the closer she walked towards them, the more they looked equally beautiful when stood side by side.

The two girls height were far above average, both were well over five feet tall, while Wang Yi-An's height was five nothing. Compared to them, she felt a little uncomfortable, as Lee Yin-Yin stood closer. If Wang Yi-An doesn't a step back a few inches, they could squeeze her in the middle.

The two girls confronted, face to face; like a fierce battle heated to a boiling point. At first, a staring-contest, a few seconds of silence as the girls stared at one another. Survival instinct kicks in; wanting to get the hell out as she could feel a bloody battle, unfolding as every second passed by. Wang Yi-An thought, "I should not stay here..."

However, as Wang Yi-An step back, Tong Yue-Yan took a step closer to Lee Yin-Yin and said, "Help You? Why would she help such a low-rank class like yourself? Can you even offer her as much money as I can?"

Lee Yin-Yin laugh out with disdain on her expression as she replied, "Low-rank? Don't you know I am now the best idol in the country? I'm more well known than you. Who's only just a mere mayor's daughter, for a small city."

Frustrated to be talked back in a bad-mannered tone, Tong Yue-Yan said, "What did you say? So what if you're a famous idol?" Tong Yue-Yan continued her abusive verbal comments towards Lee Yin-Yin as she faced her, "You are still a low-class girl; raised in a low-class family." Tong Yue-Yan lifted her index finger and point at Lee Yin-Yin's body, she kept her arrogant attitude as she pushed Lee Yin-Yin's body with her index finger, "You think because you are miss famous idol, you-you can properly match up with the Yang Family? My father is City A's Mayor! When regarding class, I'm way higher than you!"

Tong Yue-Yan's verbal attack at Lee Yin-Yin became more ruthless, as she looked down at Lee Yin-Yin, mocking her for every little detail about family background. "If this is still the Song Dynasty, you are considered a prostitute, a pretty face meant to pleasure men, who's paying you in pennies. You are nothing but a low-life, and you think you can compete with me?"

How can Lee Yin-Yin take the verbal abuse? Her body boiled up with fury as she could no longer hold in the anger. Lee Yin-Yin screamed out with anger, as she rushed towards Tong Yue-Yan and grabbed on to her hair. Tong Yue-Yan's hair was shoulder-length, so it was accessible to grab a hold on.

Tong Yue-Yan screamed as her hair got pulled, unwilling to be pushed around, she grabbed onto Lee Yin-Yin's long hair, the extensions in her hair got yanked off with force until she grabbed again at Lee Yin-Yin's real hair. The two girls pulled and tugged on to each other's hair as they screamed, shouted, and cursed at each other.

Wang Yi-An had a feeling this might happen, she felt the need to break these two apart, but she thought it would be better to find help, so she rushed outside the restroom, and cried for help. "Help someone!"

Meanwhile outside, when Yang Tian-Xu heard Wang Yi-An's voice, he rushed to her side. They met outside the entrance, the two girls voices were loud enough, their voices echoed out in the distant from inside the restroom. A few steps down towards the entrance, everyone else followed with Yang Tian-Xu. With only Wang Yi-An in his eyes, he wasn't able to hear anything else, the moment he saw her, he placed his hands on her shoulders and asked her, "Are you alright? An-An?"

Unhurt, Wang Yi-An shook her head, however, catching her breath as she ran out as fast as she can, she asked for help, "Help! Miss Tong and Miss Lee are fighting inside!" Yet, the only thing Yang Tian-Xu cared about was Wang Yi-An. After Yang Tian-Xu scanned her for any injuries, he let out a sigh of relief as he saw an unharmed Wang Yi-An.

Love, it made him blind—without a care for anything else unrelated to Wang Yi-An. Two girls fighting over for his affection? He couldn't care: as long as Wang Yi-An was safe, nothing else matters.

CHAPTER 16
That's Not Good

Worried about the two girls, Wang Yi-An cried for help, "Help! Miss Tong and Miss Lee are fighting inside!"

Yang Tian-Xu couldn't care less about those two girls. Only Jin Qi-Long cared enough to rush inside, he needed to make sure Lee Yin-Yin would be unharmed—she had become Faithful Gold Enterprise's new spokesperson. It won't be good for his company's image if the spokesperson sustains unexplainable injuries. Lee Yin-Yin's manager rushed in alone with Jin Qi-Long: he can't let anything happen to the top artist—Lee Yin-Yin was the country's top idol.

As soon as they rushed in, they could see the two girls fighting: they pulled and tugged at each other's hair, as they screamed and shouted. They cursed at one another, a chaotic scene ensued as they yanked and grabbed each other. Their clothing was a mess.

Lee Yin-Yin's manager and Jin Qi-Long tried to separate the two girls. Lee Yin-Yin's manager tried to help his artist, while Jin Qi-Long tried to hold on to Tong Yue-Yan, as they attempted to separate the two. Jin Qi-Long asked Tong Yue-Yan, "Miss Tong, let go of Miss Lee. You two shouldn't be fighting like this!" he tried to hold her back, however, her hands seemed to be glued to Lee Yin-Yin's hair.

None of them will let go, they became inseparable like someone glued their hands to the other's hair. Tong Yue-Yan cried aloud, "Why should I let go first!? She's the barbaric one!"

Lee Yin-Yin screamed as she pulled Tong Yue-Yan's hair harder, almost ripping her hair off, she shouted, "Make her let go first!"

They used every name-calling-vocabulary in the dictionary as they cursed at each other. Unpleasant to watch—the two beautiful ladies turned ugly as they continued to bicker, while they yanked at each other's hair; pulling harder as the argument became heated with anger.

Regardless of the chaos inside the ladies restroom, Yang Tian-Xu doesn't care. He turned to Assistant Tseng and said, "I will head back with An-An, you stay and handle the matter." Then he grabbed hold of Wang Yi-An's hand, and with a charming smile he said, "Let's go, leave the matter to Assistant Tseng, we have a lot of work back at the office, we should hurry back." A calm Yang Tian-Xu made others perceive him as cold-hearted— but he doesn't want to get involved in a cat-fight, he also doesn't want to get Wang Yi-An involved.

When Yang Tian-Xu leads Wang Yi-An away from the catastrophe, she said, "But!" as she turned to look at the two girls, still fighting. Yang Tian-Xu continued to pull her away by the wrist, Yang Tian-Xu was strong—unable to break herself free from his grasp—she followed along with him, he leads her away. The moment as they got out of the building, Yang Tian-Xu hailed for a taxi. The taxi was nearby, so it appeared on cue. Yang Tian-Xu opened the door for Wang Yi-An to get in first. She doesn't know what to do, or how to react towards his forcefulness, she asked, "But, what about Miss Tong and Miss Lee?"

Yang Tian-Xu squeezed next to her, making his way to have his seat next to her inside the taxi, he smiled as he reassured her, "Don't worry about them. Assistant Tseng can handle a small matter like that." Yang Tian-Xu told the taxi driver to take them to Yang Corps headquarter.

The taxi drove off, but Yang Tian-Xu's hand was still holding onto hers, she wanted to let go of his grip, but he held her tight, a sharp grip that made her conscious, "Um, President... Your hand..."

"Right... Sorry..." Yang Tian-Xu face flushed red as he let go of her hand, he felt like his heart would rip right out of his chest. He sneaked a small glance at her and realised she wasn't even looking at him. Wang Yi-An had her cell phone up, and she sent a message to Assistant Tseng. Wang Yi-An wanted an update on the situation, as she hoped nobody got hurt, and that everything was under control.

In her hand, she held an old cellular phone model, one she had used for a long time. It looked old, however, she took proper care, and all the functions still worked, she never needed to get a new phone.

Yang Tian-Xu thought, "Perhaps I should get her a new phone? But how should I give her a gift for no reason? Should I lie and say it's a company phone?" Yang Tian-Xu kept thinking of ways to gift her a new smartphone, "That might just work..." After considering for a few minutes, Yang Tian-Xu decided, and pull out his smartphone and messaged Assistant Tseng.

At the time: Assistant Tseng was busy trying to separate the two girls apart when his phone chimed. His smartphone synced together with his smart-watch, so took a quick peek at it, while he held Tong Yue-Yan as she struggled: her hands still glued to Lee Yin-Yin's hair—wanting to tear them off of Lee Yin-Yin's head.

Wang Yi-An sent the first message, "Is everything all right?" However, he ignored it, for the time being so he could settle two girls down. A brief second as they managed to have them let go of each other's hair. However, two minutes after he received Wang Yi-An's message, his phone chimed again, but this time it was a text from Yang Tian-Xu.

Assistant Tseng took another peek, shocked to the message, "Go buy me three smartphones for the interns, I don't care what the other two get, but for Wang Yi-An—I want her new phone to be the same model as mine."

"What the fu-" Assistant cursed aloud, he let go of the uncontrollable Tong Yue-Yan, and so she took her chance to jumped out at Lee Yin-Yin, she wanted to rip out Lee Yin-Yin's hair. Jin Qi-Long shouted at him, "What the hell man! Don't let go of her!"

Jin Qi-Long and Lee Yin-Yin's manager tried to get Tong Yue-Yan off of Lee Yin-Yin. At first, they managed to pull her off, but the two girls screamed and shouted trying to fight things out. Uncontrollable, it was hard for them to separate the two girls for a brief moment, and when Assistant Tseng let go, the situation repeated. The girls had a run with each other again.

Assistant Tseng was so shocked by the message, he forgot about how chaotic the situation was. The sudden action from Assistant Tseng shocked Lee Yin-Yin's manager and Jin Qi-Long, the girls rushed to battle each other in another tug-of-war. Caused both Jin Qi-Long and Lee Yin-Yin's manager to lose their balance and fall to the floor.

"Assistant Tseng!" Jin Qi-Long shouted out his name as a cry for help. Assistant Tseng snapped back to the situation and went to help the two guys to separate the girls again. No matter how much they wanted to call the police, they couldn't go because of Lee Yin-Yin's fame. He apologised and continued to hold Tong Yue-Yan back and separate the two again. The girl screamed and shouted as they cursed again, Lee Yin-Yin shouts as she pushed her manager out, and jumped onto Tong Yue-Yan, pulling her hair hard.

If the news gets out that Lee Yin-Yin fought with the heiress of the Tong Family, it will not look good for either of them.

"Stop it you two, let go!" Assistant Tseng couldn't hold it in any longer until he threatens them. "Stop it now! Or would you two ladies want to appear on the cover page of Gossipies? Oh, believe me, you will because this is one hell of a juicy story for the media!"

Both Tong Yue-Yan and Lee Yin-Yin cared about their image, so they finally stopped, however. It was only for a second until one of them started to curse the other, and so the cycle repeats itself. The guys can cry about it as they attempt to remove them from each other.

An overall chaotic day at the restaurant, yet, Yang Tian-Xu had a smirk on his face the entire time. At the backseat of a taxi, with just him and Wang Yi-An as she sat next to him in silence. They were quiet throughout the ride back to Yang Corps. Yang Tian-Xu really hoped that the trip would last forever. Even though Yang Tian-Xu wanted to talk to her, however, he cannot bring himself to open his mouth. Which was unusual for Yang Tian-Xu, he was a president of Yang Corps, a big company? Public speaking was his forte. Yet, in front of Wang Yi-An, he couldn't bring himself to engage in a conversation. Yang Tian-Xu does not want to make her feel like he was an annoying person. He sneaked a glance over at her once every-so-often and hoped the red light would stay red forever.

Wang Yi-An likes the quiet, and she remains quiet the entire ride back to Yang Corps. At 2:00 p.m., they arrived at Yang Corps headquarters where the taxi driver dropped them off at the west entrance. Yang Tian-Xu paid the taxi driver, and they walked in together. The entire ride back, Wang Yi-An thought about the two girls, concerned for them, she hoped that they would be all right. Wang Yi-An knew what they were fighting about, but she kept quiet.

Often, she sent messages to Assistant Tseng, hoping for an

update on the situation of the girls. After struggling for over half an hour, Jin Qi-Long, Lee Yin-Yin's manager, and Assistant Tseng had broken them apart for good. Assistant Tseng volunteered to take Tong Yue-Yan to a walk-in-clinic before dropping her back home; meanwhile, Jin Qi-Long and Lee Yin-Yin's manager would take Lee Yin-Yin back to her home.

Assistant Tseng replied to Wang Yi-An's message as soon as he had everything under control, "Everything's good. Don't worry about it."

Wang Yi-An let out a breath of relief, relax again after she received Assistant Tseng's message, she became cheerful again, with no need to worry about the two girls. As Yang Tian-Xu and Wang Yi-An reach the office, she jumped right back into her working mode.

Piles of unread documents and folders covered Yang Tian-Xu's desk, he had lots of work to complete by the end of the day, yet he managed to squeeze in the time to send another message to Assistant Tseng to remind him about the smartphones. Unable to bother her, he watched her from the window. Like a silly man in love, he smiled as he felt the most blissful all week long.

On the contrary: Assistant Tseng felt the most furious after he took Tong Yue-Yan back to her villa, he received the message from President Yang as a reminder. "You can give the phones to the other two interns, but for Wang Yi-An's new phone, give me the phone."

Considered being the most heartless person in the world, Yang Tian-Xu does not care for anyone else but himself. Now he only cared for one person... Wang Yi-An. Assistant Tseng cannot believe it, "How is buying Wang Yi-An a new phone more important? He didn't even bother to ask about the two girls! These two girls fought each other violently for his affection?" Assistant Tseng wanted to cry, he felt bad for the two girls, "Is it even worth it?"

A million unanswered question surfaced in his mind. Assistant Tseng continued to follow President Yang's order. He visited a mobile store in Yang Corps mall and purchased three smartphones with the business credit card. One that was the exact model as President Yang, and two random ones. By the time he finished, he had returned to the office at 3:55 p.m, he had given the two random phone to Kwon Li-Mei and Liang Shing.

Happy to receive such a gift, they thanked him, and he continued to make his way up to the seventh floor. Today was a catastrophe, he felt as if he had returned from war. Only one hour and five minutes until 5:00 p.m. Assistant Tseng wanted nothing more than to return home to his wife and cry in her arms from all the built-up stress he bottled inside.

Headed straight to meet with President Yang as he got off the elevator, he went into the office and reported the incident, "Sorry I came back so late, it was disastrous with Miss tong and Miss—"

"Yeah, yeah, just give me the phone." Yang Tian-Xu interrupted.

Assistant Tseng should know how little care President Yang had for those two girls. Assistant Tseng sighed aloud and handed over a small paper bag—with a small box inside.

Yang Tian-Xu grabbed the bag and looked inside. He checked to make sure the phone was the exact model as his. After he made sure, a handsome smile appeared from his face. "Good, good..." he said as he nodded.

One hell of a day for Assistant Tseng as he felt pain all over his body, he wanted to leave early, and so he asked, "Boss, may I please leave early today?"

"Sure, sure," he said while he shooed Assistant Tseng with one hand, without looking at him. Yang Tian-Xu placed all his focus on the smartphone: double checking the phone's specifications. Assistant Tseng felt the cold shoulders, depressed as he couldn't believe how cruel President Yang could become.

Just as Assistant Tseng turned away to leave, he heard President Yang called out, "Wait." Assistant Tseng stopped as soon as he heard President Yang's voice.

"Yes, boss!" Assistant Tseng was excited, perhaps his boss wants to hear about the crazy chaos he had been through today, but then, his excitement soon turned into disappointment when President Yang said, "You know where An-An went?"

Yang Tian-Xu saw Wang Yi-An's empty seat, he was busy reading a contract for just a minute, and she had already disappeared from his sight! He wanted to gift her the phone himself. Yet, only an empty chair in sight, he felt the anxiety, asking, "Where is she?"

Assistant Tseng shook his head, and Yang Tian-Xu walked outside the General Manager's office. He saw a random employee and asked him. "You know where An-An went?"

"An-An...? Oh, Wang Yi-An? Yeah, I saw her in the supplies room, just now." The employee pointed toward the supplies room's direction. Yang Tian-Xu ignored Assistant Tseng and the people in his surrounding as he headed straight to the supplies room. The employee stared at Assistant Tseng in confusion, and Assistant Tseng shrugged back as his reply.

His throbbing heart pounded faster, the closer he approached the supplies room's door. Yang Tian-Xu can't remember when, but he had ever felt this way before—perhaps never. But at this moment, Yang Tian-Xu felt an extreme nervousness. A small imprint formed by the bag because of his tight grip, his right palm turned red.

His nervousness made him grip tighter on to the bag, he worried more and more. Never an anxious person, Yang Tian-Xu felt a sudden queasiness. Frustrated, as he never felt this way before, he used to be so confident in himself.

Yet, his unshakeable confidence collapsed at the thought about how he would interact with Wang Yi-An. Yang Tian-Xu stood outside the door for a while, as he continued to repeat himself in a different tone, "Here An-An, I got you this phone... No! That's not good..." he paced back and forth.

The palms of his hands became sweaty and a shade redder as he squeezed the band tighter. He continued pacing outside— he thought of about all the possible things he could say to her once he sees her. Yang Tian-Xu never noticed the stares from his employees.

Random passersby would sneak a peek at him now and then. The employees would think their President was acting unusual. However, they have no guts to interrupt him because they knew how fussy President Yang can be if they did.

President Yang got lost in his thoughts often for new ideas and plans for the company, so it wasn't unusual for him to be pacing around like that. However, he remains in his office when he does pace around. Yet, today he walked back and forward in the hallway. Perhaps the problem President Yang dealing with was an extreme case so the employees wouldn't dare to bother him.

How could they know the real reason behind his unsettled restlessness? Yang Tian-Xu became so agitated and filled with nervousness today, as he tried to build up his courage. For what? For being able to gift an intern a smartphone.

Behind a closed door, unable to control his emotions. Yang Tian-Xu's expression made him seem jittery, he took in a deep breath, and exhaled slowly. Yang Tian-Xu built enough courage to open the door. As the door opened, he saw her struggling to get something above her, even with the stool she stood on—it was unhelpful.

The ceiling-high shelves were too high for Wang Yi-An. She was a shortie. At five foot nothing, she could not reach the supply she required. She struggled again as she reached her arms up higher, she tried reaching for the printer's ink-toner refill kit. The box was so high up, the more she attempted to reach out, the closer her feet were to the edge of the stool. She could fall any minute.

Inching closer to the edge, the sudden loud sound as the door opened startled Wang Yi-An: she lost her balance and was about to fall. In that split second; Yang Tian-Xu dropped the bag in his hand and rushed out to save her, his reaction was so fast, he managed to catch her in time before she tipped over.

The loud chime of the door startled her as it opened. The sound came from the access machine, it beeped as the door unlocks, and again as it shuts. Wang Yi-An twisted her head over to look and saw it was President Yang Tian-Xu, he had his arms wrapped around her as he supported her weight.

"Thank you, President Yang." She said as she gave him a sweet smile. "I can't believe how short I am." She laughed as she made fun of her height. Yang Tian-Xu remained dazzled as he kept his position.

In an awkward embracing position, Yang Tian-Xu had his arms wrapped around her waist. She had a tiny waist, but she wasn't too skinny or chubby, she was at a perfect size, like a piece of a puzzle that fits perfectly into his arms.

If he could, he'll never let her go, however, Wang Yi-An felt a sudden confusion as she had already regained her balance. Yet, President Yang's arm still wrapped around her waist! Wang Yi-An no longer needed his support anymore, so she said, "I'm alright now, you can put me down."

"No..." He said as he refused to let her go. There was a moment of pause for them both, only until Yang Tian-Xu said, "I'll help lift you up." And then he lifts her up higher, stunned by his action, she said, "It's fine!". To support her weight (although she wasn't heavy at all), he grasped tighter as he lifted her high up.

"Ah... Okay..." bewildered, Wang Yi-An didn't know what to say, and as Yang Tian-Xu held her up, her arms were at a convenient length to retrieve the box.

Wang Yi-An needed to print the design templates for Yang Tian-Xu to review first before she can send the actual design file to the manufacturer, but the printer ran out of ink. As the new intern: it was her responsibility to refill the cartridge.

When Wang Yi-An went to the supply room, she met the previous employee Yang Tian-Xu had asked for her whereabouts. She didn't think she needed help to reach the ink-toner refill kit. Now she thought about it, she should have asked for help when the employee was present.

Wang Yi-An was a little embarrassed because there was no need for Yang Tian-Xu to lifted her up like that! He could have taken the box down pass it to her as he was tall enough to manage and reach the box. Yet, he chose to lift her up, and this feeling made her blushed, and she stuttered, "Um, President... You can. Ah... Put me down now...?" she secured the box in her hands.

However, Yang Tian-Xu refused to let her go, he slides her down yet still supporting her with his body, as he held her tight. Their eyes met as he remained attached to her. Speechless as she turned her head away from his gaze. "Um... President, you can put me down now..."

CHAPTER 17

What Do You Feel About Me?

Wang Yi-An's body was average, and light weighted as he held her up, and her feet never touch the ground. Her eyes met with Yang Tian-Xu's, and he supported her body with his. They stared at each other for a brief second, still embraced in his arms, he felt his heart pound hard. Almost as if his heart could jump out of his chest, his face flushed red as his subconsciousness forced his body to lean in closer to her. He stared deep into her eyes and his mind blanked out as he became lost in her eyes.

Disregarding how Yang Tian-Xu felt and was embarrassed about her weight, Wang Yi-An thought, "Perhaps, I'm so heavy he can't seem to hold me properly?" As her body slide down lower, Wang Yi-An knew she was a little heavier than most people her age or height. Her body was at an average well-fit body mass, however, her breast was full and round.

Yang Tian-Xu could feel the fullness of her breast as she was pressed onto his body. Wang Yi-An didn't notice it and was only concern about her weight, she thought his red face was because he used his strength to keep her up. Yang Tian-Xu's face was boiling red because he could feel her breast pressed on to his chest. The feeling had aroused his desire for her.

However, Wang Yi-An still conscious about her weight, she said, "I got the ink supply now. President Yang, you can let me down."

Impossible to let her go just yet, he wanted to hold on to

her longer; much longer. Forever if he could.

Just like this...

If he died now, he'd still die as the happiest man ever, he thought. He wanted her to remain in his arms. "Isn't there anything else you'll need?" He asked, hoping that he could hold on to her for a few seconds longer.

"Nope..." she shook her head and said, "You can put me down now." Wang Yi-An felt a little more conscious about her weight every second as she remained in his embrace. She faced away from Yang Tian-Xu's eyes because she felt embarrassed.

While Wang Yi-An was concern about her weight; Yang Tian-Xu felt like he was in heaven. She had lost her balance once before, as she thought, "Perhaps President Yang worried I might fall again, he might want to be sure of my safety before he let me down?"

However, it would never cross her mind that the true reason he refused to let her go was that he wanted to remain in this intimate position. "You sure there's nothing else there? You can double check, I'll hold you for as long as you need," he asked, and if someone was to point a gun at him—he would rather die than to let her go.

Wang Yi-An shook her head, "No." Yet, Yang Tian-Xu had no other choice but to slide her down slowly; her feet touched the ground. Their bodies separated from each other as he no longer needed to support her weight. However, his arms remain rested around her waist. For a short second when Wang Yi-An and Yang Tian-Xu had stared into each other's eyes, *her eyes captivated him*. If he could, Yang Tian-Xu wanted to spend the rest of his life as he continued to stare into her eyes forever.

Unable to helped himself anymore, for a while he stared into her eyes. He leaned in closer as he closed the gaps between him and her. The distance between their lips was so close, if only he had enough courage, and if only he would lean in a few inches closer, his lips could touch hers.

Just as Yang Tian-Xu continued to close in on her, Wang Yi-An felt a little uncomfortable. "President Yang!" she cried out as she closed her eyes, "You're getting too close to my face!"

He heard her voice and snapped out of his intoxication, "Sorry... Um..." he stuttered, and all of a sudden he made up an excuse, "There was something in your eyes!"

Wang Yi-An checked as she rubbed her eyes, while Yang Tian-Xu felt safe, as his lies were believable. Telling the truth would be an impossibility, he could never tell her he wanted to kiss her! Yang Tian-Xu was a coward, the fear of rejection overwhelmed him. It was a good thing he was quick at thinking on his feet. Yang Tian-Xu had hidden his infatuation for her well.

A reasonable excused made Wang Yi-An understood the reason for his strange stares at her, as she rubbed her eyes she asked him. "Is it still there?" Wang Yi-An had a lovely voice, a little childlike but innocent and beautiful to Yang Tian-Xu's ears. He hurried to stop her from rubbing her eyes as he grabbed onto her hands. "Don't!" A smoothing deep yet caring voice as he said, "It's bad for your eyes if you rub them too much."

"Right..." Wang Yi-An agreed with him. But, whenever a person points to her that she had something inside her eyes while she could not see it herself—it bothered her! "Is it gone?!

"Not yet!" he said as he lifted both of his hands and held her head steady—he looked deep into her eyes. Only because he wanted her to stare right back at him, but with little suspicion to the true reason. Yang Tian-Xu doesn't know if he was ready to confess his love yet. However, if they remained in this position where he could look into her eyes, day and night, he would feel content.

"President Yang?" Wang Yi-An felt impatient, while he

could only see her in his eyes, she thought, "Is it gone yet?" She wondered about what the thing might have been, as she guessed, "A loose eyelash?" But she felt nothing inside her eyes, if there were something, it would itch. *Wouldn't it?*

Yang Tian-Xu knew if he confessed now, rejection would kick him hard. He can't let that happen, he looked at her one last time before he said, "It's gone." As he released her from his embrace—he distanced himself from her. Yang Tian-Xu turned to face away from her. Wang Yi-An thanked him for his help, but for a second he was unresponsive.

Fixated in her eyes, he knew she harboured no feelings for him as he was nothing more than her boss. Perhaps even worst, he was nothing more to her than a co-worker. In her eyes: it was obvious for him to see how little she felt for him. However, in his eyes: she was the only person capable enough to make his heart felt tight, *so much that it suffocated him inside.* The thoughts of unknowing how she felt for him; it was killing him slowly. Deep in his thoughts, he blurted, "Wang Yi-An, just what do you feel about me?" he blurted.

Lost in his thoughts when he blurted those words, "Wang Yi-An, just what do you feel about me?" He hated himself as he couldn't believe his words. Shocked by his own actions, he thought, "Wait... Did I just—Confess?"

Yang Tian-Xu felt like he became the stupidest person alive. It was sudden, but he had just asked her about what'd she felt about him. How does he expect her to answer? "I... I—" he panicked and mumbled his palms sweat, and he could have felt a shivering cold emerged inside his body, "Well, I—Want to know... If you—Ah... Feel—Like... Ah..." His nervousness overwhelmed him.

Think! Properly, think! Unable to think, he felt nauseated and dizzy. But then, the corners of Wang Yi-An's lips curled upward as she said. "You're a great person, President Yang! I feel like that every time you're near!"

"Say what?" Dumbfounded as Yang Tian-Xu stood there blinking his eyelids, his mind went blank. Wang Yi-An continued. "You want me to give a good rating for Yang Corps internship program right?" She asked, "Why else would you seem so tense?"

Why else? Yang Tian-Xu wanted to grab her and throw her down onto the ground and make love to her like a wild animal, but how could he act on such impulses? Impossible to tell her how he felt, Yang Tian-Xu fell to depression. It was a good thing he had a high tolerance for his own frustration and self-control. If not, what could he do? He thought perhaps her assumption was a good thing? After all, he won't have to make an excuse and lie to her again.

Not for a hundred years would Wang Yi-An thought his question was a confession. Yang Tian-Xu sighed as he articulated, "Yes, I really hope to know about your feelings for Yang Corps before you give your reviews to the board." He smiled at her charmingly.

The board was a regulation designed by the government, and it was mandatory for every secondary institutions and company that arranged internships program to hire students: companies required to submit a weekly report on students. And the students needed to submit a monthly report to the board's website every month of employment; they must submit all evaluation forms online. Wang Yi-An thought his question was regarded to her report for this month. However, only Yang Tian-Xu knew the truth. Yang Tian-Xu hated himself, he doesn't want to lie to her. However, the more he loves her, the more he feared rejection.

Wang Yi-An enjoyed working at Yang Corps, so she smiled

at him and told him, "I think Yang Corps is the best employer!" Yang Tian-Xu felt pitiful, he doesn't want to be just an employer. Yet, how could he be greedy? For now, he decided, he would watch over her just a little longer. Perhaps maybe one day, he won't be able to hold the truth in any longer? Or he need not hide his feelings for her no more—wishful thinking. Yang Tian-Xu smiled back at her, as he took a few steps back. He picked up the bag he had dropped before he rushed over to her aid—as he turned to face her—he handed out the small paper bag to her. "Have this as another plus point for Yang Corps?"

"What is it?" She asked as she stared at it, he forced it into her hands and said, "It's a new smartphone, the company gave interns a company phone."

"Wow, really?" Wang Yi-An became excited. However, for a short moment, as she looked at the phone, she paused, and she saw how expensive the brand was, and so she shook her head. "I... Can't take this."

"Why can't you?" Puzzled as he thought he saw how excited she was at first, but then she baulked at the offer.

"Someone important gave me this phone, so I can't replace it." She said, with a little sadness in her voice as she stared down at the new phone inside the bag. Her eyes teared up, and he noticed. He went over to her side and pulled her into his embrace.

His sudden movement shocked her, but she didn't struggle, nor would she push him away. In fact, she felt like he was comforting her. Wang Yi-An felt like perhaps it would be okay to cry in his arms. Yang Tian-Xu's gentle embrace made Wang Yi-An felt like it was all right for her to feel this way. She let out all the tears as she cried, silently in his arms. And Yang Tian-Xu let her cried, a silent moment with her in his arms, wordless as he held her tight. He won't ask her why, he only wanted to hold her in his arms as she cried, for as long as she needed his comfort.

Even though Yang Tian-Xu wanted to know, but he won't ask. Again, a sudden memory appeared in his mind as he remembered the first time he saw her crying. It was that time when she talked to Assistant Tseng about the flight that disappeared, people named the plane—*Medaria*. Wang Yi-An had mentioned she had someone important to her on that flight. Perhaps the worn-out old model phone she used was a gift from the same person?

"Whoever can make you feel so much sadness you had to cry out these tears? Someone, you love? A family member?" those were the thoughts inside Yang Tian-Xu's mind as he embraced her gently in his arms. He knew it was wrong to feel ill of the deceased, but he hated the thoughts that someone could make her cry this much. His heart ached whenever he saw her cry because the love he had was genuine.

Love... It made him felt a sharp pain in his heart as he saw her cried. Yet, he was happy to be by her side when she cried. Mix with emotions he could not understand. Why does he felt this way?

At 5:19 p.m. She had cried for a while, unable to stop herself. But, she had a good cry in his arms; she looked at him as she wiped her tears and she smiled at him, "Thank you. I needed that." Yet, a tear fell from the corner of her eyes.

He smiled back at her as they shared another moment of silence. Yang Tian-Xu saw Wang Yi-An smiled at him again, and he felt better. At first, when she cried in his arms, he felt a deep pain in his heart he couldn't understand why, but every time he saw her tears: he could feel the hurt. The pain was a sharp aching pain inside his heart. It was as if someone had taken a thousand needles and stabbed him with it, over and over. That aching pain, he imagined perhaps she felt that way? Maybe those feelings he felt belongs to her and not him.

Yang Tian-Xu smiled at Wang Yi-An, he lifted his right hand up and wiped the fallen teardrops from the corner of her eyes. "Anytime you need someone to talk to, or even cry too. I want to be here for you." He gently wiped the other side of her cheek with his index finger, and he continued, "I wanted to be there when you need someone, even if it's something small."

The way she stared at him, made him felt like he was dreaming. If he could hold her again, no matter what the occasion might be, happy, or sad. He wanted to be a part of everything related to her. The gentle, caring voice of Yang Tian-Xu was smoothing as he said, "I want to be a part of everything."

Perhaps she could understand the feelings he had for her now as the tears in her eyes stopped rolling out. Her eyes were red, swollen from the tears and rubbing, but he showed her how much he cared for her with his gentle gesture. He used his thumbs to feel her cheeks as he held her face with his palms. He leans in closer, "Please, let me know if you need any help at all."

"Thank you, President Yang! You are indeed a good man! An excellent boss!" She said as she gave him a cheer-up smile.

Boss? Yang Tian-Xu's feelings languished when she called him 'boss', and so he could only sigh, as he forced a smiled towards her and thought, "So I really am just a boss..." He drowns himself in his misery.

CHAPTER 18
I'm Jealous and Pitiful!

Time passed by, quicker than they had noticed, but when Wang Yi-An realised it was already 5:19 p.m. She shouted, "Oh goodness! The time passed by so quickly!" Wang Yi-An had spent over an hour inside the supply room! Wang Yi-An lowers her head slightly to apologised to him. "I'm sorry for taking up your time President Yang!"

"It's okay... It's not a problem. I love—" Yang Tian-Xu wanted to tell her that he loves her. But, he couldn't bring the courage to say it. So instead he said, "—I love to help any way I can." And then he forced the corner of his lips to curve upwards. His smile was very handsome, and she was grateful for his comfort, as she thanked him once more before she prepared to leave the supply room. Wang Yi-An held the ink-toner box in her arms as she was about to leave.

"Wait!" He said, as Wang Yi-An turned around, he took the bag with the new phone inside and walked over to her side, "You forgot this." She left the bag behind, but he brought it over for her. "Take it, even if you don't use it, I still want you to have it." Yang Tian-Xu forced the phone back into her hands once more.

Wang Yi-An had a shy personality, she didn't feel like she deserved it, but he kept pushing the phone into her hands, and told her, "Please take it!" She nodded and thanked him, then she turned back and left. Even though it was after hours, Wang Yi-An wanted to get her work done first before she returns home.

Wang Yi-An had stayed after hours for another 35-minutes before she finished printing the sample package designs. Then she submits the designs to Yang Corps manufacturer. When Wang Yi-An packed her backpack and got ready to leave. He waited for her, for the exact moment when she was about to scan her access card to unlock the door. He stopped her from leaving as he asked her, "Do you need a ride home?" The clock almost hit 6.00 p.m. in six minutes. Most employees would consider it to be late, however, for Wang Yi-An the time was still considered early for her, and she wanted to return to the Happiness Restaurant to work in the evening so she said, "No thank you, I will be fine." And left.

The office empty at 5:00 p.m. sharp, while Yang Tian-Xu stood there alone in the office, he looked at the clock on the wall as it displayed: 6:00 p.m. He glanced at Wang Yi-An's desk and noticed that she left the phone bag on her counter. Yang Tian-Xu sighs aloud, as he prepared to leave the office himself. Yet, he saw Wang Yi-An's table and stared at the phone, left behind—almost like the smartphone represented his heart—rejected before he could even confess. Still unopened and, even the plastic wrapping on the box was untouched.

The parking lot after work hours were quiet, and he made his way to his black sports car. The lights in the parking lot made the car sparkled. He was about to make his way to his car when he heard Jin Qi-Long's voice calling his name, "Yang Tian-Xu!" Jin Qi-Long cursed at him. "You damn bastard!"

Yang Tian-Xu rolled down the window and saw how bad Jin Qi-Long looked; like he had come back from a vicious battle —his hair was a mess! Pissed as he said, "Yeah! Thanks to you!" in the most sarcastic tone. Jin Qi-Long had spent his entire afternoon cleaning up a messy cat-fight. Undoubtedly for his unhappy mood, the two girls fought against each other viciously— it wasn't even for him! It was all for Yang Tian-Xu!

Jin Qi-Long's pretty face got little scratches on the left

side, it happened during the fight between the two girls. They hit him as he tried to separate them. His family had power, and it was a good thing or else the news would be all over the media, and his company image might be affected.s, his once perfect suit became wrinkled, and his face had a little fingernail scratch mark on the side, close to his chin. His overall appearance was like he had struggled to get away from hell.

"Rough day?" Yang Tian-Xu asked with a mocking voice.

"This is all your fault!" he said as he pointed to the injuries on his body.

"Me? Why is it my fault?" Yang Tian-Xu was clueless about the fight, more like he didn't care about it; also he never wanted to ask about it.

"Those girls fought each other for you! They compared with each other about who would make a better Future Mrs Yang, they nagged, and pulled me into their fight! You should have been there!" Jin Qi-Long felt hopeless as he saw Yang Tian-Xu uninterested. "You don't even care. Do you?"

"Nope." Yang Tian-Xu continued to walk over to his car. Jin Qi-Long tagged along with him, and Yang Tian-Xu stopped to ask him. "Why are you following me?"

"Oh, come on! My friend! Let's go have a drink!" Jin Qi-Long remained cheerful even after what he been through, he wrapped his arms around Yang Tian-Xu's shoulder, and as they continued their short walk to the car, Jin Qi-Long told Yang Tian-Xu. "Come on, let's go today! I need a drink!"

"Okay, okay..." Yang Tian-Xu didn't refuse him, because Jin Qi-Long looked like hell. Perhaps today had been a rough and long day for him too, but Yang Tian-Xu was considerate of his friend. Also, Yang Tian-Xu felt like he needed to have a drink himself. Perhaps this will settle the frustration he had inside.

Jin Qi-Long hopped into the passenger's seat and told him

to go to District 43. The district was the busiest district in City Y, and with lots of restaurants and clubs that were open for 24-hours a day. At first, they went to their regular club called 67. However, suddenly it seems like there have been a few drunk men who caused problems outside the club. Of course, Yang Tian-Xu and Jin Qi-Long were men of vital status, so instead of going into Club 67, they decided it would be best not to get themselves involved.

Feeling like it was his unlucky day, Jin Qi-Long couldn't even visit his favourite club for a decent drink! "Ah!" he shouted, as he screamed down in the street "Why God! Why are you so cruel to me!?" The time was 8:00 p.m. sharp, and they wandered the street looking for a decent place for a drink for the past 45-minutes. They wanted to stay as far away from the trouble outside Club 67, so they walked a bit down the street.

As a stubborn man, if he wanted a drink, Jin Qi-Long would get one. So they walked down another street passed Club 67. At that moment Yang Tian-Xu saw Wang Yi-An just outside of a restaurant called, Happiness. He stood there for a second and thought: "Am I dreaming?"

Jin Qi-Long noticed that Yang Tian-Xu had stopped, and he turned back to look at him. "Hey! Why did you stop?" And so he walked back and stood beside Yang Tian-Xu, calling for his friend who remained in a dazzled state. Jin Qi-Long looked over at where Yang Tian-Xu stared at, and he noticed that Yang Tian-Xu was looking across the street. Yang Tian-Xu's eyes were locked on to the busy-working Wang Yi-An.

She had her hair up in a bun as she worked, she liked this hairstyle because her hair doesn't get in the way. Wang Yi-An had a yellow T-shirt on with the red Happiness Restaurant's logo on the back, covered over by a red apron. She was outside in the restaurant's storefront as she changed the afternoon menu into the night menu.

Jin Qi-Long saw Wang Yi-An as well and smiled. "Let's go have a late-night snack while we drink there!" Jin Qi-Long wrapped his arms around Yang Tian-Xu's shoulders, and they crossed the street. "Hey! Wang Yi-An!" Jin Qi-Long called out her name.

She turned around to the voice that called her name and saw the two handsome fellas as they approached her. "President Yang and Mr Jin! Good Evening!" Wang Yi-An was surprised to see them, but she smiled at as she made her effort to walk closer to them.

"President Yang and Mr Jin! What brings you two here this evening?" Surprised to meet them outside Happiness Restaurant storefront, she smiled. But when she saw Jin Qi-Long's appearance, she became shocked. "Mr Jin! You look horrible! What happened to you?"

Jin Qi-Long smiled at her, "Yeah, you know it's those two girls. They sure gave me a rough day today."

"I'm sorry for not being able to help you!" Wang Yi-An felt awful when she left when the two girls fought each other. She wanted to help stop Tong Yue-Yan and Lee Yin-Yin, however, Yang Tian-Xu was the boss, and as her boss when he told her to not waste time and get back to work, she had to follow his orders; doesn't she? Even though, she felt like she should have stayed to help break the fight. Jin Qi-Long talked with Wang Yi-An casually, as he told her how much he had to suffer today, he said, "It would be terrible if you stayed behind, it's a good thing you left! The girls cursed at each other, pull on their hair, bite and scratch each other! It was like living in hell." As Jin Qi-Long complains to Wang Yi-An, he felt blessed that someone cared about him enough to listen.

In addition, Yang Tian-Xu felt a little jealous. To get their attention on him, he slapped Jin Qi-Long on the back and said, "Well, Mr Jin here is a very dependable man, he can handle anything you throw at him. An-An, you don't have to worry or feel bad about him. Handling women is Mr Jin's special ability."

"Oh..." She felt sorry for Jin Qi-Long, but she could say nothing more, she knew the reason for their fight, she was there when they first argued. It had nothing to do with Jin Qi-Long, it was because they wanted to get information about President Yang! Wang Yi-An thought it was unfair for Jin Qi-Long.

Wang Yi-An felt worse for Jin Qi-Long and the two girls, as President Yang doesn't seem to give them any attention. It made her think; perhaps Mr Jin was used to cleaning up President Yang's mess? However, Wang Yi-An was just an employee. She doesn't want to get herself involved in her boss's personal affairs.

"Would you two like to come inside the restaurant and enjoy a good meal?" she asked as she smiled at them.

Jin Qi-Long looked over at the jealous Yang Tian-Xu for a second before he gave her a big grin and said, "Oh! We want more than just a meal! Do you guys have any alcohol?"

"Yes! Of course, we do! Come in and take a seat!" Wang Yi-An welcome them into the restaurant as she gestured them in. Compared to most places they'd visited, Happiness Restaurant was a regular family restaurant. The two guys weren't used to the crowded surrounding, unlike the high-end restaurant they frequent. The internal design of the restaurant was mostly yellow, and with a red-strip followed along the mouldings of the walls. As they walked in they could see, fifty tablets or fewer, and four booths; each booth at the opposite side of the wall, these booths were near the end of the storefront.

Wang Yi-An led them to a more private area; a little further in the restaurant's back, in one of the four booths, she picked the one that was free. The noisy and loud customers laughed and enjoyed themselves, greeting Wang Yi-An as she passed by, they all looked at the two handsome men that just walked in. However, the customers took a glance and returned to their merriment.

Most of the customers there were regular, and they all call Wang Yi-An; An-An. As she passed by them, she would greet them and ask them if she needed anything. Then she continued to lead Yang Tian-Xu and Jin Qi-Long to the back. A tiny booth at the end was less rowdy compared to the front. Wang Yi-An showed them to their seat and brought them a pot of tea to enjoy first.

Yang Tian-Xu and Jin Qi-Long sat down and opened a menu. Jin Qi-Long wanted Wang Yi-An to select the food for them, and he wanted snacks that can pair well with alcohol.

"What about you, President Yang?" She said as she took their orders.

"I'll take anything you recommend." Yang Tian-Xu passed the menu back to her, and he smiled at her sweetly. Yang Tian-Xu was happy to see Wang Yi-An again.

"Okay, why don't you drink some tea while I get your order ready?" Wang Yi-An took the menus as she smiled at them and went to get their orders ready.

Meanwhile, as they waited for their orders, Yang Tian-Xu didn't expect to see her already; this made him extremely happy. However, he turned to look at Jin Qi-Long with a murderous look as he whispered to him. "Don't you try to get too close to her!"

"What? Are you jealous?" Jin Qi-Long mocked him as he grinned at Yang Tian-Xu. Jin Qi-Long didn't expect Yang Tian-Xu to respond to him. Typically, if he made jokes like that, Yang Tian-Xu would ignore him, like he always does. However, once he heard Yang Tian-Xu's response; Jin Qi-Long's face froze, and his jaws dropped.

"Yes." Yang Tian-Xu didn't deny it and admitted it straight

on. "I don't want you to get too close with her, it'll be bad if you fall for her too."

It was honestly unbelievable to Jin Qi-Long's ears! Jin Qi-Long remembered that ever since they were little, Yang Tian-Xu would always share with him all of his toys, his food, even when they had homework. Yang Tian-Xu would share everything with him. Hard for Jin Qi-Long to believed his best friend had grown up to become someone so... Jealous? Jin Qi-Long felt the need to ask him, "Yang Tian-Xu! You would pick her over our friendship?"

"Always." Yang Tian-Xu said with a straight face. Meanwhile, his replied amazed Jin Qi-Long; Jin Qi-Long could not believe his generous friend had become somebody else. Yang Tian-Xu was serious and if he had to pick between Wang Yi-An and Jin Qi-Long; he would pick Wang Yi-An in a heartbeat.

Yang Tian-Xu wasn't afraid to show Jin Qi-Long his feelings for Wang Yi-An. Jin Qi-Long sighed heavily. "I cannot believe this day had finally come." He said as he poured a cup of tea for Yang Tian-Xu.

Yang Tian-Xu took the cup, and he blew on it to cool the temperature down as he took a sip. Then Yang Tian-Xu sneaks a peek over at the counter to look for Wang Yi-An. There she stood by the bar as she laughed and chit-chats with a man.

The man was Fung Qi-Wei. Wang Yi-An had always called him Fung Da-Ge, which means; Big brother Fung. But, the way she called him, 'Fung Da-Ge', it was in such a sweet voice; it irritated Yang Tian-Xu. It might have been loud in the restaurant, but still, he heard her called him, 'Fung Da-Ge.' As she laughed along with this man. Wang Yi-An and Fung Qi-Wei looked as if their relationship was close. Perhaps a little too close?

Yang Tian-Xu never imagined himself to become someone so jealous and pitiful. And he kept staring at the two as they laughed and joke about who-knows-what and Yang Tian-

Xu cringed his eyebrows as he pretended to sip his tea. He stared at Fung Qi-Wei and Wang Yi-An.

A sudden chill creeps up his spine as he shivered—Fung Qi-Wei felt as if someone was glaring at him. And so he turned around, and for a brief second, he saw Yang Tian-Xu in the corner booth: glaring at him. While Jin Qi-Long was playing on his smartphone, he didn't seem to care about anything at all, as he patiently waited for his orders. Meanwhile, Yang Tian-Xu kept staring at Fung Qi-Wei. And Fung Qi-Wei stared back.

"Is that the boss you mentioned?" Fung Qi-Wei asked Wang Yi-An and pointed over to where Yang Tian-Xu was sitting, as she looked over at where he was pointing.

Yang Tian-Xu turned his head away the moment he saw Wang Yi-An turned her head to look at him. Yang Tian-Xu pretended like it was nothing. Wang Yi-An wasn't able to see Yang Tian-Xu's stares, and so she nodded, "Yeah, that's our company's President. Yang Tian-Xu."

"He's the direct descendant of the Yang Family isn't he?" Fung Qi-Wei asked her once more. Wang Yi-An merely nodded again.

Fung Qi-Wei saw how good-looking Yang Tian-Xu was and said, "Damn! The guy is good-looking. If I were a girl, I would definitely fall for him. That other guy isn't so bad looking either. An-An, you should try hooking up with one of those guys."

Wang Yi-An smiled at Fung Qi-Wei, "Fung Da-Ge! What are you saying?"

"I'm saying, maybe you and your boss can start a little something-something if you know what I mean." He said as he winked at Wang Yi-An.

"Fung Da-Ge! Stop joking! He's my boss!" Wang Yi-An gave him a funny-disapproving look as she rolled her eyes at Fung Qi-Wei.

"Hey! I'm just saying, employers and employees can fall in love too you know." Fung Qi-Wei loved to tease Wang Yi-An. They grew up together, and he knew her for so long, He loved her and treated her like his own little sister.

Wang Yi-An let out a big smile and jokingly hit him on his shoulder. "Stop joking!" Wang Yi-An stopped chatting with him as she heard the kitchen staff called out the orders she placed were ready for pick up. "I won't joke with you anymore, I have to go get the food now. Can you bring them their drinks?"

Just as Wang Yi-An went to the kitchen, Fung Qi-Wei grabbed a six-pack and went over to greet Yang Tian-Xu and Jin Qi-Long.

"Hello, thanks for waiting. I am Fung Qi-Wei, the owner's son. Here are your beers."

Yang Tian-Xu just stared at him and not say a word. Jin Qi-Long looked at Fung Qi-Wei and said, "Oh, hey!—I have a Qi in my name too! My name is Jin Qi-Long. Are you and Wang Yi-An close by any chance; your relationships seem to be very good."

Fung Qi-Wei smiled at them and asked, "Does it matter?"

Yang Tian-Xu was a little furious about his reply. While he was thinking to himself, "Does it matter!? Of course, it matters!!" However, he remained his cool and kept his silence.

Jin Qi-Long popped the beer cap open and downed the entire bottle. "These beers are too weak. Do you guys have anything stronger?"

"Wow. You guys can sure handle your liquor." Fung Qi-Wei said as he was amazed at how Jin Qi-Long can down two bottles of beer: like it was just water.

Jin Qi-Long laughed, "Hey, I don't want to brag, but Tian-Xu and I were known as the two best drinkers in City Y! We can drink a thousand beer bottles and still feel sober!"

"Oh? Then do you wanna try the Fung Family's secret alcohol?" Fung Qi-Wei said with an evil smirk on his face. He was so sure of his family secret homemade alcohol could knock out anyone!

"Fung Family's secret alcohol?" Surprised, as Jin Qi-Long had never heard about a secret alcohol beverage in his entire life, and he had visited many high-end bars and restaurants. He must try it out no matter the cost! "Hell yeah! Gimme one!"

"Okay! Are you sure? One small shot and it will knock you out cold!" Fung Qi-Wei warned them. However, Jin Qi-Long refused to believe it, as he was a man who had a high alcohol tolerance. Jin Qi-Long and Yang Tian-Xu can drink plenty of beers and never get drunk from it.

Wang Yi-An came out with the orders and place it down on the table as she overheard them talk about the Fung family's secret alcohol. "Don't," she warned them, " it contained an extremely high volume of alcohol. It will knock you out cold with just one shot."

"Is it really that strong?" Jin Qi-Long asked as he thought about it for a little. "Ah... It's okay! Let's do it!"

Wang Yi-An worried a little as she said, "President Yang and Mr Jin shouldn't drink it. It will knock you two out with just one shot!"

"Yeah, right!? I think I'm the only one that can handle the one shot of our Fung Family's secret alcohol!" Fung Qi-Wei laughed hard as he boasted about being the only one who could handle it, and his laughter irritated Yang Tian-Xu to the extreme.

"I'll do it." Yang Tian-Xu had finally spoken up. He wanted to show her how manly he could be too. If Fung Qi-Wei can take one shot of this so-called Family secret alcohol, then Yang Tian-Xu could too!

"Okay, but first I need you guys to pay for your bills first." Fung Qi-Wei wanted them to settle the bill because he was confident about his family's secret alcohol.

Yang Tian-Xu and Jin Qi-Long agreed, and they paid the bill. Fung Qi-Wei went behind the counter and brought out a large black jar. The large black pot looked as if it was the ones used to brew ancient Chinese rice wines.

Fung Qi-Wei opened the lid and took a bamboo spoon and poured out two shots into a shot glass. The liquor was colourless and transparent, it looked like it was just the regular rice wine.

Yang Tian-Xu and Jin Qi-Long each grabbed a shot glass into their hand. "Let's take it together." Jin Qi-Long suggested. Yang Tian-Xu nodded in agreement as they both counted. "On three."

"1..."

"2..."

"3!"

CHAPTER 19

I Like Her A Lot!

Everything was pitch black at first. Perhaps a blackout? Unable to see or feel anything at all for a minute or two, Yang Tian-Xu moved around as a sudden bright light appeared. The light had shone in so brightly as it blinded his eyes for a second. However, he readjusted, and his vision became clear again. The first thing he saw was Wang Yi-An, as she smiled at him as she called him. "President Yang."

Where were they? Yang Tian-Xu wondered, however, it felt like he was in a bedroom—maybe his own? *No*, it felt a lot smaller than his room. But, Yang Tian-Xu didn't care where he was at, as long as Wang Yi-An was with him. Only wanting to grab hold of her, he pulled her down. He held her in a tight embrace as called out her nickname, "An-An!"

When he grabbed her, she fell into the bed with his arms around her, tight; without a care in the world. He doesn't care anymore. The feelings he had for her were overflowing inside him. The emotions he had: he could not control them anymore. With Wang Yi-An on top of him, his heart raced incredibly. He felt her warmth as he touched her cheek. Wang Yi-An's skin was smooth like a baby's bottom. Soft and every time he touched he felt a desire to kiss her.

Yang Tian-Xu runs his finger down the side of her cheek. Even though, her skin wasn't perfect. However, for sure, to Yang Tian-Xu, Wang Yi-An was the prettiest girl he ever met. His slow and gentle hand stroke her hair: he ran his fingers in her long black hair. He closed his eyes and gave her a gentle kiss her. They shared a passionate kiss as they embraced each other. With her in his arms, he smelled her hair, it was like spring. A refreshing smell, even the perfume: *Grace*—was incomparable to her natural scent.

Yang Tian-Xu pulled the sheets over their heads, as he rolled her over: so she would be underneath him. The sheets were white and thin. So the light shines inside, and it was still bright even with the sheets covered over them. The lights came from the opened window from the bedroom. A breeze blew in, and it was calming. Yang Tian-Xu pinned Wang Yi-An beneath him, and won't let her go when he looked into her eyes, her eyes stared into his. A silent moment where all he wanted was to kiss her, over again, until it made her entire body weak—Wang Yi-An would return his kisses, as they continued. It was hot, and it gives him a burning sensation from within himself.

The kisses were so tender, yet sensational. Every time Yang Tian-Xu kissed her lips, it made his lust for her grew stronger. He wanted to be rough with her. But how could he? He wanted her to feel the same passion he felt. Being as much considerate of her as he could, he explored her body, bit by bit.

Wang Yi-An's face flushed a little, it made her look cute, and he revealed her beautiful shoulders as he popped open a button. Yang Tian-Xu kissed her cheek, he moved down slower. As he made his way down her neck, he kissed every inch of her. He wanted every part of her body to become his. His gentle caress made Wang Yi-An giggled, only for a little. But when his hand reached down below, he felt inches of her body as he looked into her eyes and asked her, "Tell me you like me too..."

Wang Yi-An was quiet, but let out a sweet smile, *so sweet it was gentle too*. She had her arms wrapped around his neck. Then again, Yang Tian-Xu leans his body inward for another soft and passionate kiss.

"I want you to like me too, An-An," he whispered in a soft and compassionate voice as he continued to kiss her again. Their tongues rolled around each other as he suckled her. They stopped for a few seconds for air before Yang Tian-Xu fondled her breast. It was full, and the shape fits in his hand, *perfectly*.

Gradually, he unbuttoned her top and removed her grey-shirt off. Her bra was pink, and it made her skin tone looked beautifully white. He pulled one side down and kissed her gently as he caresses her with his wet tongue. Wang Yi-An's face was rose-red as she tried to restrain her voice. He continued to caress her as he continued to eradicate her bra. Pieces of her clothing, he removed them one at a time. He was burning inside, he wanted her more than anything in his life.

When he entered her, he was a little rough. And so she could no longer suppress her voice, and so she moaned aloud. He held her into a tighter embrace as he continued to make his mark inside her.

Never could he ever like her go, Yang Tian-Xu had decided this the moment he held her in his arms. If he could stay forever like this: Yang Tian-Xu would give up everything he has—so he could be with her. Yang Tian-Xu whispered her name into her ears, "An-An..." as he continued to call her name. He caressed her entire body as he moved inside her.

Their breathing was in unison, and every touch he made, every single movement—had imprinted her inside, deep and he'll go harder if he could. Yang Tian-Xu looked at her face, and Wang Yi-An smiled at him and asked him, "President Yang. Do you like An-An?"

"Yes, I do. I like you so much. An-An." Yang Tian-Xu replied, and he leans in again for another kiss until suddenly, a strong manly voice called out to him.

"Well, you better tell her that." An intense and masculine voice shattered Yang Tian-Xu's perfect illusion. Yang Tian-Xu opened his eyes wide as he saw the image of Wang Yi-An morphing into Fung Qi-Wei.

"OH MY GOD!" Yang Tian-Xu freaked out, he panicked at the sight of Fung Qi-Wei, laid next to him on the bed. The image of Wang Yi-An turning into Fung Qi-Wei was so terrifying and horrific that he shouted and screamed.

All along, Yang Tian-Xu had been dreaming inside this perfect illusion, but when he was woken up from his beautiful dream. He found himself awaken into a real horrifying nightmare. The one when he woke up and the one sleeping next to him wasn't Wang Yi-An yet, another man: Fung Qi-Wei. For sure, his erection had ultimately been obliterated, without a need for a cold shower.

They both have an instantaneous collapse the moment they each took a shot of the Fung family's secret alcohol. At 9:00 a.m. in the morning Yang Tian-Xu woken up with a loud screaming voice as he saw Fung Qi-Wei, he lay on the bed, half-naked beside him. "Oh my God!" he repeated, as he continued to freak out as he panicked, he cursed a lot before he asked, "Why are you here!?"

Shocked to find himself in a stranger's bedroom, he looked around. A small room, compared to his maid rooms at his house, this bedroom would be the same size. However, it had three drawers; lined up against the wall. One drawer was long and placed near closed door, and a little closet inside the room with its opened door. There was still enough walking space around the large king-size bed. The bed had no frame, and the bed was positioned on the laminated floor.

Yang Tian-Xu can't remember what had happened, yet once he had finally returned to reality; he finds himself awake, laying in a stranger's bed. Semi-naked, with only his pants on. Lying next to him was Fung Qi-Wei and Jin Qi-Long. Yang Tian-

Xu was in the middle.

"You don't have to scream so loud." Fung Qi-Wei said as he cleans out his left ear, as he sat up. "Man, you were so different last night."

"Wha—What..." Yang Tian-Xu face was burning as he mumbled, "Are... You..." Yang Tian-Xu could not recall what had happened last night. The only thing he remembered was Jin Qi-Long, and he had gone to look for a place to have a drink and met Wang Yi-An working at a restaurant called Happiness Restaurant. Yang Tian-Xu also remembered he and Wang Yi-An had a passionate time together before Fung Qi-Wei's voice woke him up. Thank God, it was all a dream though, was it not?

Yang Tian-Xu looked over at the left side of the bed and saw Jin Qi-Long still out cold with his top removed. Fung Qi-Wei was on Yang Tian-Xu's right side. Yang Tian-Xu lifts the blanket up to find out that Jin Qi-Long was butt naked. Then he looked at Fung Qi-Wei, who was also naked.

"Why am are you guys naked? Where is the rest of my clothing?" Yang Tian-Xu asked as he panicked. He thought perhaps something bad might have happened last night, and he'll regret about once he finds out. Only because of the dream he had; it was such a passionate dream. Yang Tian-Xu felt so frustrated about it as he tried to recall it. However, it was impossible for him to recall what events had taken place while he was unconscious. Soon he felt disturbed by it, and Yang Tian-Xu curled his body up, as he held his head with his hands—he rested his forehead on his knees—he felt a sharp pounding in his head. "Er... My head..."

"Ah, don't worry, I did nothing to you. You might be good looking, but I'm not gay." Fung Qi-Wei said as he saw how scared and disrupted Yang Tian-Xu looked.

Yang Tian-Xu lifted his face up to look at Fung Qi-Wei and shout out aloud, "Nothing happened right?"

Fung Qi-Wei let out a mockery laugh, "Sure nothing happened, or..." and as he looked at the ceiling, "Did something happen? Or—No, nothing happened, however!—"

"However!?" Yang Tian-Xu jumped out in fright as he placed his face closer to Fung Qi-Wei's face. He felt like he was being tortured, as he demanded the truth, "What else happened!?"

"Ah, jeez, calm down! Now you are just getting too close!" Fung Qi-Wei faced his head the other way, as he couldn't look at Yang Tian-Xu anymore.

"Tell me what happens!" Yang Tian-Xu shouted out loudly as he demanded the truth again.

"Um..." Just then, Wang Yi-An opened the door, with a tray that had their clothes on. Wang Yi-An brought them their clothes after she washed and folded them. However, as she came in—she saw them in an awkward position.

The sight of Yang Tian-Xu on top of Fung Qi-Wei had caused her to blush. The two men faced toward each other: so close it looked like they were kissing—both topless—it seemed like they were... *intimate*? It was a quick glance, and Wang Yi-An turned around fast as she became shy and her face flushed redder.

"I'm sorry, for interrupting! I brought you your clothes— I'll just leave it here!" She said as she placed the tray down on top of the drawers and rushed off while she continued to blush.

The drawers were near the bedroom entrance, it didn't take long for her to placed the clothing down, and rushed off. Wang Yi-An shut the door as she went out. Her face still beet red, as she felt a burning sensation. She placed both her hands on her cheeks, as she tried to cool her face down, however, it wasn't helpful. She fans her blushed cheeks and couldn't believe what she had witnessed.

An awkward silence inside the room left Yang Tian-Xu's body frozen stiff. Unknown that Wang Yi-An would barge in like that as she caught him at an awkward position with another man! Yang Tian-Xu felt like he would die from the embarrassment. Fung Qi-Wei was a sharp man. It was like he could tell what Yang Tian-Xu was thinking about, as he patted Yang Tian-Xu's right shoulder. "There, there. You should get dressed, and I'll fill in the blanks."

Still frozen from the event, for a moment he stood still, then he suddenly jumped out of bed. Grabbed hold of his clothing from the counter and dressed up in prompt time. Jin Qi-Long was still sleeping in the bed, unaware of his surroundings.

"Hurry up and tell me!" Yang Tian-Xu demanded again as he buttons up his suit.

"Well," Fung Qi-Wei got up as he grabbed some new clothing in his drawers and got dressed. However, he told Yang Tian-Xu in a calm voice, "you kissed her did you remember that?"

Yang Tian-Xu's eyes popped out wide as he heard it. "I kissed her?"

A billion thoughts appeared in his mind, and Fung Qi-Wei's words replay in his thoughts. "You kissed her... You kissed her... You kissed her..." Yang Tian-Xu's eyes remained opened wide for the longest time. Then he turned his head to face Fung Qi-Wei. "I did what?" he asked, as he became confused. Too shocked to believe it, as he thought, "Who did I kiss?"

Fung Qi-Wei's voice sounded calm, it was like he could read Yang Tian-Xu's thoughts, and said it like it was not a big deal. "You kissed her, Wang Yi-An."

Once again, Yang Tian-Xu's body froze. He couldn't move, his mind went blank, as he could recall what had happened last night. Yang Tian-Xu felt like his world had crumbled down before his eyes. It's not that he didn't want to kiss her, he wanted it to be more romantic. Not when he was drunk!

The worst part was that he had failed to remember it, their first kiss! He had everything planned out, roses, presents, and he would have already confessed his feelings for her, but no. It wasn't like how he wanted it to be. Yang Tian-Xu buried himself in his thoughts. He tried his best to recall last night's memory. Yet, It was fruitless.

"Oh my God!!!" He screamed as he ruffled his hair and paced around in a circle. "What did I do!!!!?" Yang Tian-Xu wanted to pull out all of his hair. Then suddenly, he heard a subtle laugh, he stopped to look over at Fung Qi-Wei as he saw the guy; trying to hold in his laughter.

Fung Qi-Wei cleared out his voice, and he said, "Ah, don't worry. It wasn't that bad."

It wasn't that bad? Those words were worse than he could imagine. A shattered dream, broken to little pieces. Yang Tian-Xu was a romantic, he wanted to have a perfect first kiss with the woman he loves most in the entire world. Wang Yi-An.

"Please..." Yang Tian-Xu had never thought he would beg anyone in his life. Yang Tian-Xu was a man born and raised in an authoritative household. The Yang family had everything; power and wealth. He never needed to beg for anything in his life. But now, he; Yang Tian-Xu, had lowered his head and begged a stranger for the truth. In a soft, and low volume voice, he begged Fung Qi-Wei, "Please, tell me what happened..."

With the sincere expression on Yang Tian-Xu's face, Fung Qi-Wei could no longer make fun of him. Unexpected for Fung Qi-Wei to see a wealthy and powerful person like Yang Tian-Xu: begging him.

Even though, Yang Tian-Xu wasn't on his knees to beg.

However, his pleading words make Fung Qi-Wei felt like Yang Tian-Xu was a sincere man. He took a deep breath and told him the truth.

"Well, after you drank the shot. You blanked out for a while. You didn't even move. An-An became worried about you two boys, so she walked over to check and see if you guys were all right. But then you—"

However, just as Fung Qi-Wei was about to get to the crucial details, Wang Yi-An had knocked on the door. "I'm coming in." She said as she opened the door. She saw the two of them standing in one place, and in her hands held another tray, with two hot bowls of ginger soup.

Then for a second as her eyes met with Yang Tian-Xu, she blushed and turned away. Wang Yi-An tried to avoid direct eye contact with him. As she remembered about the previous position he was in with Fung Qi-Wei. Wang Yi-An placed the tray next to Jin Qi-Long's clothes, "Um… Drink some ginger soup. It should help with the hangover." And then she walked out as she closed the door behind her.

The entire time, Wang Yi-An avoided Yang Tian-Xu's eyes. It gave Yang Tian-Xu a thought, "Did I do something bad?"

Certain he had done something wrong without realising it, he wondered. "Did I confess to her while I was drunk?" Frustration filled his thoughts with doubts, "Did I force myself on to her?" He screamed and shout as he won't be able to forgive himself if he had done anything to hurt her. He felt fear, afraid of finding out the truth. Worried that he might have forced himself on Wang Yi-An, he can't live with those thoughts. He'll hate himself forever!

As Yang Tian-Xu screamed, while he drowns in his misery, he grabbed onto Fung Qi-Wei's shoulders and shouted, "Tell me what happened!"

Fung Qi-Wei smirked and continued as Yang Tian-Xu gave him a violent shake. "You fainted and collapsed on top of her."

Yang Tian-Xu stopped and paused for a moment as he let go of Fung Qi-Wei and thought out loud, "That's... That's all?"

"What else were you expecting?" Fung Qi-Wei looked at Yang Tian-Xu and smirked at him. "Well, when you fainted on top of her, your lips touched her cheek." He said as he pointed to his right cheek.

Both of Yang Tian-Xu's cheeks turned red as he saw Fung Qi-Wei gestured. Yang Tian-Xu thought, "I kissed her cheek?" He covered his mouth with his hands and thought again. "I... Kissed... Her..."

Yang Tian-Xu's flushed red cheeks had made Fung Qi-Wei certain about one thing. "You must really like An-An." Fung Qi-Wei was direct about it when he asked Yang Tian-Xu. "How much do you like her?"

Without hesitation, he nodded as he blushed, "I do. I like her a lot!" he was red as a beet.

It was obvious, and Fung Qi-Wei noticed how Yang Tian-Xu felt towards Wang Yi-An. Fung Qi-Wei was sharp and wise, he could easily figure out Yang Tian-Xu's feelings from last night when he glared at her. Fung Qi-Wei knew it from the first time he saw how Yang Tian-Xu kept staring at Wang Yi-An.

However, even though Yang Tian-Xu made his feelings towards Wang Yi-An obvious, believing is one thing, yet, he felt the need to warn Yang Tian-Xu. He had a serious expression on his face as he said, "An-An is a simple girl. She lives a simple life with her mother, and she'll want nothing more in her life than a happy home."

Yang Tian-Xu stood still and listened as he cools down his embarrassed emotions. He looked up at Fung Qi-Wei and listened to his words with great interest. Fung Qi-Wei continued as he stared at Yang Tian-Xu in the eyes. "You are somebody; your world is different compared to hers. Could you truly bring her happiness?"

"What do you mean?"

Yang Tian-Xu paused for a moment as he thought about Fung Qi-Wei's words. He wanted to tell Fung Qi-Wei that he can be certain he'll be able to make Wang Yi-An happy, but... Could he honestly guarantee it?

Fung Qi-Wei looked at how serious Yang Tian-Xu looked, as he stood still in one place, unmoving. Yang Tian-Xu had an earnest expression on his face, it made Fung Qi-Wei smiled at Yang Tian-Xu and said, "I'm sure your parents or family members would prefer you to marry a more suitable heiress. An-An is nobody."

"But.."

The only three-letter words he could let out of his stunned emotion. He wanted to say so much more. He wanted to say, "But, I only have feelings for Wang Yi-An!" or "She's the only one I love!" However, he can't seem to say anything else, and remained silent and listened to every word Fung Qi-Wei had to say.

"Mr Yang, you're not just wealthy but also a handsome man. I'm sure the feelings you think you have for An-An now is love. But, what about the future? What if later you realised that all the feelings you thought you had for her were only because you wanted to try something different? She's new and entertaining for you now because she's different compared to all the heiress you met. If that were true, you'd only be toying with her heart."

"I'm not like that!" Yang Tian-Xu shouted out. He was confident he isn't someone like that!

CHAPTER 20

I'm Not Like That!

Often in movies or dramas, the rich men would always experiment with the regular girls. Only because she was different, compared to most girls that surround them. Often these rich men would fool around with women born and raised in a poor family. Or they end up eloping, but the man would soon realise it was a mistake and leaves the woman for another rich woman, with a strong family background: Fung Qi-Wei worried about this truth. It happened in movies and drama because sometimes they show a small reflection of this truth.

Fung Qi-Wei knew this same story because his father and mother were like that once. They eloped for two years until his father ran back home because he couldn't stand being poor. The Fung Family was also a wealthy family back in City B, he knew the real story, even though Madam Fung lied to him saying his father died in a car crash. Fung Qi-Wei pretended to be an ignorant man, but he knew why he grew up without a father.

Uncertain if he could bring Wang Yi-An happiness or not, however, Yang Tian-Xu was 100% certain of his feelings for Wang Yi-An, they were most definitely love. The look in Yang Tian-Xu's eyes as he told Fung Qi-Wei. "I am not like that!" He wasn't only sincere, and he was honest with himself. Yang Tian-Xu was sure that his feelings wouldn't change. No matter what!

Toy with her heart? He'll never do that! Yang Tian-Xu believed that even if he had to give up everything he owns just to be with her. *He would!* He would never want to hurt her!

There was a sense of determination in Yang Tian-Xu's eyes as he looked at Fung Qi-Wei. "I am sure of my feelings for her, and I will never change." Yang Tian-Xu held a sincere and honest stare—without a doubt to his heart. He knew he would never change, not when his feelings for her were this strong.

However, Fung Qi-Wei felt that Yang Tian-Xu was way out of Wang Yi-An's league. Not only was he handsome, wealthy, but he was masculine too. It made Fung Qi-Wei feel unbelievable, and he couldn't get his mind over it!

They stood still for a moment until Fung Qi-Wei sat down on the floor; like his legs had given up on him, and he asked Yang Tian-Xu. "Why do you like An-An?"

Yang Tian-Xu was silent for a short while, and Yang Tian-Xu was still an arrogant rich-boy he was, as he looked away from Fung Qi-Wei's stares, he answered him. "I'm not obligated to tell you that—am I?"

It wasn't an answer that could satisfy Fung Qi-Wei's curiosity. Also, it was one of those answers that get him on his nerves. However, Yang Tian-Xu was right. He doesn't have to tell Fung Qi-Wei anything. Still, Fung Qi-Wei treated Wang Yi-An like she was his little sister. If someone was to hurt or toy with her feelings, he won't stand around and watch!

Fung Qi-Wei was feeling mad and irritated by Yang Tian-Xu's response. However, Yang Tian-Xu continued, "Once I tell her myself. You can ask her yourself and find out the answer from her."

Yang Tian-Xu spoke in an arrogant tone, however, it brought a sense of peace to Fung Qi-Wei's worried heart. "I can only hope so," he said as glared at Yang Tian-Xu's eyes. A sudden change in his expression as Fung Qi-Wei let out a relaxed smile, "To me, An-An is like my little sister." as his expression changed into a serious appearance: it was murderous and chilling as he warned Yang Tian-Xu. "If you hurt her. I will murder you."

"I definitely won't hurt her!" Yang Tian-Xu felt like he had just received an elder brother's blessing; until he thought about it for a short second before he said. "Wait... Little sister?"

"Yeah, I treat her like my little sister." Fung Qi-Wei said in a proud voice. Fung Qi-Wei was five years older than Wang Yi-An, and he remembered when her mother was in labour, he was also there in the delivery room. She grew up in his arms as he cared for her like she was his younger sister.

To Yang Tian-Xu surprise, he couldn't believe he heard it right, "You're... Not in love with her?" The truth was a lot different from what he had imagined. However, he was happy that Fung Qi-Wei wasn't his love rival, and it shows on his face as he couldn't stop the grin on his expression.

Confused as Fung Qi-Wei watched the grin on Yang Tian-Xu's face. At first, he couldn't understand why someone like Yang Tian-Xu would fall for Wang Yi-An. To Fung Qi-Wei, Wang Yi-An was an average looking girl. If Fung Qi-Wei had to be completely honest with his feelings, he felt that Yang Tian-Xu was too good for Wang Yi-An.

Fung Qi-Wei believed there must be something wrong with Yang Tian-Xu's head, or else why would he fall for such a plain and simple girl like Wang Yi-An? He said, "Dude... There is a lot of pretty girls out there... Only you have such a unique taste."

However, Yang Tian-Xu wasn't mad at his comments, he remained with a smile on his face, as he laughed out loud. "I guess I do?" For a moment there, Yang Tian-Xu and Fung Qi-Wei had developed a bond of brotherhood.

A memory reoccurred in Yang Tian-Xu's mind; at first, he couldn't bring himself to ask, but he couldn't stop thinking about it.

"One more question," he asked, as Yang Tian-Xu uttered up the courage to ask. "Why were we naked before?"

"Well, last night your friend threw up everywhere." Fung Qi-Wei answered him as he recalled what had happened last night.

Fung Qi-Wei remembered about last night and felt too disgusted to recall. However, he continued, "He threw up all over you, me, and himself. It was disgusting. You were semi-lucky, he only vomited on your suit and shirt, and not your pants too." Fung Qi-Wei felt disgusted as he recalled those memories from last night when Jin Qi-Long had regurgitated all over him. "Me? I wasn't so lucky..."

"I'm sorry to have caused you the trouble." Yang Tian-Xu felt the need to apologised. Just hearing about it had somewhat disgusted himself. He couldn't have imagined what the trouble it was for Fung Qi-Wei.

"Oh, it wasn't that much trouble, poor An-An. She ended up cleaning the mess though. Also, it was hard for me to bring the both of you back to my house alone, so, An-An helped by taking you back here, but then you fell on her and kissed her cheek."

"She... She brought me back here...?" Yang Tian-Xu blushed a little as he thought about how could Wang Yi-An and her small body able to bring him here. She must have to hold him tightly if she had to support his weight. Which means, she had to lean in close to his body. Just the thought of their bodies interacting was enough to make Yang Tian-Xu blushed.

While Yang Tian-Xu's filled his mind with thoughts of Wang Yi-An, little did he know; trouble was stirring back at home.

The young heiress to the Tong family, Tong Yue-Yan was

angry. She had the entire Tong family fortune at her toes, her father was the current mayor of City A. Yet, Lee Yin-Yin got away with assaulting her? Impossible. She paced back and forward in front of her aunt. "Unbelievable!" she chewed on her nails as she tried to suppress her emotions.

Her aunt sat in their grand villa's living room as she sips on her morning tea. Aunt Tong acted relaxed and calmed, however, she was boiling with frustration inside. Mad that Yang Tian-Xu allowed a mere singer to hurt her dearest niece. "Don't worry Yue-Yan, auntie will make sure anyone who hurts you would suffer greatly." She grinned.

"Aunty!" Tong Yue-Yan shed tears at the corner of her eyes, as she came over to Aunt Tong. "I can't even sleep last night!"

"There, there." Aunt Tong patted her niece's back as she comforted her. "Don't you worry. Today, just stay at home and rest."

Every morning at 6:00 a.m. Tong Yue-Yan would pay a visit to Grandfather Yang and join him for his morning tea, a walk in the Tian-Bo-Fu's garden. However, that morning she made a decision not to contact the Yang family. It was her subtle way of rebelling, she wanted to enervate Grandfather Yang's schedule.

Grandfather Yang became accustomed to having Tong Yue-Yan visit him every day at 6:00 a.m. He became worried for an entire hour, without the sight of Tong Yue-Yan. "Perhaps the child had an accident, or was she not feeling well?" He thought as he sat under the family gazebo. He called her after waiting impatiently for the child to visit him.

Tong Yue-Yan's phone rang as she cried in her aunt's arms. It was a call from Grandfather Yang, at 7:00 a.m. sharp. The aunt and niece duo—sat in their living room as they waited for the Yang family to make the first move. They smiled when they received the call from Grandfather Yang.

Tong Yue-Yan had a trickster's mind as she passed the phone to her aunt to answer. As Tong Yue-Yan smiled she said, "Auntie, can you pick it up for me?" and her aunt let out a grin on her face as she replied, "Of course."

The phone rang again for a few moments, unhurried to answer the call. Aunt Tong let the phone rang two more times in her hands before she finally answered it. She cleared her throat and swiped the virtual button, and she pressed the speaker-mode button on the phone, and she said, "Hello."

Aunt Tong flicked her hair to the side as the emotion on her face changed completely. Like she was an actress on stage, and so she immersed herself in her role as the disappointed aunt; someone of unimportant status had bullied her niece.

Aunt Tong had Grandfather Yang on the speaker, so his voice was loud enough for them to hear him when he said, "Hello, Is this Yue-Yan?"

"No, this is her aunt. Is this Grandfather Yang?" Aunt Tong sounded polite, however, her eyes and expression were not the same as her voice. Her face showed an arrogant and disdainful expression.

Grandfather Yang had the phone up to his ears as he smiled with a cheerful tone in his voice, "Yes, yes." and soon, he showed his concern towards Tong Yue-Yan as he asked, "Is Yue-Yan not feeling well today?"

"Yue-Yan? How can she feel well after what happened yesterday? The poor child cried herself to sleep!" Aunt Tong sounded serious like she was angry at the unfair treatment her niece received yesterday.

"What happened?" He asked, it was the first time he heard about such an event, Grandfather Yang became curious. The tone of Tong Yue-Yan's aunt sounded like she was angry at him.

"Our Yue-Yan is the future heiress to the Tong's family

fortune, and my older brother only have this one child! Yue-Yan has plenty of suitors waiting in line for her! Who does your grandchild think he is? How dare he ignore her when that Lee Yin-Yin bullied her!?" The tone of Tong Yue-Yan's voice was getting louder and angrier as she spoke.

"Bullied?" Surprised as Grandfather Yang thought, How could Tong Yue-Yan get bullied by someone? Lee Yin-Yin? Wasn't that the name of the new famous idol? She was on TV as the most popular singer in the Country.

Grandfather Yang doesn't know what to say or do, and so he listened to Aunt Tong venting out her anger. "If it weren't for my niece's begging me not to say anything. I would have reported this incident to my older brother the moment I saw her wounds yesterday!"

Wounds? Aunt Tong made the situation sounded much worse. Tong Yue-Yan had a few scratches here and there, but it was not extreme. However, to a rich spoiled girl like Tong Yue-Yan, a small cut would be the end of the world.

Grandfather Yang sat under the gazebo inside Tian-Bo-Fu's courtyard as he listened to Aunt Tong's voice on the phone. The phone was up to his ears, but he felt like the voice became distant to him as he wondered. "Who is this Lee Yin-Yin?"

Underneath the gazebo, Grandfather Yang would enjoy his casual morning tea every day, however, his mood today was less jolly than he would be any other day.

"Do not worry, and I will not let Yue-Yan suffer any hardship." Grandfather Yang responded to Tong Yue-Yan's aunt. "I will swear—on my family's name—I will sort this out and bring justice back to Yue-Yan. I will not let my future granddaughter-in-law suffer from any grief."

Tong Yue-Yan and her aunt smiled as they heard Grandfather Yang's voice. Then her aunt replied, "I would look forward to what kind of justice you can bring back to my niece." the call ended after a brief farewell. Ending with a huge smile on Tong Yue-Yan's face as she said to her aunt, "Did you hear what he called me? Future granddaughter-in-law!"

Moments after the call between Grandfather Yang and Aunt Tong ended, Grandfather Yang speed dialled Yang Tian-Xu's cell number. The phone rang as it vibrated on the dining table in Fung Qi-Wei's home. The phone used to be in Yang Tian-Xu's pocket until Wang Yi-An removed it and place it on the dining table. She wanted to clean the soiled clothes, and so she emptied their pockets and left them on the table in plain sight.

Like a regular home in the neighbourhood, with three bedrooms, Fung Qi-Wei's house wasn't grand or huge. The interior similar compared to Wang Yi-An's home. However, the only difference was the third bedroom was on the main floor, instead of upstairs with the other two bedrooms.

Fung Qi-Wei and the two guests; Yang Tian-Xu and Jin Qi-Long were in the bedroom downstairs. The downstairs bedroom was of a decent size, on the same floor as the kitchen, living room, and the front door. Every morning when Fung Qi-Wei left the bedroom, he could reach the living room in two steps. Another five steps and he'll make his way into the kitchen and dining table.

Wang Yi-An left Yang Tian-Xu and Jin Qi-Long's belongings on the table so they could see it the moment they opened the door and walked into the living room. She left their phones and wallets in plain sight.

At 9:30 a.m, Grandfather Yang had already ended his call with Aunt Tong. He spent a two-and-a-half hour listening to Aunt Tong's complaints. Grandfather Yang had only heard about the dispute between Tong Yue-Yan and Lee Yin-Yin from Aunt Tong's side of the story. However, the story told by Tong Yue-

Yan's aunt made it seemed like Tong Yue-Yan was the victim, and the bully was Lee Yin-Yin.

When the call did not go through, unable to reach his grandson, Yang Tian-Xu; Grandfather Yang called Assistant Tseng.

Assistant Tseng jumped out of his seat as he saw the caller's ID. It was from the chairman. He felt his hands sweating, as he shivered uncontrollably like his heart was about to drop out of his chest! He answered it promptly, without letting the phone ring again for a second time.

"YES, SIR!" Assistant Tseng shouted loud into the mic as he answered the call. The nervousness caused his sweat glands to be clogged with sweat.

Grandfather Yang knew how much pressure he exerted on a mere assistant, so he wasted no time and went straight to the point. "Tell me what happened between Tong Yue-Yan and the singer Lee Yin-Yin. I want to know everything."

Grandfather Yang was the company chairman, his status made Assistant Tseng nervous to the extreme. He told Grandfather Yang everything he could about the fight at the restaurant. He reported details, times, locations like he would inform a business contract. However, he left out the most crucial detail. The girls were fighting, and President Yang completely ignored them and left with Wang Yi-An. But how could he say those words when his loyalty lies with President Yang?

Grandfather Yang was sharp, and he knew something was off. In an authoritative voice, he asked Assistant Tseng, "Where was he when the event happened?"

"Ah... An important matter has to be taken care of at the company, and the president needs to return ASAP! Sir!" Assistant Tseng lied, and he felt the cold sweat dripping down his forehead as he held onto the phone, shaking.

The air condition was on—high—yet inside Assistant Tseng's office, he felt hot. The cold sweats dripped and soaked his suit. Assistant Tseng had worked for Yang Tian-Xu for a long time. Assistant Tseng was a smart man, and he knew one day Yang Tian-Xu would become the future chairman of Yang Corps. However, would it still be wise for him to lie to the current chairman? He took a gamble and hope he had jumped onto the right boat.

"Where is he now?" Grandfather Yang asked as he took Assistant Tseng's word for it.

But, how could he know the whereabouts of Yang Tian-Xu? He hadn't shown up all day! Assistant Tseng did not understand where President Yang was because he didn't see him in the morning. He wasn't in his office, nor was he in the manager's office on the seventh floor.

Assistant Tseng thought perhaps President Yang had something important to do, which sometimes he would do before he appeared at the office. Although Assistant Tseng had no idea where President Yang was, he made an excuse and said, "President Yang is currently in a business meeting with Mr Jin. Sir!"

Even though Assistant Tseng knew that lying to the chairman might come back to bite him later, however, the one he maintained his loyalty to was still President Yang. He crossed his fingers and hoped he did the right thing.

Grandfather Yang didn't ask anymore and was ready to hang up, but before he did, he reminded Assistant Tseng. "Tell him to call me when he's out of his meeting."

"Yes, sir!" He exclaimed as he waited for Grandfather Yang to hang up the phone first. Later, he wiped the sweat off of his forehead. Assistant Tseng hurried and called President Yang to warn him about the upcoming trouble President Yang might face later on.

Time went by quickly; Wang Yi-An had cooked them some hangover ginger soup and left them on the counter before she left for work. Yang Tian-Xu looked over at the two bowls of hot ginger soup and took one in his hands. He enjoyed every last sip and felt all tingly inside; warm and filled with happiness, and so he let out a silly smile.

Yang Tian-Xu was never a fan of ginger, in fact, he disliked ginger. However, he finished drinking all of Wang Yi-An's ginger soup. He eyed the other bowl, he picked it up and finish drinking it all and didn't even bother saving a drop for Jin Qi-Long.

Fung Qi-Wei laughed at Yang Tian-Xu's immaturity. "You're not going to save that bowl for your friend? He might need it when he wakes up." Fung Qi-Wei asked as he saw Yang Tian-Xu drank the second bowl.

"Qi-Long? No, he doesn't need it." Yang Tian-Xu wanted all of Wang Yi-An's ginger soup; all to himself.

"Need what?" Jin Qi-Long was stupor as he had finally woken up. The time was 9:35 a.m. "Holy Mother..." He realised that one shot knocked him up cold. "Damn, that's one heck of a strong family recipe you got!" Jin Qi-Long complimented and looked around the room. "I like it! I will become your number one regular from now on!" Jin Qi-Long chirped as he gave Fung Qi-Wei a thump-up.

Yang Tian-Xu always ignored Jin Qi-Long, even though he also wanted to visit the restaurants, but only on days when she had a shift at the restaurant. Hence, Yang Tian-Xu requested her work schedule from Fung Qi-Wei.

Fung Qi-Wei felt happy that a magnet like Yang Tian-Xu was interested in Wang Yi-An, and so he disclosed Wang Yi-An's schedule. He wanted to play cupid for Wang Yi-An and Yang

Tian-Xu. Deep inside his heart, he hoped that they won't end up like his parents. With Yang Tian-Xu reassuring him about his feelings for Wang Yi-An, he thought he could give his trust in Yang Tian-Xu. Fung Qi-Wei wasn't just a brother to Wang Yi-An, but he would try to stand up for her like a father would for his daughter.

For a while, Yang Tian-Xu and Fung Qi-Wei had gotten along well, as he and Fung Qi-Wei talked about Wang Yi-An's favourite things. Fung Qi-Wei decided he would give pointers on how to win over Wang Yi-An's heart, as he told Yang Tian-Xu her likes and dislikes, Yang Tian-Xu would keep a note in his mind. He would forget nothing related to her.

Their entire chat, not wanting to bother them Jin Qi-Long sat at the corner of the bed, as he watched how concentrated Yang Tian-Xu was on the subject. Jin Qi-Long knew Yang Tian-Xu so well, and so he went to put on his clothing and sat back down on the bed as he listened. Patient for the entire hour until Jin Qi-Long warned him, "Ah, Tian-Xu it's almost 11 a.m. now, shouldn't you be back at Yang Corps?"

Surprised to realise they had been talking with each other for another hour before they saw the time, displayed 10:45 a.m. "Well, I guess we should go now, thank you very much for your care, and I apologise for last night." Just as he reached out a hand to shake Fung Qi-Wei's hand, he gave him a slight smile.

Fung Qi-Wei took Yang Tian-Xu's hand for a shake. Nevertheless, he felt like this once arrogant man had suddenly become someone so polite and mannered—he had to ask him. "You're only so polite because of the pointers I'd shared you about what An-An's likes and dislikes, right?"

"Yes..." Yang Tian-Xu was honest, and perhaps he was a little too honest that he somewhat hurt Fung Qi-Wei's feelings.

Still, Fung Qi-Wei would prefer to be on good standings with someone who was the current heir to the Yang Family rather than being on bad terms with him.

A coincident when they walked out Yang Tian-Xu's phone was ringing continuously. Assistant Tseng had called him non-stop for the entire hour! Yang Tian-Xu saw the name and along with a bunch of missed call notifications on his phone. He finally picked it up.

"PRESIDENT YANG!!!!" Assistant Tseng shouted as he continued, "Chairman called! And he asked about your whereabouts! He told me to notify you as soon as I can!"

"Yeah. Okay." Yang Tian-Xu had always brushed off Assistant Tseng's emotions. All the while, Assistant Tseng had panicked on behalf of Yang Tian-Xu, what did he get in return? Two simple words that were literal and carried no feelings.

Assistant Tseng felt hurt, however, he still reported about his conversation with Grandfather Yang. Yet, when Assistant Tseng asked him, "When do you plan to return to the office, boss?"

"In a bit—First, I want to ask An-An if I can give her a lift to work today." He said as let out a sly smile. Jin Qi-Long and Fung Qi-Wei both felt like they wanted to hurl.

"Um... President Yang, Wang Yi-An is already here at the office." Assistant Tseng felt awkward as he wondered. "Why offer her a lift to work when she's already here?" At 9:15 a.m. Wang Yi-An had already started her shift at Yang Corps. Wang Yi-An had messaged him she would be late and perhaps she might show up at 9:30 a.m., however, she made it to her desk at 9:15 a.m.

"Say what?!" Yang Tian-Xu shouted into the phone. The shout was so loud, it could have damaged Assistant Tseng's eardrum.

CHAPTER 21

It Is Yours To Keep Forever

When he realised that Wang Yi-An had already left without him. He became shocked, for sure he hoped she would wait for him: he wanted to arrive to work together like a couple. Yang Tian-Xu felt his heart shattering into pieces. Unable to hear anything else. "My An-An already left me?"

Both Jin Qi-Long and Fung Qi-Wei remained quiet to themselves as they thought, "Your An-An? Since when did she became your An-An?!"

Assistant Tseng was still on the other line, he could hear everything. So he had the same opinion—although his answer was entirely different from his thoughts, "Yes, boss. She is at her desk finishing up the illustrations for the—"A beep came from his phone that cuts him off.

Assistant Tseng found out his President Yang had already hung up on him! Even when he had so much more to say, Assistant Tseng had wanted to remind President Yang to hurry and call Grandfather Yang. How could he do so? Without a chance to continue his sentence, Assistant Tseng soon felt a headache: a sharp pain pounding in his head.

The situation became worst for Assistant Tseng when his cell phone rang again. He looked down and saw the caller; it was none other than the chairman himself. Assistant Tseng wanted to cry as he picked up the call. "YES, SIR!" Assistant Tseng was so nervous he started sweating again.

Assistant Tseng's loud voice almost deafen Grandfather Yang's ear, he pulled the phone away from his ears for a second. Grandfather Yang cut to the chase, without wasting time, "Tell Tian-Xu I will drop by to have lunch with him today."

"YES, SIR!" Assistant Tseng's sweat was like a build-up pool. He couldn't believe the president would be on his way soon enough. He hurried as he tried to call President Yang again. However, none of his calls went through, Yang Tian-Xu had ignored them. Perhaps even blocked him?

When Yang Tian-Xu hung-up on Assistant Tseng, he rushed outside of Fung Qi-Wei's home. Yang Tian-Xu stood still outside as he looked back and forward, and then he pulled out his cell phone to call a cab back to take him back to his vehicle.

Jin Qi-Long tagged behind the moment the cab driver arrived. The cab driver took no longer than five minutes to come. The two got in the taxi in a hurry, and the cab driver drove off as Yang Tian-Xu told the driver, "Step on it!"

Yang Tian-Xu's car was only five minutes trip away from Fung Qi-Wei's place. When they got to the parking lot, they got off the taxi, and Jin Qi-Long wondered, "Tian-Xu, why are we in such a rush?"

"It's almost 12 p.m., and I have to get back in time to ask An-An if she wants to go out for lunch with me." Yang Tian-Xu's replies made Jin Qi-Long froze with shock.

"Don't you want to have lunch with me?" Jin Qi-Long stressed as he opened the car door before he let himself inside Yang Tian-Xu's car.

"No." Yang Tian-Xu said bluntly and got into the vehicle himself. Jin Qi-Long reaction was priceless as his mouth dropped. He couldn't believe his ears. He stood there dumbfounded for a moment before Yang Tian-Xu shouted at him. "Are you coming in or not?"

"I'm coming! I'm coming!" Jin Qi-Long could not believe Yang Tian-Xu's impatience over a mere intern. "Jeez, you are totally obsessed with her!"

"So what if I am?" Yang Tian-Xu retorted as he could not care less about what other people's opinions. The infatuation he had for Wang Yi-An was something he would expect no one to understand, nor does he want anyone else to know, but her: Wang Yi-An. Yang Tian-Xu didn't wait for Jin Qi-Long to let himself inside the car, Yang Tian-Xu was about to drive off without him. However, Jin Qi-Long hurried as he hopped in, while Yang Tian-Xu drove off. He barely had the time to fasten the seatbelt.

Yang Tian-Xu slammed on the gas pedal as soon as Jin Qi-Long got himself inside. It was too sudden and fast, Jin Qi-Long wasn't even able to shut the door properly. "Dude! That was dangerous!" He shouted, the high velocity of the vehicle with his door remained opened startled him. Jin Qi-Long closed the door as fast as he could.

Yang Tian-Xu's drove fast, and with his expensive white sports car, the horsepower on his vehicle could easily rival a race car. Just as Yang Tian-Xu was pulling out of the underground parking-lot; the street was packed, and it appears to be crowded.

The wait made Yang Tian-Xu became a little more impatient, and he wanted to return to Yang Corps in time, so he could ask Wang Yi-An out for lunch. Moments after he could pull out of the underground parking lot, he reached a pedestrian-crosswalk.

The crosswalk was at a sharp curved corner, and so Yang Tian-Xu's vision was obstructed. However, because Yang Tian-Xu was in such a hurry, so he did not bother to check for any pedestrians, and as he turned the sharp curved corner, he almost hit a lady; about to cross over.

Not that Yang Tian-Xu was speeding or anything. However, he wasn't able to see her only until he completed the right turn. It was fortunate that he stopped on time and the lady sustained no injuries. However, when Yang Tian-Xu stopped so suddenly as soon as he spotted her. The loud screeching sounds of his wheels startled her.

Instead of getting out of the vehicle to check if she was hurt or not, he merely rolled down the window and asked, "Hey! Are you all right?"

The lady was an older woman, whom Yang Tian-Xu could have never imagined it was Wang Yi-An's mother. Mother Wang may be old. However, she was still a beautiful and attractive older woman. How could Yang Tian-Xu have imagined that she would be Wang Yi-An's mother?

Mother Wang became angry at the man, whom she thought was another well-off and arrogant rich-boy. She assumed he was someone with no respect for others. She kicked his car by the wheel and demanded him to get out.

"Get out of your car! Now!" She shouted and screamed as she continued to kick his car.

The sudden scare had taken Mother Wang by surprise; as she fell to the ground and scraped the palm of her right hand. Mother Wang was so mad when the driver only had rolled down his window to ask her. "Hey! Are you all right?"

The tone of Yang Tian-Xu's voice makes it seem like he was ready to leave if she said, yes. However, Mother Wang got up and screamed at him. "Get out of your car! Now!" She kicked the wheels of his car. Mother Wang screamed, shouted while she kicked Yang Tian-Xu's white sports car. Mother Wang hated nothing more in the world, than arrogant, good-looking and well-off boys, she carried with her a biased opinion. She believed them to be people who think they own the entire world and shows no respect for others.

Yang Tian-Xu felt quite annoyed, he felt he won't make it in time to ask Wang Yi-An out for lunch. "Okay, old woman. You can stop abusing my car now! I barely even touched you!"

Naturally, Mother Wang was furious with his remark. "How dare you call me old? I'm not even 45 yet!" She yelled at him as she continued to hit the windshield with the palm of her right hand, she purposely smeared some of her blood onto the windshield. "Get out right now!"

If money could solve the issue, the issue was not a problem. Yang Tian-Xu was the only heir of a big company. Arrogance came to him by nature. However, he still tried his best to respect his elders. However, Yang Tian-Xu could see that this older lady was disrespectful towards him. He couldn't stand the smacking and shouting she caused.

Even the windshield of his car had traces of her blood on it. It disgusted Yang Tian-Xu as he opened the door and stepped out, he wanted to reason with her. Jin Qi-Long also got out, and he said, "Look, lady! We won't waste time arguing with you, just tell us how much you want already."

Mother Wang let out a scornful laugh, and she stared at them with disdain as she told them. "You, don't you have any respect for people! You think money can solve everything?" She pointed at them with her right index finger.

"I do have respect. But, only to those that deserve it." Yang Tian-Xu retaliated, he showed no emotion toward someone who he felt inferior to him. Perhaps, if Mother Wang hadn't kicked and screamed at him, and he wasn't forced out of his vehicle. Yang Tian-Xu might have been a little more respectful to her.

Mother Yang's endless shouts as she lectured had irritated the two boys. Yang Tian-Xu pulled out his wallet from the pocket of his suit and pulled out a bunch of cash. "Here. Now, can I go?" Yang Tian-Xu said as he waved the wad of money in his hand in her face.

Mother Wang hated his attitude even more. Then she took out her phone to take a picture of his license plate, and then she took a picture of the little blood stains on his windshield. Finally, Mother Wang told him. "I'll see you in court! Pretty boy!" She later turned around and took more pictures of the surroundings.

Yang Tian-Xu felt insulted; however, he still decided that catching up to Wang Yi-An would still be his top priority. He left the mad women alone as he and Jin Qi-Long got back into the car before they went, Jin Qi-Long shouted out some inappropriate swear words at her. "Good look, Old hag!"

The time was already 11:57 a.m. when he had gotten back to the Yang Corps Building. Yang Tian-Xu dropped off Jin Qi-Long at the entrance and told him. "Call your driver to pick you up! I need to go see An-An."

Yang Tian-Xu rushed inside the building—without bothered to greet anyone—his expression became serious as he frowned his eyebrows. Yang Tian-Xu made his way to the elevator, and the elevator-lady greeted him when she first saw him. "Good afternoon, President Yang."

However, he ignored her and pressed the seventh-floor button himself, he repeatedly pressed on the button until the door closed. The ride up was fast, but still he became agitated as he kept checking the time on his phone. Yang Tian-Xu got off as soon as the door reopened. The elevator-lady could only feel nervous and wondered if something important had happened, but how could the elevator-lady know the truth? President Yang's impatient attitude was because of a mere intern. Yang Tian-Xu rushed to Wang Yi-An's seat as he saw her. Still, she stayed for a little longer until she goes on her lunch break, as he saw her, this time he would be sure to ask her, "An-An!"

Wang Yi-An turned around and saw him and let out a

smile, "Good afternoon, President Yang!" The tone of her voice was so gentle and sweet, and Yang Tian-Xu felt nervous. However, she returned to focus on her screen again. Yang Tian-Xu felt hurtful, a sense of rejection as he saw the new phone he gave her, still untouched and remained unopened on her desk.

He thought, "Perhaps she doesn't like the same phone model as his?" He took a minute or two to build the courage to asked her. "Do you not like the phone?"

"Oh?" She was surprised and looked at it, "I still don't want to change my phone yet. I'll do so once my old one dies on me. Is that all right? Or is the phone only available to me during my internship?"

"No!" He shouted, his shout had startled her a little because he was too loud, until he continued, "No... It is yours to keep for life."

"Oh... Thank you very much then. I will do my best to take good care of it." Then she gave him another sweet smile that melted his heart.

Yang Tian-Xu wanted to use this chance to ask her, as he had already mustered all the courage he had to speak to her. He might as well asked her now. "Would you—"

"President Yang!" Assistant Tseng shouted as he interrupted Yang Tian-Xu.

As soon as Assistant Tseng saw Yang Tian-Xu, he called him. Assistant Tseng passed by the office to remind Wang Yi-An of her lunch breaks, because he knew sometimes Wang Yi-An would forget to take her lunch breaks. But when he saw President Yang, he felt the urgency to pass the chairman's message to him.

For a second, Assistant Tseng was happy to see President Yang, as he was unseen all day! However, President Yang was unhappy, as he got interrupted by Assistant Tseng's shouts. Yang

Tian-Xu turned his head slow, as he glared at Assistant Tseng. Gradually, he stared at Assistant Tseng with the expression that he would eat him up alive if he doesn't shut his mouth.

Assistant Tseng gulped. "President Yang! The chairman had requested for you to have lunch with him today! SIR!" He squealed as he closed his eyes for a second, praying he could survive President Yang's rage.

"Grandfather said he would come?" Yang Tian-Xu clarified the matter with Assistant Tseng, "Today?"

"Yes, sir!" Assistant Tseng confirmed it with him, "Today, he will arrive shortly."

"Why didn't you tell me sooner?" Yang Tian-Xu felt irritated. His irritation shown on his face as he felt like he couldn't ask Wang Yi-An out on a peaceful and quiet lunch with just him and her any more. Today was not his lucky day.

"Ah... I apologise, boss!" Assistant Tseng felt fear when he saw President Yang's irritated expression.

Assistant Tseng wanted to say, "I tried to call you, but you won't pick up the damn phone!" But Assistant Tseng would never have the guts to say those words out loud, and so he only daydreamed about what it would be like to say, "Next time don't ignore me!" Yet, Assistant Tseng could see the irritation on Yang Tian-Xu's expression. He felt like his end was coming nearer.

Yang Tian-Xu sighed as he felt depressed. "I'm sorry for interrupting your work, An-An. But, please have a good lunch today."

"Thank you very much, President Yang. I almost forgot that it's twelve now." She said as she removed her ID card from the computer. She gave him a slight head bow before she smiled at him and said, "Have a good lunch too." And so she got up from her seat and went for her lunch break.

Yang Tian-Xu could only watch her as she passed by him. Each step she took, their distance became further, and further apart. A tightness inside his heart as he watched her go. Then, his phone pinged him, a notification about a new message he received from his secretary, Geng Yi-Jun.

The time stamped on the message was at 12:01 p.m., he read the message out of all the other in which he had received from Assistant Tseng—asking about his whereabout. Among those messages there were missed calls notification, and he ignored all the notifications from Assistant Tseng and only read the most recent message he received from Secretary Geng.

"The Chairman is already here at the Yang Corps entrance right now! Are you there at the office yet?"

Yang Tian-Xu hurried as he rushed towards Wang Yi-An. He hoped he could make it in time to ride the elevator down with her. "Wait! An-An!" He shouted for her name as he saw her turn around.

As Yang Tian-Xu passed by Assistant Tseng, he stood there as he wondered. "Seriously? Why are you calling out for her?" Curious as he followed behind President Yang.

Wang Yi-An turned around when she heard someone called her. "Yes, President Yang?" She said as she saw Yang Tian-Xu approaching her at a quick paste, Wang Yi-An was a little confused as she thought, "Does he need to shout my name?"

Yang Tian-Xu stood still to look at her, and then he gave out an attractive smile at her. "I have to go down too. Can we go down together?"

"Ah, sure." confused as ever, Wang Yi-An thought, "Does he need to ask me that?" However, her emotion remained inexpressible.

Assistant Tseng's thought were different, as he watched President Yang, who stood there with a charming smile, almost as if he was begging for something. He thought, "What? You rushed to catch up to her, just so you can take the elevator down with her? Shit! For real!? Boss! Why are you acting like this!?" However, he only kept these thoughts in his mind, and not let it out. He had a wife and a baby on its way, he needed to keep his job.

It took no longer than ten steps to reached the elevator, and Yang Tian-Xu pressed the up-button first.

"Um. President. I need to go down." She looked at him as she wondered. "Is he still drunk?"

"Oh! Right, sorry, what was I thinking?" Then Yang Tian-Xu finally presses the button to go down. There were two elevator shafts. One goes up, and the other down. The one going down had another greeter. However, the person had already gone on a lunch break.

The moment the elevator door opened, he grabbed her by the arm and pulled her inside, he had his hands on her shoulder as he dragged her inside, "It's here, let's go!" When she got inside, he pressed on the button for the door to closed faster.

"Wait! Boss, I didn't-!" Assistant Tseng were only two steps behind them. The door closed before he could even get inside, he reached his hand out to stop the door from closing but he was too late.

Wang Yi-An heard and saw Assistant Tseng as he tried to reach out to stop the closing doors. However, it shocked her how President Yang could close the door on him like that before Assistant Tseng could get in. "President Yang, Assistant Tseng haven't gotten in yet." She said as she tried to pressed the button to reopen the door.

Yang Tian-Xu rushed to stopped her hand, he said, "It's okay. He might have something else he needs to do. He can take the next ride down later."

"Okay..." Then she distanced herself from him. But of course, Yang Tian-Xu won't try to push his luck and remained an appropriate distance between him and her. With only Yang Tian-Xu, and Wang Yi-An left in the elevator, alone. Yang Tian-Xu could only pray that the elevator would break down, this way he could be alone with her for a while longer.

Every single second it took for the elevator to go down a level lower. Yang Tian-Xu could only dream of having a power outage. These few precious seconds he spent with Wang Yi-An alone felt like the heaven had finally shown pity on him.

Yang Tian-Xu wanted to ask her a question before the elevator reaches its designated floor at the ground level. "Do you have any special plans for lunch today?" He asked her finally. However the trip was short, perhaps too short. The doors opened, and she stepped out. Yang Tian-Xu followed her and then she turned to look at him with a bright smile. "Yes! My mother and I will have lunch together today!"

"That's good." Yang Tian-Xu forced out a smile on his face, and could only hope that one day, he could meet her mother. They walked past the security, and Wang Yi-An had scanned her card. While Yang Tian-Xu was the President, Yang Corps belonged to his family, and so he doesn't have to scan through the security checkpoint, and went straight into the lobby area. Yang Corps had a tight security system, and the building was incredibly vast, when employees' family or friends came to visits, they would need to go to the reception desk first.

Mother Wang came to pick up Wang Yi-An for lunch, she wanted to surprise her daughter, so she arrived early, however, she was delayed by a certain someone that had frustrated her, and she was still angry. She wanted to tell her daughter she was almost hit by a rich and obnoxious boy today. But, how could Mother Wang imagined the man who caused her to be so angry today, was walking side by side with her precious daughter, Wang Yi-An.

CHAPTER 22

How Can I Bring You Happiness?

Mother Wang was furious as she saw the man who had almost hit her. He looked like he was up to no good with her daughter as he kept a close distance from her. Mother Wang could only hope that the man following her was only trying to ask for directions.

Immediately, Mother Wang came up to Wang Yi-An. Wang Yi-An saw her mother approaching, and she jogged to her mother with opened arms, and her mother embraced her. "Mom!" She shouted.

Shockingly, Yang Tian-Xu stood still, as he thought: "That woman is her mother?! Shit!" Yang Tian-Xu recognised the lady he had a little misunderstanding with today. He panicked—of course— he panicked! Quickly, he rushed out and tried to hide from them.

"Mom, I would like you to meet my boss, President Yang." Wang Yi-An said as she turned around, but only see nobody behind her, President Yang was nowhere in sight. "Ah... that's weird, and he was just behind me a moment ago." Wang Yi-An ponders for a second, "Oh, well, maybe he was busy and had to leave first. Next time I'll introduce you to him. The Yang Corps president is a really nice boss!"

"Yeah?" Mother Wang wondered the tone of her voice was sarcastic, yet curious. She could somehow guess that the man she met earlier was President Yang. However, she said nothing to Wang Yi-An.

Mother Wang thought perhaps it would be better to drop the strife she had with him today. Now she knows he was in fact, her daughter's boss. Mother Wang prefers not to start a conflicted relationship with her daughter's boss. Mother Wang doesn't want the man to take revenge on her by hurting her precious daughter, and so Mother Wang could only believe it must have been her unlucky day.

Wang Yi-An noticed that her mother's hand wrapped up in a band-aid. "Mommy! What happened to your hand?" She was worried when she saw it. Wang Yi-An held onto her mother's injured hand and inspected.

"It's nothing. I just tripped today. It's okay, don't worry about it." She replied as she tried to reassure her daughter it was not a big issue.

Wang Yi-An was still a child at heart, even though she was already 22 years old. She blew onto her mother's wound and said, "Pain, pain fly away!" Her mother could only laugh as she told her. "An-An! You silly girl!" Yet, Wang Yi-An smiled at her, as she linked arms with her mother, and placed her head to leaned against her mother's shoulder.

Yang Tian-Xu had quickly taken a few steps back, to hide behind a beam. The beam was ceiling high, and it would need two people to hug the beam completely—for every ten feet apart a beam placed there to support the enormous building of Yang Corps. The architecture structure of the building was built to withstand an earthquake of a 9.0 magnitude. However, Yang Tian-Xu had used it to hide from the two. The shaft was broad, and it was a perfect hiding spot for him as he stood behind it while he stalked them.

The high and mighty Yang Tian-Xu have now become a stalker. Wang Yi-An and her mother decided they wanted to go to the food court. The food court located inside the mall, and there they will have their lunch together. As they head towards the Mall's direction, Yang Tian-Xu had circled the beam, he remained hidden from their sight. He watched them as they walked further and further away.

Yang Tian-Xu focused his attention to stalked the two, so how could he notice the look on the security guard's face when the guard watched him. The security guard ignored it and minded his business: Yang Tian-Xu was the company's president—so the guards weren't paying much attention to him—and let him be.

The guard noticed how suspicious the president acted. When Yang Tian-Xu circled the beam with small steps, he hasn't noticed that his back faced toward Yang Corps's main entrance. Yang Tian-Xu stood there as he continued to watch Wang Yi-An. He couldn't possibly notice that Grandfather Yang had arrived and saw him there, hugging the beam.

"Tian-Xu!" Grandfather Yang called him. Yang Tian-Xu heard Grandfather Yang's voice, and in an instant, he turned around and saw him. Grandfather Yang just arrived at the building, but he didn't come alone. Grandfather Yang had decided that today, he would return Tong Yue-Yan her justice. So he went to the Tong family's villa with his driver to pick her up. Also, he had apologised on his grandson's behalf. But, how could Tong Yue-Yan waste such a good chance? She immediately agreed to follow along with Grandfather Yang to get her revenge.

As soon as Yang Tian-Xu saw the two, he greeted his grandfather. "Good afternoon, Ye-Ye." He said as he slightly bowed to his grandfather. Then he turned to greet Tong Yue-Yan. "Good afternoon, Miss Tong."

They didn't waste time standing around chit-chatting, they travelled to a restaurant nearby to have their lunch together. The restaurant they went to was inside Yang Corps' mall.

Yang Tian-Xu wanted to follow Wang Yi-An and her mother. However, he was stuck with Grandfather Yang and Tong Yue-Yan.

The busiest time for the restaurant was at lunch-time, the restaurant carried a regular Chinese cuisine menu, with a slight western twist. Yang Corps owned many businesses, and this restaurant was one of their 258 locations. The employees greeted the Chairman and the President as soon as they saw them walked in. A manager rushed over to greet them and led them to a VIP area. The restaurant might be a part of Yang Corps. However, it was one of the lower-tier restaurants that belong under the Yang Corps name. It was a simple and ordinary restaurant with no private rooms.

The staff had set up a private area for the three special guests in the far corner of the place. Separated by two Shoji screen—it divided them in a different sector compared to the rest of the customers. They sat down, and the waitress came over to greet them and gave them a choice of menus to select. A unique trait about the restaurant was because it carried a multi-cultural selection of food choices. However, Grandfather Yang was such a traditional Chinese man, he had to choose the Chinese Menu.

Most of the customers knew their high status and importance. The Chairman and President of Yang Corps were well known as they were all over the media. At such a busy time as lunch hour, most customers would have to wait for a table, they could only envy Grandfather Yang and Yang Tian-Xu as they walked in without waiting for a table. Tong Yue-Yan strolled in with them, she looked like she owned the place. She wasn't a nobody, and most people could recognise her as the heiress to the Tong family.

After they ordered a few side dishes from the Chinese

Menu, and the waitress went to place their orders. Grandfather Yang cut to the chase, "I want you to apologise to Yue-Yan first. You had ignored her when that vicious woman bullied her."

Even though Yang Tian-Xu felt annoyed by it, he stood up and did as he was told. "I apologise on behalf of Yang Cooperation and Faithful Gold Enterprise's spokeswoman." Then, he sat back down.

Tong Yue-Yan was dumbfounded, as she thought, "Did he think this is a business matter? Why is he treating it like it is?"

To Yang Tian-Xu, it was all business and nothing more. Lee Yin-Yin had signed a contract with Faithful Gold Enterprise: his best friend's company. The two companies were in good terms, he can't let anything happen to their image. So Yang Tian-Xu felt the need to help protect the image of their spokesperson. Apologising for artists' bad behaviours were always a part of being a president.

Grandfather Yang was also dumbfounded and curious, but Yang Tian-Xu's response made him questioned. "Why do you make this issue sound like it was just a business matter?"

"Because it is, Ye-Ye." A blunt response as he said, "Lee Yin-Yin is our business partner's current spokesperson. If she offended anyone, it would be my responsibility to apologise on her behalf."

"Then remove her position as the spokesperson, that way it won't be an issue." Grandfather Yang said, in a clear and strict voice. Grandfather Yang wanted Yang Tian-Xu to remove Lee Yin-Yin from her position as the spokeswoman. However, Yang Corps and Faithful Gold Enterprise had just signed a contract with her. How could he change the spokeswoman without Jin Qi-Long's permission?

Yet, Yang Tian-Xu never wanted to explain about whose idea it was to have Lee Yin-Yin as the spokeswoman was Jin Qi-

Long. Yang Tian-Xu honestly said, "I will not remove Lee Yin-Yin's position as the spokesperson.

"Why not?" Grandfather Yang expressed a curious look on his face, and when he looked at his grandson's expressionless face there was an unsetting emotion inside of him as he thought, "Could he be dating this Lee Yin-Yin?"

A simple response was all Grandfather Yang could squeeze out of him as Yang Tian-Xu never felt the need to explain his reasons. Not even to the chairman. "Because the reason to remove her is foolish."

"Foolish you say? The woman used violence on Yue-Yan!" Grandfather Yang raised his voice as it became loud, showing his displeasure. Grandfather Yang thought his reason was more than enough. He asked his grandson. "She will ruin our business' image if she continues to be our spokeswoman! Good enough reason for you?"

"I'm afraid that isn't true." Yang Tian-Xu disagreed with Grandfather Yang, as he continued to give him the reason. "Lee Yin-Yin is an internationally famous artist. She's known as our country's number one idol. How could any other celebrity compete with her fame?"

Yang Tian-Xu paused for a moment as he stared at Tong Yue-Yan and he continued, "Also, it wasn't just Miss Tong who was injured. Miss Lee sustained an equal amount of abuse, but she never complained about it, and she hasn't even called in to change her schedule for the filming on Friday."

"How can you compare her with Yue-Yan, Lee Yin-Yin is just a singer!?" Grandfather Yang's voice was authentic when he asked Yang Tian-Xu. "What is your relationship with Lee Yin-Yin?"

"Ye-Ye! If you question my decision on using Lee Yin-Yin, you might as well question my ability as Yang Corps' President!"

Yang Tian-Xu shouted back, as he was feeling irritated. Yang Tian-Xu could not believe his Grandfather would blindly side with Tong Yue-Yan. He felt that his grandfather was too biased, the anger made him speak his thoughts out loud, "Ye-Ye, you have not heard the entire story, and yet you are already siding blindly with Miss Tong."

Yang Tian-Xu's words were sharp and clear. So clear, it left Grandfather Yang speechless, as he quietly agreed about his biased behaviour.

They were quiet for a moment as their orders rolled out. The waitress came with their food orders on a rolling cart and one dish at a time, she laid them on the roundtable

For the short minutes as the food came out, Yang Tian-Xu thought of only one thing: Wang Yi-An. Even with Lee Yin-Yin status as a world famous idol. Grandfather Yang still sided with Tong Yue-Yan.

What about Wang Yi-An? She was someone with no social status, Wang Yi-An was only an intern. If she were to compare with Lee Yin-Yin—Wang Yi-An would be nobody. Would his grandfather be so biased and unfair towards her as well? Yang Tian-Xu's heart aches as he thought to himself. "How can I bring you happiness?"

Others could feel the tension in the air, the waitress strolled in with the cart of food, and she felt the intensity in the air. She remained quiet as she posed the food and left once she completed her task.

The food was laid out neatly on the table, but no one had touched a single piece yet. Tong Yue-Yan can feel the intensity of the conversation.

Tong Yue-Yan thought maybe it would be a safer idea for her to behave more mature and said, "Ye-Ye, it's ok, we should forget about it altogether. Tian-Xu is correct." She stated as she gave him a sweet innocent smile.

"It wasn't entirely Miss Lee's fault, and we had a few misunderstanding, my aunt was just overreacting. Let's forget about it and not cause any more problems." She said as she tried to loosen the tension in the air.

Grandfather Yang felt like Tong Yue-Yan was such a good child. She put in a few kind words and said it wasn't entirely Lee Yin-Yin's fault, and she too was to blame for the misunderstanding.

Grandfather Yang was a little angry at his grandson's behaviour. How could he have foreseen that his grandson would defend a mere singer? If Tong Yue-Yan wanted to forget about the incident with Lee Yin-Yin; Grandfather Yang would not continue to pursue the issue. He might as well just follow along with her request.

"If Yue-Yan said she no longer wishes to pursue the unfortunate incident, I too—will break it off." Grandfather Yang said as he looked at the quiet Yang Tian-Xu.

"Thank you very much, Ye-Ye. You are indeed such an admirable man." Tong Yue-Yan said as she took the chance to suck-up to Grandfather Yang. "Ye-Ye, thank you very much for your support. I honestly appreciate it and truly hope you can be my real grandfather."

Yet, Yang Tian-Xu remained quiet. With only one thought on his mind: How could he make grandfather likes Wang Yi-An just as much?

Grandfather Yang laughed and told Tong Yue-Yan, "Once you marry Tian-Xu, I can be your grandfather then."

However, how could Yang Tian-Xu sit there and let his grandfather decided his marriage? He slammed both his hands on the table hard—sudden and loud—it was such a brassy sound as it startled everyone.

There was utter silence for a second or two as Yang Tian-Xu stood up. "I will not marry her, Ye-Ye!"

"What are you saying? Yue-Yan is the only girl that can match perfectly with you! Who else can you marry that would conform to the Yang's name and worthy as the Yang Family's bride?" Grandfather Yang's voices rose once more. This time, he couldn't help it: as he got angry.

"Fitting or not, is something I should decide myself, Ye-Ye! My heart can only love just one woman, and that woman is definitely not Tong Yue-Yan!" Yang Tian-Xu raised his voice. He couldn't bear it any longer.

How could he sit here and do nothing when his grandfather was so dead set on having Tong Yue-Yan as his future wife? What about the woman loves?

Grandfather Yang felt the anger in his chest. He was a healthy old man. Even though he's angry, he won't get a heart attack from this. Then he stood up, "I will not accept this behaviour of yours, Yang Tian-Xu!"

Yang Tian-Xu shouted back, "Ye-Ye!" Yang Tian-Xu was ready to dash out of their sights as he pronounced, "You said no matter who I have fallen in love with, you will support me. Have you already forgotten what you had said once before?"

Grandfather Yang was quiet because he remembered what he had said to his grandson that day. He couldn't believe his words could come back to bite him. Grandfather Yang could only express his regrets about the words he had promised that day.

"I hope that you can keep your word." Yang Tian-Xu gave Grandfather Yang a farewell bow as he turned his back on them and bolted out of the restaurant. He could no longer stick around in that location any longer.

The only one who he wanted to spend his time with was

Wang Yi-An. He felt the need to see her, and it was like he had became addicted to her.

Grandfather Yang didn't stop his grandson from leaving, he sat back down and said, "Let's enjoy our meal. One day he will understand, give him some time, okay? Yue-Yan?"

Tong Yue-Yan nodded and smiled back at him. Then he smiled back, and they had their meal. Tong Yue-Yan believed in Grandfather Yang's words. She will one day become Yang Tian-Xu's wife, and then she thought, "Just you watch Yang Tian-Xu. One day I will own your heart!"

Meanwhile, in the food court of the Yang Corps' Mall was a busy sight. There were plenty of chatters and laughter as many citizens enjoyed their time at the Mall. Although, it was a Tuesday afternoon Yang Corps' Mall was always a busy shopping centre.

Wang Yi-An and her mother were sitting at a table as they enjoyed their takeout meal together. Wang Yi-An loved to talk with her mother about her day; and so, Mother Wang would listen to her. However, suddenly she asked. "Is your boss the type to hold on to grudges?"

"Hm?" Wang Yi-An was both shocked and curious about why her mother would ask such a thing. "I know little about him. But he looks like a decent guy. Why?"

"If you suddenly get mistreated, you better quit and get a different internship somewhere else! Okay?" Mother Wang felt worried for her daughter.

CHAPTER 23

I Am Restless Without You

No matter what time of the day, Yang Corps mall was always filled with shoppers. With Wang Yi-An and her mother as they sat in the busy cafeteria. Wang Yi-An was confused, for a second; she thought she misheard her mother's words. Yet, she knew she heard it correctly as she thought her mother was worried she might get bullied.

Wang Yi-An was a poor child, from a single home. In school, she was often teased and bullied, but it made her stronger. She smiled at her mother and said, "Don't worry mom. My boss is a decent man. He treats his employees really well!" Still, the innocent smile on her face worried her mother more.

The table was at a corner in the cafeteria, and it was one of the smaller tables. Only enough room for them as they sat across face to face, and Mother Wang and Wang Yi-An each have their red-tray of food in front. They ordered it themselves at a different fast-food joint. Mother Wang liked to have rice for lunch, but Wang Yi-An preferred stir-fry noodles.

Mother Wang sighed as she told her, "He's only nice for now." And then, Mother Wang held her hands and said, "Remember you can't always trust people. Remember the idiom; You can see a person's face, but not their hearts."

"Yes, Mommy! If I start ever get mistreated at Yang Corps, I'll find another company to work at, Okay? It's only for another two or three months anyway, and I'll be fine." Wang Yi-An tried to reassure her mother's worried, as she gave her a big warm smile. She went back to finish eating the stir-fry noodles she had ordered from a fast-food stall.

Mother Wang forced out a smile as she sighed, "You must like working at Yang Corps."

Wang Yi-An paused and stopped eating for a second and asked, "Would you rather I work for Pan Holdings?"

"I didn't say that!" Mother Wang let out an honest smile; filled with concern and sincerity, "You work wherever you feel happier, okay?"

"Hm!" Wang Yi-An nodded and smiled back at her.

"Okay," Mother Wang patted her daughter's hair and points to her food. "Hurry up and eat."

"I have a two-hour lunch! Lots of time! We can go shopping later!" Wang Yi-An chirped as she continues to eat, Mother Wang would sometimes take a few pieces of food off her plates and gave them Wang Yi-An. With her mother by her side, she felt the happiest.

They laughed and talk as they enjoyed their time together as mother and daughter. Later, when it was time for Wang Yi-An returns to the office, she kissed her mother on the cheek like a little child. Then, Mother Wang would hug her once more, and leave the Yang Corps building after.

In the Manager's Office, Yang Tian-Xu sat down impatiently as he waited for Wang Yi-An to return. He ate nothing all day. However, he does not feel hungry. He looked everywhere for Wang Yi-An and her mother the entire lunch-break.

Yang Corps was just too big, and he felt depressed when he couldn't find them. He spent two hours searching for her. However, he needed to return to the office. Yang Tian-Xu was becoming more and more impatient as he sat in his chair for a while. Then he stood up and pace around, and then he tried to focus on his work, but how could he? He only wanted to see Wang Yi-An as she remained in his mind every second.

Finally, Wang Yi-An returned, and she waved to her other coworkers and greeted them. And as he heard someone called her name, he bolted out the office. He was like a watch-dog waiting for her to return. Yang Tian-Xu rushed outside and saw her as she approached her workstation.

"Hello, President Yang." She smiled at him and gave him a slight bow.

Yang Tian-Xu's feelings of excitement burst and over-flowed when he saw Wang Yi-An. He couldn't say anything and just smiled at her. He twisted around as he felt his face boiled, and then he rushed back into his office as he slammed the door.

"Ah, dammit all!" He thought as he lifted his head up to the ceiling. He closed his eyes and felt frustrated. Like he might rush outside and grab onto her. He took a deep breath as he tried to calm down his emotions.

Yang Tian-Xu felt powerless, as he continued to stare at her as he hides from behind the window blinds. All Yang Tian-Xu wanted to do was watch her all day. He would ignore his calls and when Assistant Tseng came by to collect his signed documents. Yang Tian-Xu ignored him, while he had neglected his duty as the President of Yang Corps.

"Ah... Boss... What are you doing?" Assistant Tseng watched him, as he stood behind Yang Tian-Xu. When he saw that Yang Tian-Xu was busy stalking Wang Yi-An; he let out an awkward smile. "Boss, you are just too obsessed with her! You need to finish signing these contracts! I need your signature urgently!"

Assistant Tseng's constant nagging didn't bother him as

Yang Tian-Xu said, "Okay, okay." Then he reached out to grab the document and signed it, without looking at the papers.

"Boss!" Assistant Tseng shouted, and his voice was so loud, it startled him.

"What!? God, you are loud." Yang Tian-Xu said as he glared at Assistant Tseng for a few seconds, and then he returned to stalking Wang Yi-An.

Assistant Tseng wanted to cry—as he let out a sigh—he thought, "Why are you like this, boss? Oh, the amazing Yang Tian-Xu is now... Such a girl." And then he left as he felt so depressed to see his boss becoming someone: so odd.

Just like that, the time passed by, and soon the clock hits 5:00 p.m. Yang Tian-Xu rushed out of the office, and he begged her, "Please! Allow me to take you home!" Then he paused for a second and continued, "I mean, please let me give you a ride home."

"Ah..." Surprise took Wang Yi-An, as he came by and asked her so suddenly, she doesn't know how to answer him.

But before she could say anything, he said, "Oh, I also wanted to drop by and thank Fung Qi-Wei as well for today. So I would be in the area."

"Oh..." Wang Yi-An finally understood, then she smiled at him with a slight head bow. "Sure! Thank you in advance!" Her smile was the sweetest one he had ever seen, and once again her smile had melted Yang Tian-Xu's heart.

There was a slight tightness inside Yang Tian-Xu's heart, as he stared at her blankly. He waited weeks for this day to come, and he imagined it many times, and every time she rejected him: a little more of his faith goes down the drain. But now she finally said yes? He had been depressed for a while now, but her acceptance of his offer made him felt happy.

Yang Tian-Xu thought perhaps he was dreaming. He stood still as he blanked out for a second, and then he thanked her sincerely, "Thank you for allowing me to do so.

Yang Tian-Xu's words of thanks made Wang Yi-An stunned, as she thought, "Wait, did he just thanked me for giving me a ride? Wow, why is he so polite?" Yet, she replied, "Oh, no. Thank you, President Yang."

On their way to his car, Yang Tian-Xu hoped they could walk slower. However, Wang Yi-An was used to walking at a fast pace. As for Yang Tian-Xu, he had longs legs and slowed himself down to match her speed.

Wang Yi-An had short legs, but still, she was fast. Then before he realised it, they had already reached his vehicle. They got in, and he slowly started the car. Wang Yi-An didn't have work today, and so he took her home.

There was no need for Wang Yi-An to tell him the address as Yang Tian-Xu had already memorised it by heart. The ride to her house wasn't as long as Yang Tian-Xu had hoped for. And sometimes he would pretend to take the wrong turn so he could drag on their time together, even for an extra ten minutes: he was satisfied.

Wang Yi-An felt that perhaps he had a problem finding her house. "Are you sure you don't need me to give you the address? I can punch it in the GPS."

"No, it's okay. Don't worry about it, and sorry I took the wrong turn. My mind gets a little preoccupied sometimes. Sorry if I had caused you any problems." Yang Tian-Xu said as he wanted to tell her he wanted to spend more time with her. However, he was afraid he might make her feel uncomfortable if he said that, so he kept quiet.

Wang Yi-An smiled at him, and shook her head, "Oh no, thank you very much for giving me a lift."

"Anytime. If you want, I can give you a lift every day."

Wang Yi-An laughed, "How can that be possible? Did you and Fung Da-Ge bonded today?"

"Well, sort of?" Yang Tian-Xu wanted to tell her, "I only became friends with him because of you." However, it was impossible for him to say those words out loud and thought in secret as he smiled at her.

Yang Tian-Xu wasn't lying, it was the truth, as Yang Tian-Xu's mind was preoccupied with thoughts about her. Also, for a second or two; he thought perhaps he should see Fung Qi-Wei and have a chat with him.

Perhaps, he could and asked him for his advice on what Mother Wang would like as gifts of apology. However, for now, he let that matter go, and only wanted to enjoy his time with Wang Yi-An. Throughout their ride together, he would sometimes try to talk to her. However, Wang Yi-An just replied to him with simple short answers.

Yang Tian-Xu asked random questions like, "Have you worked at the Happiness Restaurant long?"

"Yes." A straightforward reply with no intention to carry on the conversation. However, Yang Tian-Xu won't give up, and he wanted to know more about her from her mouth, and not from a third-person like Fung Qi-Wei.

"What do you like to eat." He continued to question her.

"Everything." She replied as she smiled at him. Still, she didn't ask him in return, because she wasn't curious about what he likes to eat.

Yang Tian-Xu felt like he should at least try to pry into her thoughts about Fung Qi-Wei. He thought, just because Fung Qi-Wei thinks of her as a sister—doesn't mean she doesn't have feelings for him. "You and Fung Qi-Wei seems to get along really well, do you considered him as an older brother?"

"Sort of." Wang Yi-An replied the tone of her voice seems to have another meaning.

Yang Tian-Xu was not satisfied with her replies, and he felt like perhaps she doesn't like to talk much? And so, Yang Tian-Xu asked her one last question. "How long have you known him?"

Once more, she answered him with a simple answer. "A long time."

The only remark Yang Tian-Xu could say was, "I see..."

The ride back to her district by bus would take Wang Yi-An one hour during rush hours, and if there were no traffic, it would take about 45-minutes. However, for Yang Tian-Xu he had purposely taken wrong turns here and there, and so they were together in the car for an hour and a half.

Wang Yi-An felt like perhaps it would have been better for her to take the bus home? However, Yang Tian-Xu apologised and said, "Sorry it took so long, next time I would be faster, I promised. I hope I could give you a lift next time as well."

Wang Yi-An wasn't sure how to answer him, perhaps it would be faster next time? Wang Yi-An pondered for a second and said, "Maybe? You might be busy. I wouldn't want to bother you so much."

When they arrived at her house, Yang Tian-Xu shouted, "Wait." Of course, Wang Yi-An remains seated and wait as she unbuckled her belt. Yang Tian-Xu got out of the car and dashed over to her side, and he opened the door for her. Wang Yi-An thought, "Ah, you told me to wait just for that?"

An awkward feeling she had as she said. "Thanks..."

Wang Yi-An got off, and he closed the door. Wang Yi-An was ready to go inside, she gave him a slight, polite bow. However, it seems like Yang Tian-Xu doesn't want to leave. He stood there for a moment.

There was an awkward feeling in her as she thought, "Shouldn't he leave already? Doesn't he need to meet up with Fung Da-Ge?" Then she waved to him and said, "Thank you again for the ride. I hope you have a nice day." As she twisted her body around, she never turns her head back to look at him once. Still, Yang Tian-Xu stood there as he watched her getting inside her house.

Mother Wang was home earlier than usual that day. She was in her room as she heard a car drove by, it was like she was expecting a guest. She peeked outside her bedroom window and saw the entire scene unfold down below. Her daughter with that man, Yang Tian-Xu. She worried about her daughter as soon as she recognised the man. Once Wang Yi-An came inside, she rushed downstairs to see her daughter, "An-An." She called her.

"Mommy!" Wang Yi-An exclaimed as she was so excited to see her mother returned home before herself. Lately, it was rare for her mother to be home early. "You're off work so early today!"

Mother Wang smiled and told her, "My boss can't make me do overtime forever. That would be slavery."

Wang Yi-An smiled back and jumped in her mother's arms. While she hugged her mother as if she was still a baby, and her mother cradled her. Wang Yi-An felt a gentle warmth as she remained in her mother's arm, so she smiled. To Wang Yi-An's mother, Wang Yi-An would always be her baby girl, no matter how old she turns. Her mother would do the best she could to spoil and love Wang Yi-An—because Mother Wang was a great mother.

Mother Wang never had to worry much about Wang Yi-An because she always behaved like a good girl she always been. Wang Yi-An always listened to her mother's words. Still, Mother

Wang remembered how she spotted Wang Yi-An with that rich-spoiled youngster awhile ago. Mother Wang continued to worry as she said, "Was that man outside just now, your boyfriend?"

"What?" Wang Yi-An was both shocked and confused. "No. Why would you even think about that? He is my boss, not my boyfriend." Then she let out a small laugh. "How could you even thought about that?"

"Right." Mother Wang held on to her hand, and they walked over to the wooden four-chair dining table and sat down. Once they were comfortable, Mother Wang continued. "You still remember what I told you right?"

Wang Yi-An nodded as she still remembered. "Trust no one. You can see a person's face, but you can't see their hearts. I remember! Mom, you don't have to worry about me." Then Wang Yi-An patted her mother's hand as she tried to reassure her.

Wang Yi-An and her mother were by themselves in their small kitchen-living room. Wang Yi-An's mother still kept her hands on her as she said. "I know I kept repeating myself, but..." then Mother Wang paused for a second as she breathed in and out heavily, "I just don't want you to end up like me."

Mother Wang's expression shows both concern and pain, she worried for Wang Yi-An and said, "I had poured out all my heart to love a man, who wasn't even worth my love."

"Mom," Wang Yi-An squeezed tightly onto her mother's hand, and said, "Don't worry, he is my boss. President Yang said he would be in the area, and so he was kind enough to give me a lift today. That's all. Also, President Yang seems to be like a decent man."

"How can you tell?" Mother Wang asked, her voice was strong as she made her point. "He finds excuses to take you home. His intention could be because he wanted to get close to you."

Wang Yi-An giggled, "Why would he want that?"

Mother Wang gave her a frivolous stare, "He only wants what every other man wants."

She doesn't know what Mother Wang was hinting at, so she became curious, and she asked, "What's that?" while she had an innocent expression.

"Sex." Mother Wang voice was sharp and clear, and she warned her, "And once he is finished playing with you, he'll get bored and throw you aside, and—"

"Mom!" Wang Yi-An interrupted her as she was a little upset, "You're over thinking."

Mother Wang hastily replied, "All those rich young masters are all the same, I just want you to be careful and…"

"And not to fall in love? Yes, yes, Mom. I know. Mom, I told you. He was just kind enough to give me a ride home."

Therefore, Wang Yi-An gave her mother another sweet and innocent smile as she said, "Besides, he already has so many beautiful girls fighting for him, beautiful women surround him every day, why would he have any ill intention towards me?"

"It's because you differ from those girls he's used to." Mother Wang gave her an answer, "He wants to find something different for his entertainment, like a toy, and that new toy of his is you. So, just be careful, okay?"

Wang Yi-An was lost for words, and she knew what her mother was trying to say. She wouldn't want anything to do with "rich young masters" herself. Wang Yi-An nodded instead of saying anything more to her mother.

Wang Yi-An was always careful and always tried to distance herself from Yang Tian-Xu. It was the reason she turned him down when he offers to take her home, but tonight was different. Wang Yi-An was tired.

Last night, she carried Yang Tian-Xu back to Fung Qi-Wei's house. Wang Yi-An was strong, but she was still petite. To support Yang Tian-Xu's body was a miracle.

Jin Qi-Long was covered in vomits at the time he regurgitated everywhere. Wang Yi-An had to clean up whatever Jin Qi-Long's disgorged. She was already so tired, and it was already morning by the time she finished.

Wang Yi-An went back to her home, and it was a five-minute walk from Fung Qi-Wei's home. Wang Yi-An prepared herself for work, came back to check on them, and cook them the ginger soup before she took the bus to Yang Corps. She finished a lot of work today, and Wang Yi-An felt exhausted. She wanted to return home quickly and rest.

Yet, the ride offered by Yang Tian-Xu took her longer to return home than the bus, perhaps next time she should continue to refuse President Yang's kind offers? This way, maybe her mother's uneasiness would also be lifted?

CHAPTER 24

One thing She Has

A surprised Fung Qi-Wei stood by the door as he saw Yang Tian-Xu three feet away from him. Fung Qi-Wei heard the doorbell ring as he went to open it. And when he saw who it was, he became surprised. Yang Tian-Xu waved at him and let himself in.

Yang Tian-Xu came to visit him after he took Wang Yi-An home. Fung Qi-Wei's mother was the owner of Happiness Restaurant, and he helped out as much as he could. However, on his days off he wanted to enjoy his peace at home. After he spent an entire night struggling to clean the two drunkards.

It amused Fung Qi-Wei as he saw Yang Tian-Xu returned to visit him so soon. "Did you forgot something here? Or you came back because you missed me?" He asked as he joked around.

Therefore, Yang Tian-Xu came up to him and placed his hands on Fung Qi-Wei's shoulders, and he begged him, "I need your help. Please help me!"

At first, Fung Qi-Wei was a little confused. However, he still let Yang Tian-Xu explained himself. They went into the living room together, and Yang Tian-Xu explained everything to Fung Qi-Wei in details.

After Fung Qi-Wei heard the entire story: He laughed out loud as he slapped his palms on his thighs. "You almost ran Mother Wang over with your sports car!"

Yang Tian-Xu felted like he was being teased. "Not funny... Please tell me how I can get her mother to like me."

"Well--An-An gets her stubbornness from her mother. If you sincerely apologised to Mother Wang. I'm sure she'll forgive you." He paused for a second and Yang Tian-Xu would let out a smile of hope.

However, Fung Qi-Wei added, "Or not!" Then he laughed out loudly again. Fung Qi-Wei felt so amused by Yang Tian-Xu's reaction. The expression on Yang Tian-Xu's face was just so amusing to him--Yet Fung Qi-Wei soon felt terrible for him.

Yang Tian-Xu had a genuine look on his face. Just as sincere as when he told him his feelings for Wang Yi-An--which was why he wanted to help him.

"Look." He said and paused as he grasped on to Yang Tian-Xu's attention. "Mother Wang might be stubborn, but she is also very soft hearted. Just visit her at her office every day to apologise once she knows you are sincere. She will forgive you. Who knows? She might even like you enough to allow An-An marry you."

"Rea... Really?" Yang Tian-Xu blushed when he thought he could get permission from Mother Wang. His face lit up, and Fung Qi-Wei could only click his tongue and said. "You need some serious help..."

Help? Yes, Yang Tian-Xu needed lots of support. Not with the situation with Mother Wang, but with his brain. Fung Qi-Wei thought, "What does he sees in An-An? Is she that pretty?" Still, he could only get the answer from Wang Yi-An after he confesses his love to her. Yet, when would that be?

"When do you plan to tell her your feelings?" Fung Qi-Wei asked as he poured himself a cup of tea. The teapot placed at the centre of the small coffee table in the living room; it was at the perfect drinking temperature. He took a sip of his tea and waited for Yang Tian-Xu's answer.

"Hmm..." Yang Tian-Xu hummed for a while and then he smiled at Fung Qi-Wei as he said, "Not telling!"

Suddenly, Fung Qi-Wei felt teased and knew he won't be getting any answer from him. He could only wait, hoped that he would still be alive for that day, then he could finally tell Wang Yi-An. "This guy is crazy about you."

Fung Qi-Wei let out a smile as he thought, "That would definitely be a fun day to tease them both!" He watched Yang Tian-Xu rushed out of his house after he received a message on his phone. Although he felt used, he still felt happy for Wang Yi-An.

Days and weeks went by, and Yang Tian-Xu had visited Mother Wang's workplace every day. Every day he came to apologise to her, bearing fruits baskets day after day, one early in the morning at 6:00 a.m., and another at night time at 10:00 p.m., before she gets off work. The reception desk at the clinic she worked at was filled with them. She gave a few to customers and her coworker.

The first day she ignored him as much as she could but for four days straight, Yang Tian-Xu was determined, and he would never give up! Not until she forgave him for his poor behaviour. Then on the fourth day, Mother Wang gave in. She told him. "I'm not mad about the car accident anymore! Go away already! I forgive you!"

"Really!?" He was excited when she told him she forgave him. However, Yang Tian-Xu had to push his limitation. "May I please date your daughter?"

Mother Wang was stunned, she fell off her chair. Thank God it was 6:00 a.m. in the morning and no one was around to witnessed her clumsiness.

Yang Tian-Xu tried to help her up, but she refused his help, and when Mother Wang got herself up—she yelled, "What did you say?!"

"I would like to date your daughter," he repeated.

"No—Oh, hell no!" Mother Wang refused to have this rich boy playing with her daughter's heart. "You better leave her alone!"

"But, please! Mother-in-law! I'm sincere! Allow me to date your daughter! I intend to marry her!"

He left her speechless for a long while, she stood there stunned. She couldn't believe her ears, and she had to clarify it again as she asked him, "*You* want to marry my An-An?"

"Yes!" his voice was sharp and sincere. He had a heart filled with sincerity. He believed one day Mother Wang could see the honesty in his heart and understand these feelings he had for her daughter were real.

All while, Yang Tian-Xu was trying his best to win Mother Wang's favour and adoration. Rumours were spreading around in the Yang Corps building, perhaps over the media. They gossip about Yang Tian-Xu standing up against his grandfather for Lee Yin-Yin. The reason was that they were currently dating!

The rumours had started by random customers that were there at the restaurant that day, eavesdropping on their conversation. Yang Tian-Xu had argued with his grandfather about Lee Yin-Yin, and he stood up for her.

However, he only stood up for her because he felt like it was unfair. Still, in the eyes of many bystanders; they thought perhaps Lee Yin-Yin, and Yang Tian-Xu were probably a couple.

Lee Yin-Yin heard about the rumours herself, and she felt

delighted, as she let off a happy smile on her for days. Lee Yin-Yin was staying at her apartment, with floor to ceiling high windows, and she looked outside the busy street of City Y below her.

In Lee Yin-Yin's right hand she held a wine glass, and she smiled as she imagined the look on Tong Yue-Yan's face when the president of Yang Corps had stood on her side, even against his grandfather, Chairman Yang.

At that moment, Lee Yin-Yin let out a big grin on her beautiful face. Lee Yin-Yin believed that every man would fall in love with her. They had to, she was the current nation's number one idol. All men drooled for her. And Yang Tian-Xu? He was like any other wealthy young masters, and Lee Yin-Yin believed she could easily hold him in the palm of her hands like he was her object.

The long-awaited day of the photo-shoot had arrived, and they were to photograph pictures for the promotional poster. Lee Yin-Yin took a few days off of work from her other project because of her fight with Tong Yue-Yan--she felt better--and she made a promise to herself that she would one day get her revenge.

Lee Yin-Yin arrived at Yang Corps early at 9:00 p.m. on a Friday. The injuries she sustained had healed, leaving no scars on her beautiful complexion. Thus she wanted to see Yang Tian-Xu and thank him for siding with her. Also, she wanted to apologise for causing a misunderstanding between him and his grandfather.

Lee Yin-Yin walked into the Yang Corps building with her manager. Appearing at her best, she wore a stunning long summer dress. It was hard for the other clients of the Yang Corps mall to not fixate their eyes on her. Also, there was a rumour spreading around about her and Yang Tian-Xu dating.

The media and paparazzi were all over Yang Corps building. They knew Lee Yin-Yin's schedule and were camping out to interview her. She had no other option but to enter through the underground parking lot. When she reached the entrance, two security guards stopped her.

It was a sunny day today, she and her manager both had their shades on as they walked in. Of course, the security told them they must remove all face accessory rendering anyone unable to hide their faces before could enter Yang Corps.

Lee Yin-Yin was a very respectful lady. Even though she was famous, she still abide the rules, and she removed her sunglasses. Lee Yin-Yin's beauty amazed the security guards. He recognised her and he let her in. The lift operator were inside, ready to greet them as they walked in. Standing beside the nation's top idol made her feel nervous inside. The lady suppressed the impulse to solicit for a picture or a signature.

Soon enough, they arrived at the fifth level. The fifth floor was where all the Yang Corps films and photography studios were located. Yang Corps worked on many projects and multiple companies at once, filming and photographing for promotions daily. Public Relations was also a big department for Yang Corps. It was Lee Yin-Yin and her manager's first time at the studio, and the place was massive as they head toward the studio at the far left end of the wing. There were about twenty-five crew members working on the set. As soon as they saw Lee Yin-Yin walked in, they greeted her.

Lee Yin-Yin was known in the industry to be someone of extreme courtesy and kindness. Often she helped out many new artists that were just starting out. They had known her as the role model, and she deserved the title as the nation's number one idol.

Lee Yin-Yin came from a mid-class family. Her parents were not rich people, and she worked hard to get her wealth and fame herself, as she treated people with respect. Even after she became famous that personality of hers never changed.

If anyone treated her poorly, she would return the favours in the worst way possible, a belief she carried with her since childhood. Anyone that treated her with kindness and respect, she would repay ten times more in return. The first thing she did as she came in, she brought coffees and doughnuts for the entire staff and crew members.

Everyone cheered as they thanked her, and Lee Yin-Yin took a portion for Yang Tian-Xu. She looked everywhere for him. Only to find him busy sharing a document folder in his hand with the director, he ordered him. "Make sure all the equipments are double checked before you start."

The director left to complete his task, and he went pass Lee Yin-Yin he greeted her with a slight bow, and Lee Yin-Yin would reciprocate. Then she walked inside the small break-room, compared to most rooms on the upper floor level the room could fit about six or seven people at once; it was the studio's multipurpose room. The director had heard the rumours so, he left quickly the moment he saw Lee Yin-Yin approaching them. He closed the door behind them as he left.

"Hello, President Yang. I brought you and the staff coffee and sweets. Here's your share." She said as she handed him the coffee and a doughnut. She extended her arms out to hand him the food.

However, Yang Tian-Xu ignored her, unbothered to care about what she brings him, he left Lee Yin-Yin's hands still suspended in the air.

"It's okay. You can have it." Unintended to accept her gifts Yang Tian-Xu continued to ignored her.

Lee Yin-Yin placed the coffee and snack down on the table for him, then she approached him, and came to a halt as she only an inch away from him. "But I brought them for you. Take them as my gratitude." Lee Yin-Yin wanted to place her hands around his arms, but only if he initiates the intimacy. But how could that be possible? Yang Tian-Xu avoided her her like she was someone with an incurable illness? Like she was contagious, and he needed to stay away from her.

"Gratitude? What for?" Yang Tian-Xu said as he remained a considerable safe distance from her.

Lee Yin-Yin won't push it after seeing his reaction. She halt at two feet away from him and said. "You know, for defending me when your grandfather wanted to fire me."

"Oh... That's nothing. It was a justified act, and you don't have to thank me for that." A casual reply as it carried no bigger meaning to him than it did for her. For himself he felt that if he did not clarify, Grandfather Yang could still be adamant on matchmaking Tong Yue-Yan and him.

"But I should show you my gratitude, and thank you properly, so. Thank you." Lee Yin-Yin held her hands together behind her back, she fidgeted with her fingers. Her nervousness was clear. She studied Yang Tian-Xu's appearance to a great extent. Taking peeks at his beautiful sharp eyes. His nose bridge was at the perfect height, a clear and exquisite feature of his jawline. She had never met such a fine-looking man, even the other popular actors won't be able to compete against his ravishing good looks.

"Okay, You are welcome. I need to get back to work and discuss with my staff about a few scenes..." Yang Tian-Xu said as he wanted to keep his distance, he was about to leave the room. His hand position on the door-knob as Lee Yin-Yin shouted. "Wait!"

Her loud voice stopped him and he turned around and asked her."Can I help you?"

"No, I..." She wanted to ask him about the rumours. Was

it true? Did he like her so much he would confront his grand-father? However, it would be improper and embarrassing for her to ask such a question and she became a little shy thinking about it.

Still, she wanted to know why he defended her. Being it as a justified act of right or wrong, doesn't make it reasonable enough for her. She wanted to know if he carried any romantic feelings for her.

Lee Yin-Yin had mustered all her courage to ask him. "Is it true? The real reason was because you like me? If you liked me. I want to know."

"What? Oh, hell no. I don't like you." Yang Tian-Xu was blunt about his reply. "I have someone else I like."

"You mean Tong Yue-Yan?" Lee Yin-Yin showed an un-happy expression on her face as she frowned. Her first reaction was to find out who this person might be and hoped that it won't be the spoiled rich-brat, Tong Yue-Yan.

"No, it's someone else." He professed in the open, smiling as he thought about Wang Yi-An.

"May I ask who she is?" Lee Yin-Yin was dying to know, just who was it, that could be better than her and that bratty-heiress Tong Yue-Yan?

"Well..." At first, Yang Tian-Xu was unwilling to tell her. However, he wants none misunderstanding from her stand-point. He must cut all hope she would ever have or harboured. "She's my intern. Wang Yi-An."

"What?" She stood in disbelief, as she thought perhaps she heard it wrong? Or Maybe she heard the wrong name? Wang Yi-An? "You like Wang Yi-An?" she disproved herself as she asked again, "You like Wang Yi-An? The same intern I met that day, Wang Yi-An?"

Lee Yin-Yin's eyes became blurry as she saw Yang Tian-Xu blushed, "Yes, but don't tell her. I haven't confessed yet. So, I want to tell her myself."

Briefly, she wanted to faint from all the blood rushing towards her brain. She couldn't believe it still, yet Yang Tian-Xu stood in front of her smiling like a fool. "It must be his excuse!" she thought and brainstormed, then she concluded he was only using Wang Yi-An as an excuse, and she said, "You're lying!"

"I'm not, and I'll tell her one day." Yang Tian-Xu was serious and determined as he continued. "And for sure she will become my future wife." He smiled to himself again, like a fool.

Lee Yin-Yin still couldn't wrap the thoughts of her losing to an ugly girl like Wang Yi-An. So she disproved and asked, "If it wasn't a lie, why did you tell me first and not her?"

Lee Yin-Yin was still sceptical and couldn't understand why he had chosen Wang Yi-An as she thought, "He must be lying! Yeah, that's it. That's why he doesn't want me to tell her, and he's just using her name as a cover!"

Yang Tian-Xu's answers were not what Lee Yin-Yin wanted to hear, "The reason for me to tell you first is that I hoped that you could sing for us on our wedding day. I noticed that she loves your singing and your songs, so on our wedding day, I want you to perform so I can surprise her."

Lee Yin-Yin slightly shuddered her head as she let out a chuckle of sarcasm. "You want me to sing at your wedding?"

"Yes." Yang Tian-Xu said in a simplistic tone.

"Your wedding?" She doesn't know if she should laugh or cry, Lee Yin-Yin thought everything she heard was a nightmare. "With that girl?"

"Yes." In the same tone as he answered her again. His facial expression remained motionless towards her. Unable to tell if he was joking, or being serious. Lee Yin-Yin felt like her world had fallen apart.

"Wang Yi-An?" Lee Yin-Yin repeated herself. She couldn't help herself—she became desperate to know the truth. "The intern?—Who's plain, have no background? Who has nothing at all: and nothing but a mere intern?"

Once more Yang Tian-Xu had replied the same way. "Yes."

Lee Yin-Yin scorned as she asked, "Why?! What does she have and I don't? Yang Tian-Xu! That's enough bullshit!" Lee Yin-Yin felt like Yang Tian-Xu was talking nonsense on purpose. She felt like he was trying to reject her and shouted. "If you want to reject me, just say it! Don't make some bullshit lies!"

However, Yang Tian-Xu had enough, as he said. "I love Wang Yi-An and that--is not a lie. I can't understand why it would be so hard for you to believe in the truth."

"The truth?" Lee Yin-Yin laughed, it was bitter and sour. However, she continued to make her point. "There is no way you would like her and not me?" Lee Yin-Yin felt like he had crushed her pride: her eyes filled with anger.

"Why you? But not her?" Yang Tian-Xu felt like Lee Yin-Yin was wasting his time. "Look, if you can't believe it, don't." He opened the doorknob and told her. "I need you to leave, please Miss Lee. My An-An is on her way here so I can brief her on today's activities. Also, this room is a restricted area for employees on--"

"Why?" Lee Yin-Yin interrupted him, as she refused to leave without an answer. "Why is it her?" She demands an answer from him. Anger was in her eyes as she teared up. She tried to calm her emotions down as she continued, "I'm of equal match against Tong Yue-Yan. But no, you pick a normal intern over us?" Lee Yin-Yin felt futile and thought about all she'd been through were for nothing, she let out a hysterical laugh.

Still, Lee Yin-Yin became more annoyed as she continued, "I have fame, I have beauty, I have everything she couldn't possibly have!" Lee Yin-Yin needs to know. "Why her?"

"Even if I lose to Tong Yue-Yan, I would understand. But to Wang Yi-An? What does she have and I don't?" Lee Yin-Yin stared at Yang Tian-Xu's emotionless eyes towards her. "I can't accept that without a good answer!"

"You want a truthful answer? Fine, I'll tell you." Yang Tian-Xu stared into her eyes, with all seriousness in his expression as he pronounced. "Right, She has no family background, no beauty, no fame, no power, no money, nothing! Perhaps in her entire life, you have everything she could never have."

In an instant, when Lee Yin-Yin listened to Yang Tian-Xu, she felt like he somehow knew who would be the better choice for him. Despite that her emotions were wretched, and she felt bitter as she heard him continued, "But there is one thing she has that you don't, and can never have."

"What would that be?" Lee Yin-Yin was sure that whatever-it-was, she could get it too. His answer was harsh and heart-wrenching.

"My heart."

Once Lee Yin-Yin heard his response, she could no longer stay, she declared: "One of these days. You will regret it." And then she paraded passed him, wiping her tears away as she thought, "Yang Tian-Xu, you are not worth my valuable tears!"

Just as Lee Yin-Yin walked through the small alleyway, she bumped into Assistant Tseng and Wang Yi-An. They made way for her to pass through. However, they could tell that she was having a bad day. Still, they couldn't do anything about it but continuing with their duties.

CHAPTER 25

Someone Worthy of Your Love

While Lee Yin-Yin walked passed them, she gave a scornful look at Wang Yi-An. But, only Assistant Tseng had noticed it, and he wondered. "What happened here?"

Just as Wang Yi-An and Assistant Tseng walked into the break room, they saw Yang-Tian-Xu as he stood by the entrance. The door was opened wide.

Perhaps something had happened between them? Wang Yi-An had also heard the rumours, but she wasn't one to pry, and so she minded her business.

Assistant Tseng knew his boss too well and thought, "He must have rejected her. Oh! The nation's top idol, I can't imagine what would happen if her fans find out. That is not good for her image."

"Hey, boss!" With a cheerful expression, Assistant Tseng greeted Yang Tian-Xu. However, the only person in President Yang's eyes was Wang Yi-An.

"An-An! You came so early!"

"Early?" Assistant Tseng wanted to cry. At 9:15 a.m., she was fifteen minutes late. How could that be early? However, Assistant Tseng remained quiet.

"I'm sorry for being late! I got lost." Wang Yi-An had a good memory. However, it would be impossible for her to memorise a place she never been or seen before. She saw a map of floor seven. But, floor five was different, and nobody gave her a floor plan beforehand.

"Don't worry about it: the photo shoot doesn't start until 10 a.m. You're still early." Yang Tian-Xu smiled at her, and she smiled back.

When Assistant Tseng called her, she was all the way in the other wing. He realised she was lost and had to come to find her.

Sure enough, Assistant Tseng didn't tell President Yang that she was lost. If Yang Tian-Xu knew—Assistant Tseng believed President Yang would drop all of his work and rush to her side. President Yang needed to discuss with the staff and crews about the stage set-up. How could Assistant Tseng let President Yang go?

Yang Tian-Xu pulled a chair over to his side so that Wang Yi-An could have a seat beside him. Yang Tian-Xu looked at Assistant Tseng for ten seconds to ask him. "Go check if the stage would be complete in time for the photographers and film crews by 10:00 a.m." Then he returned his attention to Wang Yi-An.

"Okay..." Assistant Tseng was stunned, "Do I need to take Wang Yi-An with me?" Assistant Tseng thought it would be a good experience for her if she could see how the stage was set-up.

"No, she'll stay here with me until we shoot." Yang Tian-Xu wanted to be alone with her as he continued, "And I'll explain everything to her."

Clear for Assistant Tseng to see, what he wanted, but he had already briefed Wang Yi-An on the process. "I already did that on our way here, sir."

Yang Tian-Xu became annoyed as he told him. "Well, I want you to double check they didn't leave out any important details okay, now go." Yang Tian-Xu, he hinted that he wanted to be alone with Wang Yi-An.

Assistant Tseng got the message as he received the look from President Yang's face. He let out a heavy sigh as he closed the door behind him before he disappeared from their view.

Wang Yi-An stared at the documents that were laid out on the table. It was a template of the storyboard, in script form. Yang Tian-Xu sits there with Wang Yi-An as he explains to her all the shortcuts of the script. It was simple and easy to understand, and Wang Yi-An had no question.

Yang Tian-Xu and Wang Yi-An sat at the table, with just them alone inside the room. He made an excuse to keep her there with him. He acted like he wanted specific details about the animation part of the commercial.

Wang Yi-An would add notes on her copies. When the actual filming of the commercial begin, she won't be the only one to work on such a big project. However, she was the only one discussing with President Yang, and she thought it was weird.

"Um, where is everybody, shouldn't we wait for everyone to come first?" She asked while she pondered.

"No need, I already briefed them earlier today. Everybody has different tasks to complete. Don't worry too much about it. Let's continue." he said, but it was just an excuse he used so he could spend time with her alone.

Yang Tian-Xu had secretly planned this. He had purposely hoped that she would become lost. Allowing him time to finish the meeting without her.

In a big Company like the Yang Corps, there would be a hundred people working on set. Yang Tian-Xu wanted to have alone time with her, so he explained to her the duties of each department unrelated to hers, and he kept information about her tasks to the end.

Wang Yi-An felt like it was unnecessary to know all those information he gave her. However, he said, "Its good knowledge for you as an intern."

Wang Yi-An nodded and agreed. It was a valuable experience and practice to understand each department. She won't be collaborating with these departments, but it was still a good knowledge to have.

The commercial needed plenty of work, and with plenty of employees with their tasks. Wang Yi-An sat in the chair beside him, and he was hovering over her shoulders as he pointed at the documents and explained to her about every single one.

Out of the Blue, he thought about his family and her family. He tried to apologise to Mother Wang early this morning before work. Again, for the fifth time, Mother Wang refused to give Yang Tian-Xu her blessing.

He failed yet another time this morning, as he remembered what Mother Wang told him, "Stay away from my daughter, I don't want you to be with her." But, how could he?

It was sudden, but he still needed to ask her. "If the parents of the person you love object you two from being together, what would you do?"

Wang Yi-An doesn't understand why President Yang would ask her that. "I would..." Still, she considered the question before she answered him. "I would still love." She said as she paused for two seconds.

"I would use all my heart to love the person." Wang Yi-An's eyes remained glued to the papers while she stared at them and continued. "Even if I have to endure all the hurt, the pain, the bitterness, and even the hatred of everyone else. I would still endure it all even if I have to wash my face with tears in secret. I would continue to love him."

With another pause, Wang Yi-An turned to face him

straight on. Her eyes were full of determination as she said. "I will not regret it." Then, a gentle smile appeared on her face. "Because that man is worth my love."

For a moment they shared a look. Wang Yi-An waited for Yang Tian-Xu to response to her answer. His heart was moved, The fluttering feeling inside his heart imprisoned his gaze.

Wang Yi-An looked at him with a puzzled expression. Yang Tian-Xu continued to stare into her eyes passionately as he thought, "I am definitely the man worthy of your love." Then he smiled.

In the small room, Yang Tian-Xu remained entrapped in the woman's gaze whom he loved so dearly. Every time he looked into her eyes, he found himself—*lost* and all he wanted was to keep his stare. Silent, as Wang Yi-An had no clue what was going on in his mind, she wondered why he asked her such a question.

For reference perhaps? Maybe it's a theme for a new commercial product? Could it be because his relationship with Miss Lee was complicated because of his family's objection? Was that why Lee Yin-Yin looked unhappy the last time she saw her? Wang Yi-An felt heartache for the two lovers. However, how could she had known, the one Yang Tian-Xu loved and worried about wasn't Lee Yin-Yin but her? Still, Yang Tian-Xu wanted to make it clear. "I—"

Interrupted by Assistant Tseng again, with his loud voice as he said, "Boss, it's time for the shooting to start."

How could life be so easy for Yang Tian-Xu? The interruption irritated him severely as he turned his head around in slow motion as he stared at Assistant Tseng with a murderous glare.

The way how President Yang looked at him had made him gulped. "Ah..." Chills, running through his spine, like his neck was ensnared, strangled, and snapped in two. He shivered, and said, "Well, I gotta go now!" He fled the scene, as he was running for his life. Assistant Tseng felt like he might get killed later if he stayed any longer, his instinct told him to run.

Yang Tian-Xu sighed as he wanted to continue to tell her his feelings. How would it be possible? Wang Yi-An stood up from her seat and said, "We should get going too."

Yang Tian-Xu sighed again and said, "Yeah. Let's go to the stage and watch the filming." Yang Tian-Xu could only hold on to his thoughts and sighed once more, then he followed her outside of the break-room.

They walked out and headed to the stage that was completed and well prepared. Assistant Tseng had himself standing further away from them as he could. Staying away from danger was the best choice for survival. However, Assistant Tseng had received a call from the chairman.

"YES, SIR!" He screamed into the microphone, because of his nervousness and every time he felt pressure, his voice became extremely loud. Grandfather Yang's ears felt like it might have gone deaf, as he said in a distinctive voice. "Put him on the phone."

"YES, SIR!" Assistant Tseng couldn't be frightened anymore. At this point he needed to give the phone to President Yang: the chairman was still the big boss.

Assistant Tseng made his way over to where Yang Tian-Xu stood, with his hand, he covered the microphone and said, "President Yang, Chairman Yang would like to speak with you."

Even when Yang Tian-Xu knew what his grandfather wanted to say, he still took the call. "Yes, Ye-Ye?"

The stage was in the middle of filming, Yang Tian-Xu needed to step outside and not interfere with the filming.

Once Grandfather Yang heard his grandson's voice, he told

him, "I know you are busy, I won't beat around and ask you sincerely. Are you and Miss Lee Yin-Yin dating?"

Yang Tian-Xu doesn't want to deal with the rumours. Still, the scandal had reached Grandfather Yang's ear. There was no way Yang Tian-Xu could avoid it, and hope that perhaps everything would disappear on its own.

"No. Ye-Ye. Miss Lee is not my girlfriend."

"If she is not your girlfriend then why won't you consider Yue-Yan?" Grandfather Yang found the opportunity to suggest Tong Yue-Yan in the conversation. That annoyed Yang Tian-Xu even more.

"Grandfather, I already told you I—"

But, just as Yang Tian-Xu about to tell his grandfather, "I don't like Tong Yue-Yan." A loud scream screeched out and interrupted him, followed by a loud crash; sounds of shattered glass followed the loud rumbling sound. Suddenly, the stage became noisy, louder as people shout, "Oh my God!"

Yang Tian-Xu rushed back to see what happened, and he saw a devastating scene. A large stage-lamp had fallen from the ceiling. The loud crash he heard was the sound of the glasses of the light bulbs shattered onto the floor. Underneath, that broken lamp was Wang Yi-An.

The broken stage-lamp have bits of the shards shatter all over the ground. The small shards cut Wang Yi-An's legs, and she bled. Next to her was Lee Yin-Yin, who was unharmed, but laid there on her buttock.

The two girls were in a sitting position on the ground, and Lee Yin-Yin was shy of an arm's length away from the accident. Too close by where the broken lamp had fallen on, Wang Yi-An were closer to it, only a two inches more and she could have been beneath the lamp, crushed. What on earth had happened?

Those who had witnessed the event rushed over and the staff and crew members all crowded Lee Yin-Yin. They surrounded her and inquired about her injuries, which she had none.

Nevertheless, Wang Yi-An's leg was injured. The blood was dripping out of her wounds. The glass shards had shattered, and the velocity of the impact of the drop had lunged the broken pieces of the glasses into her left leg.

Usually, Wang Yi-An wore long dress pants. However, the weather for today was boiling weather for her. Wang Yi-An thought it would be better to wear shorts. How could short pants cover her entire legs? And the shards of broken glass injured both of her legs, her left leg was in the worst condition.

When Yang Tian-Xu saw her on the ground surrounded by broken glass. Yang Tian-Xu thought his heart would stop. He quickly rushed over as he pushed through the crowd to get to her.

All the staff were surprised. At first, everyone thought the person that Yang Tian-Xu was so worried about would be Lee Yin-Yin. However, he did not even bother to look at her. Nor did he even bother to mention her name. The only words that came out of Yang Tian-Xu's mouth were, "An-An! Are you hurt?"

When he sprinted over to her side, everyone was shocked, and they all share the same thought. "An-An?"

The expression on Yang Tian-Xu's face was filled with concern and worries, he looked at her injured leg and saw all the shards remained stuck inside her cuts. Yang Tian-Xu felted heartbroken and felt like how useless he was when he couldn't even protect the woman he loved.

CHAPTER 26

I Don't Like You

The stage was set, and the staff and crew members began production at 10 a.m. They prepared a scenery a sanctuary; the scene was where Lee Yin-Yin was to act like a Goddess from high in the Heaven. Like a beautiful angel, she descends from Heaven. Surrounding her was a forest—she flew down from above. The set had a green background for the animators to add in the effects using computer graphics later on after the film. The photographer was standing on the side as he took shots of different poses as the film crew rolled their camera.

Lee Yin-Yin's handmade costume made her beautiful, every eye was fixated on her. However, only Yang Tian-Xu didn't even bother to look at her. His eyes were on Wang Yi-An's amazed expression as she seemed excited to see the live-filming in person.

Yang Tian-Xu felt contented just watching her. However, his moment of happiness was once again, interrupted as he received the phone call from his grandfather. Yang Tian-Xu took the phone from Assistant Tseng and took a few steps outside the door. He stood just a few steps outside the door while he listened to his grandfather questioned him about his relationship with Lee Yin-Yin. How could Yang Tian-Xu possibly have any feelings for Lee Yin-Yin? Just as he was about to tell his grandfather, "Grandfather, I already told you I—".

The accident happened, perhaps when they reset the

lightings for the stage, a screw from the high-up ceiling light-lamp become loosen. When they moved the lamp back and forth, the gravity took a troll onto the heavy lamp. The metal frame made a screeching sound before it dropped, as one of the staff had witnessed it fall so suddenly, the lady screamed.

Just as when the light lamp was about to fall on top of Lee Yin-Yin. Everyone could only respond to the situation with a shout, "Be careful!" or screamed. But, only Wang Yi-An who's response was fast enough to rush over to save her. Wang Yi-An was quick, she sprinted over just in time to pushed Lee Yin-Yin out of the way.

In the nick of time, the lamp fell down on and almost hit Wang Yi-An as after she had successfully pushed Lee Yin-Yin to the side. The glass shattered to the ground and some pieces bounced off the floor and cut Wang Yi-An's legs. It was fortunate that the lamp didn't crush her.

Everyone present panicked as they all came rushing over to see if Lee Yin-Yin was hurt or not. No one paid any attention to Wang Yi-An. After all, compared to a famous Singer like Lee Yin-Yin. Who was Wang Yi-An? Wasn't she just a nobody?

The countless person that had asked if Lee Yin-Yin was okay or not wasn't so unexpected. It was utterly surprising as Yang Tian-Xu's reaction was once he saw the scene, he rushed over to Wang Yi-An's side. Yang Tian-Xu sprinted over to her side and yelled out, "An-An, are you hurt!?" with a worried expression on his face. His voice was loud, and everyone could hear him. He didn't wait for her to respond, and quickly he lifted her up princess-style as he carried her outside the studio.

Everyone was stunned, shocked, and couldn't believe what they saw. The instant when everyone was concerned about Lee Yin-Yin and thought perhaps President Yang would do the same. Yang Tian-Xu couldn't care less about Lee Yin-Yin.

The only person he cared for was Wang Yi-An. Assistant Tseng and Lee Yin-Yin knew why, as they thought to themselves, "He must really love her..."

With Wang Yi-An in his arms as he walked into the corridor, she was both confused and shocked. "Um. President Yang... I think you had carried the wrong person. Miss Lee is—"

"How can I mistook you for someone else?" He interrupted her.

Wang Yi-An was shocked. Overly astounded to say another word, with a blank expression on her face as she thought, "What's happening?" She remained silent in his arms, carried like a princess. Wang Yi-An was petite, and Yang Tian-Xu could easily carry her with no effort.

Instead of taking Wang Yi-An to the clinics; Yang Tian-Xu wanted to treat her wounds himself. The thoughts of someone else's hands touching her was enough to make him go crazy. He felt the need to take her someplace quiet, alone, where they won't be interrupted again. The top floor in his Presidential Office was his first choice, and Wang Yi-An had no clue where they were heading towards, as she thought he would take her to the clinic downstairs and simply drop her off.

When he carried her inside the elevator, the life operator's eyes and her mouth dropped and wide open. She was too shocked that she didn't even press the button, only until Yang Tian-Xu told her. "Top Floor."

"Yes, President Yang! Top floor!" She hurried to press on the button for the top floor.

"Um... President Yang... The clinic is on the 4th floor." Wang Yi-An was a little curious. Why the top floor when there were three different walk-in clinics on the floor down below?

"Walk-in clinics are always busy at this time of the day, I'll treat your wounds in my President Office." He said as he smiled at her. Yang Tian-Xu had first-aid training, emergency care, and he knew how to treat her wounds. Yang Tian-Xu's secondary education was in medicine. He had a good understanding of emergency medical care so Yang Tian-Xu wouldn't want anyone else to touch her when he could treat her wounds himself.

As they stood inside the elevator, Wang Yi-An gave a slight nod to show she understood his reasoning, but she opened her mouth and said. "Um... President...?"

"Yes?" He answered her with all his attention as he looked at her.

Wang Yi-An felt like she was in an embarrassing position in his arms. He was carrying her like a princess, and she couldn't help it; she wanted to get off. "You... Can you put me down..." her voice was shy and soft-spoken as she looked over to the elevator girl. The girl pretended not to look at her, but Wang Yi-An knew she was being stared at like a zoo animal.

With Wang Yi-An being carried like a princess in the President's arm. The elevator-lady got a little jealous, she felt even more jealous when she heard him said, "It's better if you don't walk for now. I'll treat your wounds first."

A few seconds later, the elevator door opened. Yang Tian-Xu left the elevator with Wang Xi-An cuddle up in his arms. Even when Yang Tian-Xu wanted the ride to be longer. That way Yang Tian-Xu could have his love in his arms longer. But he knew he should treat her wounds as soon as possible.

A locked door prevented anyone other than Yang Tian-Xu from accessing the Presidential Office. He carried her all the way to his office, his real office. Not his temporary office downstairs, where it was so small, but a huge office that could double up as a single room apartment if he needed to stay the night. Yang Tian-Xu placed his finger onto the access pad, and it automatically opened, the only person who has access to this office would be him.

Few people with authority worked on the top floor. Yang Tian-Xu had Wang Yi-An in his hand and went inside his office with only two people who saw them. One was Vice-President Ma, and the other the vice-president's secretary. However, they were too busy to care about what happened and minded their own business.

As soon as Yang Tian-Xu got into his office, the massive size amazed Wang Yi-An. The presidential suite was more than just a simple office, it was larger than both her living room and kitchen combined. Much more massive compared to the manager's office. The two closed doors made her wondered what could be behind them as she took a glance.

Yang Tian-Xu sat her down slowly on the sofa and hurried to look for the first-aid kit inside his cabinets. When he found it, he rushed over to her side, and Wang Yi-An remained silent because she didn't know what to say. She sat there on the comfiest sofa she had sat on before. Still a little confused as she thought, "Wasn't it be better to visit the clinic instead?"

Yang Tian-Xu kneels and opens the first-aid case beside her. He had prepared a small bowl to place the broken shards aside. First used a clean cloth to wipe away the blood on her legs, she felt a little uncomfortable and told him. "It's okay. I can do it myself." And she tried to take the cloth from his hand, yet he stopped her.

How could he let her? He placed his hand over hers and said, "It's better if I do it." and then he continued to clean her legs. There were little bits of fragments of the glass caught inside her skin, but for Wang Yi-An—the pain wasn't as bad as it looked. Big and small cuts were everywhere on her legs, the new cuts were made from the broken glass, but she had old ones all over her legs.

The biggest cut was on her left leg, Among all the little cuts were three or five other small cuts that had small bits of shards stuck inside. The blood dripped all over Yang Tian-Xu's clothing as he rested her leg on his lap. He tried to be as gentle as he could when he wiped the blood off, cleaning both her legs, removing the shards slowly so he won't hurt her. He inspects them to check if there were any more cuts and glass-fragments left that needed treatment.

Yang Tian-Xu was gentle and caring as he looked at them with his entire focus. Wang Yi-An was embarrassed, she wasn't sure of how to react, or what to say when he touched her legs. She couldn't understand the feelings she felt inside, but it was the first time another man, who's a stranger to her had touched her legs.

While Yang Tian-Xu was cleaning her legs, removing bits of the dried blood—dried on their way here. He saw more glass shards stuck in her cut, and he was trying very hard to be as gentle as he could to remove them. Somehow he felt the pain in his heart. "Doesn't it hurt?" he asked, his face was full of concerns as he tried to take the shard out.

Wang Yi-An shook her head. "No, it's okay. This is nothing." Just as Yang Tian-Xu tried to be so gentle, she said, "Here, let me." she took the tweezer and pulled it out of her wounds, without a change in expression. Like it didn't hurt her at all.

"You're really—" He wanted to say "brave." But the words don't seem right, and he couldn't say it because if it was his leg? He would probably be screaming in pain, but he realised that those cuts weren't the only ones she had. Both of her legs were filled with old scars, new cuts, and even bruises. It looked like her legs had been abused.

Yang Tian-Xu gently glide his finger on the older scars on

her legs, "How come you have so many cuts and bruises?" he couldn't help himself, he had to ask.

She looked at them and smiled. "Those are nothing. I got them from doing hard labour works at the mayor's garden last month."

"Garden work?" Yang Tian-Xu suddenly became confused, he knew she worked part-time at the Happiness Restaurant, but to work part-time as a gardener as well? It was impressive for him to hear more about her, not from Fung Qi-Wei, but from her.

"Yeah, I didn't have a well-paying job yet, so I worked as a gardener to pay my tuition fees while I was in school, the mayor pays better than my wages at the Happiness Restaurant." She smiled, and he looked up and finally their eyes met. They were quiet for a long while, with no words, he stared into her eyes. And Wang Yi-An? At first, she waited for him to reply, but later she felt self-conscious.

"Did my scars and bruises disgust you?" Wang Yi-An asked as she looked away from his gaze. Yang Tian-Xu snapped back and immediately he said, "No! I—" he looked down at her legs, and took out some disinfecting wipes and wipe her left leg as he said, "I think you're very admirable."

"Me?" She turned her head to look at his handsome face, and then she looked back down on her legs.

"Yes, you are a very hardworking girl. Your mother and father must be very proud of you." He said, but when he said, "father" her expression changed.

Wang Yi-An's expression became sorrowful and looked away from his face. Yang Tian-Xu looked at her expression as it changed, and the corner of her lip curled up. Sorrowful, painful, and heart-aching when she said, "I don't have a father." But then she smiled as she continued, "But I'm sure my mother is very proud of me."

For the first time in Yang Tian-Xu's life, he wanted to understand this girl, Wang Yi-An. He wanted to know her life story, her background, everything about her life. Before he'd never cared to learn about other people because he was never interested. He stared at her, and when she looked up, she caught his glance. "My mother is a single mom. But she really loved my brother and me."

Surprised to find out one more thing about her, Yang Tian-Xu asked, "You have a brother?"

"Yep!" she smiled, then her expression changed, and tears flowed out of her eyes. Her tears were like a sword that jabbed his heart. How could she smile one second and cry the next?

Yang Tian-Xu sat next to her as he pulled her in for a hug. The embraced was shocking to her, she never expected it. The shock paused her for a moment. She didn't know what to do, but she quickly snapped back to her senses and pushed Yang Tian-Xu out. "President! If you keep showing me kindness like that, I'll misunderstand!"

Wang Yi-An's word surprised him. He couldn't believe he had heard it. He had to ask her. "Misunderstand what?" Yang Tian-Xu needed to know. What would she misunderstand?

"I'll... Well... You..." Wang Yi-An blushed. "You're too nice to me. People might misunderstand and think you (like) me, or something, people get weird ideas—"

"Well, I don't like you—" Yang Tian-Xu said in a clear voice.

For a second, Wang Yi-An's emotions had cool down, and she wanted to tell him. "You should only treat the girl you like with such care and kindness."

However, to her surprised. Yang Tian-Xu continued. "I

love you."

"I don't like you. I love you." Those were the words that caught Wang Yi-An by surprise. With just Wang Yi-An and Yang Tian-Xu alone in the president's office. A moment of silence enclosed them with feelings of uncertainty.

For Yang Tian-Xu the feelings that stopped became feelings of eternity. He felt like he could kill himself if he gets rejected. However, for Wang Yi-An—it was a feeling of uncertainty. The three words he said were his true feelings.

Feelings that made his world stop—time had stopped for him—only until she gave him an answer. And her reply? He would wait for as long as his heart still beats.

To be continued...

AUTHOR'S NOTE

Many times I dreamt about becoming an author. This is my first time publishing a novel—even though it's on Amazon (it's still available in print!). But I felt that I had accomplished a lot more than many who thought about writing and not *actually writing*. I would like to thank the people who make it possible for me to write. They encouraged, supported, and (bash) my writing. But with all respect to them, I couldn't thank them enough! Only when you understand how important it was for me. I had spent countless (sleepless) nights writing, editing, and formatting this novel, I hope that my readers would be able to understand and enjoy this novel as much as I had—when I write, edit, and format this novel.

We all have dreams. We all have our goals—we want to accomplish. Sometimes we don't start because we fear rejection. I had that fear for sometimes now, (*laughs*) but now I felt better about my writing voice. And if you have dreams of becoming an author yourself, go for it! Find your voice and write! We have the Internet now!

And I want to thank the readers from the world wide web (where I had posted the rough drafts), you guys were the ones that made me more confident in my writing voice. Thank you all very much for your support in purchasing a copy of My Obsession Volume One. I know I end it in a cliffhanger, but please don't hate me for that!

Look forward to the next volume! I hoped you all enjoyed reading this novel. Again! Thank you very much for your purchase!

About the Author

Who is D2D or Dare2Dream? A person with a dream? Someone—who likes to hide behind his/her imagination? Dare2Dream is willing to write anything to get a best seller. Romance, Fantasy, Erotica, Horror, Science Fiction, and *basically anything*. D2D started writing novels in 2018 and hide behind the shadow of the pen-name; D2D-Dare2 Dream.

Daring you to dream!

Dare2Dream
information@d2d-dare2dream.store
www.d2d-dare2dream.store

Ordering Information:
For details, contact the publisher at the email address above.
Please order at visit www.d2d-dare2dream.store

Credits
Cover Illustration and Design Copyright © 2019 by
Jesse Samra
Book design and production by Dare2Dream, www.d2d-dare2dream.store
Editing by James Chew

ISBN paperback: 978-1-9995770-2-5
ISBN eBook: 978-1-9995770-1-8